A Gryphon's Trial

Kathryn Brown

The Quill and Claw Series

Book One: A Gryphon's Journey

Book Two: A Gryphon's Trial

Book Three: A Gryphon's Mercy

Copyright © 2021 by Kathryn Brown

Published by Kob Publishing

Illustrated by Jen Elliott

Edited by Bridgit Davis

ISBN: 978-1-7363046-3-1

ACKNOWLEDGEMENTS

With a huge thank you to Amber Mielke, Danielle Lincoln Hanna, and Yadira Perez, who were liberal with their encouragement, wisdom, and friendship when I needed it the most.

I also wish to thank Travis Trazor for his valuable feedback, Jen Elliott for her never ending patience with my requests, and Bridgit Davis for her wonderful insights. And of course, a last thank you to my family, who have always encouraged me in my writing endeavors.

CONTENTS

APPENDIX OF CREATURES

Gryphon: Diurnal, carnivorous predators that boast eagle-like heads and lion-like bodies. Possess wings and can live solitarily, in small units, or in large flocks.

Strigigryph: Nocturnal, carnivorous predators. May or not possess a crest. Have owl-like heads and lion-like bodies. Possess wings and are capable of nearly silent flight. Typically live in small groups, with larger flocks being extraordinary.

Ardeigryph: Crepuscular, piscivorous predators. Opportunistic feeders. Possess crested, heron-like heads, long legs, and lion-like bodies. Typically live in large flocks.

Alicorn: Diurnal herbivore possessing the body of an equine, with pale coats, wings, and a single horn. Have the innate ability to manipulate magick, and are long-lived and peaceable, with the tendency to live in herds.

Hydra: Crepuscular, serpentine carnivores possessing wings and five heads. Have the ability to spout acid from four heads and flame from one. Venomous. Territorial, long lived, and solitary.

Basilisk: Crepuscular, serpentine carnivores that are largely opportunistic in their feeding habits. Capable of paralyzing prey with their piercing gaze. Solitary and territorial, with most living according to a basic hierarchy.

Aquila: Diurnal, predatory raptors possessing the ability to form storm clouds and harness the electricity therein. Typically live solitarily or in pairs.

Tweeter: Diurnal, feathered insectivores.

Fae: Diurnal, nocturnal, or crepuscular depending on their type. Possess wings and a basic ability to manipulate magick. Reserved and aloof, they are typically peaceful and live in colonies.

Tusker: Diurnal, mid-sized omnivores possessing two tusks that curve upward on either size of their snouts. Distinct for the grunting sounds with which they communicate. Typically live in small herds.

Peryton: Crepuscular, deer-like herbivores possessing wings and cloven hooves. Males grow antlers during their breeding season. Typically live in small to large herds.

Longear: Crepuscular, small herbivores that possess large ears and soft fur. Common in many environments, and typically live in small colonies.

Pegasus: Diurnal herbivore possessing the body of an equine, with pale coats and wings. Live in herds and, while generally peaceable, are highly territorial.

Pixie: Nocturnal carnivores that typically live

in colonies. Possess wings, horns, and bright red hair. When able, forms a mutualistic bond with a host creature for both protection and increased chances of finding food.

Brimel: Diurnal herbivores that possess large incisors for gnawing. Possess coarse coats and a stocky body, and prefer to live near water. Typically solitary, with small groups not being uncommon.

Squileap: Diurnal, ground-dwelling herbivores that possess large, bushy tails and the ability to climb when needed. Typically live in small groups.

Fangjaw: Nocturnal carnivores that prefer to hunt by stealth. While preferential to hunting smaller prey, they are capable of predating creatures many times their own size. Possess sizeable claws, crushing jaws, and hind legs that are longer than their front legs, giving them considerable jumping ability.

Kirin: Diurnal herbivores possessing thick manes, cloven hooves, long, tufted tails, and bodies that are covered in scales. Have the innate ability to manipulate magick, and are long-lived and peaceable, with the tendency to live in herds.

Bonebrancher: Crepuscular, herbivorous, and solitary. Possess massive antlers, cloven hooves, rough coats of fur, and are well-muscled. Prone to aggression.

Mermaid: Diurnal, aquatic, and piscivorous. Social. Possess a scaled body, sharp teeth, powerful tail, and webbed fingers, as well a pair of fins at the shoulders. Typically found in large bodies of salt water.

Sea Serpent: Nocturnal, carnivorous, and solitary. Found in large bodies of salt water. Possess whiskers that help detect prey, a long, muscular body, fins, spines, and serrated teeth. Long lived, with the ability to continuously grow throughout their life span.

Phoenix: Diurnal, long lived, and typically solitary. Have the innate ability to manipulate magick, and to rebirth at the end of their life cycles. Raptor-like, with fiery plumage in varying shades of red, gold, or orange, as well as notably long tails.

Cockatrice: Nocturnal, solitary, and territorial. Capable of paralyzing prey with their piercing gaze. Large and unflighted, with an upright stance and the ability to run at great speeds. Possess both scales and feathers, and rely on stealth to track their prey.

Kelpie: Crepuscular, predatory shape-shifters that prey on the essence of others. Possess the ability to manipulate magick. Distinctly equine in appearance, with skeletal features in various stages of decay. Inhabit dark pools of water.

CHAPTER ONE

The sea stretched out in all directions. There was no land in sight. Hlaena, the last surviving Alicorn mare of her herd, still led the group of Gryphons, Strigigryph, and Ardeigryph on their perilous flight. The claws of fatigue were sinking into them all.

Arias's eyes watered under the light of the sun. There were no trees or clouds to block the rays of sunlight, no shelter for his albino eyes. He resorted to keeping them closed as much as possible, following the sound of the wing beats around him for direction. He tried, unsuccessfully, to ignore the pounding headache that had etched its way into existence behind his eye sockets. The world had long since faded from recognition, and was now a tangled blur of sea and sky, made hazier by his exhaustion. He hadn't been injured as badly as many others had been in the battle between the Gryphs of the two eyries they'd left behind, but convincing his wings to continue flapping was still becoming a difficult task.

What had originally started out as a compact group of individuals hurrying to flee from a home blighted by basilisks was now a scattered group of weary souls that stretched out across the ocean. Arias swore that he could taste the dust on his tongue, and the sea looked more and more tantalizing the longer he went on. The Ardeigryph had warned everyone that it wasn't to be drunk from under any circumstance, but that didn't keep some individuals from learning for themselves. Those that swallowed the brine quickly discovered that they shouldn't have.

The group had flown all through the night, and now the sun had reached its full zenith. It would be a long time until night fell again… and brought with it its own special terror. Arias watched his companions drift lower and lower in the sky, some scraping claws with the whitecaps in the ocean as they lost the will to continue. What would it be like to fall into depths that were as dark as night itself, never to rise again?

There were things in the deep, beasts the likes of which most Gryphs had never seen before. The ones that appeared and vanished in the surf were massive wrigglers that breathed through the tops of their huge, blunt heads as they crested the waves, their forked tails slapping at the water. They seemed as curious of the Gryphs as the Gryphs were of them; some even leapt into the air as if to get a better look. It was hard to imagine how many of the creatures lurked below, just hidden from view.

Arias's ears flicked upward as he detected something new in the beating of the wings around him, and he lifted his head and squinted, watching as a group of Gryphs veered off course to his right. His heart leapt in his chest when he saw them all rise in a lazy spiral a murm later. An air thermal! It was the first they'd come across in a while. He angled over to where the air current was drawing his companions upward, and he relaxed a bit as the warmer air allowed him to soar high without flapping his wings. It was as close to resting as he was going to get.

From his new orientation in the group, Arias was able to pick out a fiery orange coat just across from him. Brynne. She was as tired as anyone else, but did a good job of hiding it. When Arias edged over to be nearer to her, she gave him a look out of the corner of her eye and said nothing.

"How are you doing?" he asked, and she snorted.

"Fine. I am surprised you haven't fallen into the ocean and drowned yet, though."

Same old Brynne, Arias thought. *Just a bit meaner than the cubhood version of herself.* Not that he blamed her after what she'd been through. Having one's homeland and loved ones ripped away all at once would change anyone.

"We should have fought those basilisks," Brynne continued. "At least then we would've either died for certain or won back our territory. Who knows where or if this ocean ends? I'd rather die in a good roasting than by drowning. It's a coward's death, to drown after running away. I don't know why I followed you all out here."

"There's no way any Gryph is winning against a basilisk," Arias said. "And either way, what's better about dying fighting a battle you can't win? I'd take a coward's death over a fool's one. Because I can guarantee you that you wouldn't have won. At least this way, we have a chance."

Brynne's eyes flashed. "You would defend the path of the weak. You may have fought well back there, Arias, but deep down, I always knew that you'd stay a coward." She flapped hard to ascend above him. He didn't follow her.

The Strigigryph travelling in the group were at a disadvantage, as their short, broad wings didn't lend well to long distance flight. They had also taken heavier damage in the battle between Arborochre and Oceanside, having been on the losing side, and were the first to succumb to the effects of the journey. The air thermal gave out at around twilight, and droves of them started to sag toward the ocean. A few of the worst-off ones dipped into the ocean, and they ignored the calls of their comrades to continue on. Arias could see it in their eyes. They had given up.

Tybrake, an Ardeigryph keythong who towered above even his other already incredibly tall flockmates, struggled to pull a few from the sea, but all but one he'd hefted skyward gave up again shortly thereafter. The Ardeigryph were used to travelling over the ocean, just not this far into open waters. They had huge, narrow wings that allowed them to soar and exploit air thermals to their full advantage, but even they were starting to tire. Arias cast a quick glance around to check that Alissi, a Strigigryph hen from Arborochre that he was particularly fond of, was still on the wing. Then he found Tybrake with his eyes and shook his head. The keythong gave him a withering look.

"You can't save them all," Arias called out, not caring who heard. It was true.

Tybrake's gaze grew from withering to horrified. Arias didn't understand the look, until he realized that the keythong wasn't staring at him. He was looking past him.

Arias's eyes trailed downward until he was looking at a group of the big wrigglers from before. Only now, there was something massive swimming in their midst. Its combined length easily made up six of the smaller forms around it.

"Hlaena!" Arias yelled, but his parched voice was unable to project the volume needed to reach the Alicorn mare at the front of the group. He fought his way to reach where she was, but when he finally caught up and looked down again, the waters below were empty. The Strigigryph that had fallen into the surf were gone, too.

"There was something—" he began, but the

Alicorn mare was already nodding.

"By the time I looked it was gone, but I sensed it," she said. "Something ancient lives in these waters, older than even my kind. I don't know if it's aggressive or not, but let's hope it has passed us by."

"Considering that the Strigigryph that fell in aren't there anymore, I'm worried that it may stick around."

Hlaena's face was grim, but she said nothing more.

The sun's light slipped quietly from the horizon, like the last sigh of a dying beast. Despite their fatigue, the group grew anxious. The thin sliver of crescent moon that rose only served to exacerbate the feeling, making the darkness seem impenetrable. Arias had returned to flying next to Nanchu, a blind Ardeigryph hen, and Larin, a mute Gryphon hen he'd met in Arborochre. He'd hardly settled in next to them before Nanchu suddenly snapped her head up, sightless eyes wide.

"What was that?" she asked.

Larin and Arias both looked at her, confused. Larin clicked three times, the inflection questioning.

"Didn't you hear it?" Nanchu said. "There's something big moving through the water."

A chill shot through Arias. He peered down, but couldn't make anything out below. He started to ask a nearby Strigigryph if they saw anything, on account of how good their night vision was, when something smooth and silvery slid into view below. He watched it trail bubbles with a hissing sound, and then it vanished again. Every Gryph watched anxiously, their timid warbles filling the night. And then, without warning, a jet of water shot through the air in a wide arc, sweeping unsuspecting Gryphs from the sky.

Cries of alarm rose as a pointed, whiskered head rose high above the waves, its mouth opening to reveal rows upon rows of glistening, serrated teeth that gleamed in the faint moonlight. Its body was a coiling monstrosity of scales and muscle, long and interrupted by jagged spines. It snaked toward where the fallen Gryphs were struggling in the surf and dove into their midst, snapping and ripping them asunder. Those that escaped the first attack cried out, and then were silently sucked under the waves a murm later.

Hlaena's command to spread out was lost in the panic as the creature launched itself from the water and snatched a few more Gryphs from the sky. Arias caught sight of its tiny, sunken eyes as it fell, its jaws streaming with feathers. They were totally opaque like Nanchu's, and its dead-on accuracy despite the darkness began to make sense.

"It can hear us!" he yelled. "Fly higher! It's our only chance!"

His feeble voice, like Hlaena's, was drowned out in the commotion. Larin hissed as a small crowd of alarmed Gryphs flew backwards through the flock, trying to separate themselves from the bulk of the group. The monster below made another lunge toward the front of the group, where Hlaena was, but when it closed in on her position, it deviated at the last murm. It centered its attention on the Alicorn, and despite its lack of discernable expression, it seemed quizzical.

Hlaena's mouth was moving, although Arias couldn't make out what she was saying. The sea serpent's whiskers twitched and reached up toward her, like they were hungry to sense the words she spoke. The blind eyes of their owner never blinked. The Gryphs mostly quieted, watching the exchange. The creature spread giant fins, previously hidden, on either side of its head as it waited for her to finish whatever she was saying. After a time, it whipped its head to the side, agitated.

"Meinsin sun-itsu..." it said in a low, rasping voice, then parted its jaws to send another jet of water streaming upward. Frightened Gryphs scattered in all directions, trying to escape.

Adrenaline overrode the fatigue in Arias's reluctant body, and he started to ascend in earnest. A fleeing Gryphon barreled into him, and he tumbled backward into a hen he thought was Larin, but the Gryphon who shoved him back was an unfamiliar stranger. He realized that, in the fray, he no longer saw anyone he recognized.

8

"Arias!"

He heard Nanchu's voice, but couldn't find her either. A cry of fear escaped him as the sea serpent launched itself and tore through the flock again, and he had to lurch sideways, hard, to avoid meeting its teeth. He stabilized with effort, and for a murm he thought he'd caught sight of a streak of black and white, but in the tangled mass of feathers and fur, he wasn't sure if it was actually Nanchu or not.

The Ardeigryph were already nearly out of range of the monster, their huge wings carrying them aloft faster than any other Gryphs. Arias fought to catch up to them, still searching below for Nanchu.

Larin materialized to his right, along with a number of other Gryphons. Most of the Strigigryph were struggling to gain any altitude, putting them at risk, while Arias and the high-flying group had reached a range where they could easily avoid the predator's attacks. A few Strigigryph managed to drag themselves to the upper reaches of the sky, where they were encouraged and supported as best the others could.

Arias almost felt relief as he realized that his life was no longer in danger, but then his eyes locked onto a particular figure in an isolated group toward the water's surface. Too tired to climb, the Gryphs hovered above the waves in an anxious bundle. Arias blinked, the black and white markings unmistakable. Nanchu was following the wrong group, having lost him and the others in the commotion. The water below them bubbled with the promise of death.

Arias angled his wings and dove, intending to knock Nanchu away from the group before the sea serpent could attack again. From his vantage point, he could see the monstrosity moving beneath the waves, its body whipping from side to side like a sheet of moss in a windstorm. Arias narrowed his eyes and focused all of his strength into reaching the Ardeigryph hen. He leaned greedily into the dive, determined to outpace the beast below him. Nanchu half turned, her keen hearing picking out his approach over the rest of the cacophony. There was confusion on her frightened face as she turned her sightless orbs towards him. He extended his talons and ripped her away from the group as a massive splash brought the sea serpent to the surface again. Its shining body rose, twisting, so close by that Arias could see his reflection in its oversized scales. The screams of the other Gryphs cut off almost as soon as they'd begun. All that was left behind was an eerie patch of water littered with the feathers and fur of the fallen.

"Climb!" Arias barked. Then hen didn't need to be told twice. Her huge wings took her soaring past him, and Tybrake called out from above so she could fall into line with him and Larin. They watched the waves with apprehension until Arias finally caught up, and Nanchu wasted no time in thanking him again and again as soon as he did. Tybrake and Larin averted their eyes.

"I should've been down there," Tybrake said. "I saw what was happening, but I couldn't move. Forgive me, Nanchu."

Larin added an apologetic click, but Nanchu was already shaking her head.

"I wouldn't have expected either of you to risk your lives to save mine. That's what makes it so incredible that Arias did. I got confused when the group started to break up. I couldn't tell where you went. That thing... it's huge. I never knew such horrors existed."

Arias hadn't debated whether he could've saved Nanchu or not. There hadn't been time to do so. The idea of failure hadn't crossed his mind in the murm, and he was glad it hadn't, or he might not have made it. He closed his eyes and tried to ignore the exhaustion spreading in his body. He told himself over and over that an air thermal was only a couple of flaps away. It was the only way to force himself to continue on.

***

In the long murms that followed the flock's escape to a higher altitude, the sea serpent constantly poked its head up to look for stragglers, long whiskers feeling through the air. However, the Gryphs had a renewed sense of survival after seeing the terrible fate of those who'd been eaten, and no one, not even the remaining Strigigryph, lagged in their flight. When the sky started to lighten with the promise of dawn, the mammoth creature surfaced one final time, shrieking its unintelligible, gritty language into the salty air. Hlaena glanced down, but she didn't try to speak with it again. After a time, the beast slipped into the watery graveyard it called home, vanishing without a trace.

A collective ripple of relief ran through the flock at the departure of the predator that had filled the night with murder. Without the reminder to stay aloft, the price of their lengthy escape became evident. A few Gryphs sank toward the sea, as if they'd only made it this far so that they could die by drowning. Arias found himself sinking, too. He even caught himself thinking that maybe it was a fine ending to drown, perhaps even better than being eaten. And then the wind cupped beneath his wings, and the strongest thermal he'd ever encountered sent him sailing back into the sky. It was as if Halada herself had heard his thoughts, and disapproved. Mere murms later, an Ardeigryph at the front of the group cried out excitedly.

"Ey, there's something up ahead!"

The tense waiting after hearing those words seemed to stretch on forever as every Gryph strained to see. Arias looked, too, but in the hazy light of the rising sun, he couldn't see very much at all. Still, his spirit jolted as he heard Tybrake begin to cackle wildly. Hope spilled over him as the big keythong roared,

"Bless the winds! Land!"
***

The island was huge, with long, sandy fingers that combed out over the ocean as if to beckon

12

weary travelers to its shores. Every Gryph called out happily as they drifted down to the sand bars, rushing to lie among thin trees with leaves that hung in vibrant green blades. A great majority of them immediately fell asleep, either not caring to scout for danger or trusting those who remained awake to attend to the task.

The firm earth felt alien under Arias's talons as he finally landed. His wings felt as if they were no longer attached to his body, and he let them hang limp at his sides instead of immediately tucking them away. He mentally took note of everyone that was on the beach. He'd seen Bala, Tybrake, and Lue. Alissi was huddled near a group of other Strigigryph, and Larin was watching him from some distance away. Brynne was taking stock of her own group, the Pale. They were a tough bunch, and seemed to look out for one another.

Arias looked a bit more, wondering if he'd forgotten anyone, and with a start he realized that he hadn't seen Brint, the Ardeigryph keythong who'd scouted on one of the original missions to defeat Shadowbane on the mainland. If he were honest, however, he couldn't pretend he was too torn up about it. He'd hardly known Brint, but he still felt bad that he'd only just now noticed his absence.

Arias sought out one last individual, and found her further inland, by herself. Hlaena was lying down, gazing off into the distance. She had an uncharacteristic frustration about her, and she flattened her ears when he drew near, surprising him. Seeing his reaction, she softened her demeanor.

"I'm glad you're unharmed little one," she said quietly, turning back to stare out over the ocean again.

The silence threatened to stretch, and she added, "I always knew there was something out there. In the ocean."

Arias followed her eyes. "Hlaena, you couldn't have known—"

"I had hoped it was intelligent. I saw the hope painted on the faces of your kind when I tried to speak to it, and it actually stopped. I was hopeful, too. But its speech was so ancient... I could only understand a fragment of what it spoke. All except what it screamed just before it finally left us."

Arias waited for her to repeat whatever it had said, but it was soon clear that she had no intention of doing so. He still couldn't suppress the shiver that ran along his spine at the cryptic implication of her words. "It wasn't your fault," he said.

"I was the one who lead you all across the ocean in the first place."

"We would've had to cross the ocean one way or another. It was either that or face the basilisks, which would've been nearly the same as certain death," Arias said. "Or starve in a burned, trampled land with no prey surviving on it.

Sometimes bad things just happen, Hlaena. It's not always someone's fault."

"It wasn't your fault, either, you know."

Arias looked back to her, not expecting to hear the words. Her voice was halting.

"It's hard to imagine a world without Xio and the rest of the herd. It's even harder to actually live in that world. I'd be lying if I said I haven't fantasized about how it would have been better had you left me to die with them. But... I like to think that I'm here for a reason. And I'm happy to be here for you, right now."

Arias drank in the words of forgiveness, feeling a little appalled at himself for how quicky he did so. Hlaena lifted a wing and he shimmied underneath it, feeling like a tiny cub again as he rested against her shoulder.

Sleep wasn't hard for him to find.

CHAPTER TWO

The sunny days on the island bled into balmy nights, and it wasn't long before everyone began to feel at home. There hadn't been any sightings of the sea serpent by any Ardeigryph casting out at sea, and they began to fly out even further for bigger wrigglers, boasting with one another about their catches. The winter was much milder here than on the mainland, and spring was hurrying to settle itself in. Bountiful prey saw everyone rested and well fed, despite the fact the peryton were smaller than the ones everyone was used to from the mainland. They made up for their tiny size by being ridiculously easy to catch; one could practically walk up to them before they decided that fleeing was an idea worth entertaining. Water existed in the form of a small, bubbling spring toward the center of the island, and the only alternative was to break open the small, hard fruits that adorned some of the trees to drink the tepid liquid within them. Everything was a welcome respite after all that the Gryphs had been through. Or at least, it was for nearly a moon… and then it wasn't anymore.

***

"We're running out of food," Brynne said, lying on her back with her paws in the air.

Arias frowned, turning. "What?"

"We've been hauling in less and less by the day. There's been a sharp decrease in prey over the last three days."

"The wrigglers, too?"

Brynne shook her head. "No, but not all of us eat those things."

Arias thought in silence. It made sense. This island had probably been thriving without major predators for a long time before they'd arrived. And they'd arrived in huge numbers relative to the island's size.

"Well," he said. "There's only one thing to do. Eating less isn't feasible; we're so many that we'll still run out. We have to leave."

Neither of them liked the prospect. But if the choice was between either a slow death of starvation or a swift end with whatever that *thing* out there was, Arias knew which one he'd pick.

"The idea won't be a popular one," Arias said, "but if we can get the leaders and influential Gryphs on our side…"

"The stragglers will fall into line," Brynne

finished. She stood up, shaking the sand from her coat. "Right, then. I'm on it. Let's have a meeting.

***

Bala, Brynne, and Alissi all joined Arias in a wide semi-circle in the sand. Larin, Tybrake, Lue, and a few assorted Strigigryph lounged off to one side, preferring to listen instead of taking an active part in the discussion.

Arias began by saying, "It's become apparent that we have an issue. Food is running short. Inaction is obviously not an option, so… let's talk about what we're going to do about this."

"My flock hasn't complained," Bala said, glancing toward Lue and Tybrake.

"That's because it isn't the wrigglers that are becoming sparse, it's the preymeat," Arias said. "Even if we consumed less—"

"Which would probably start a riot in the Pale," Brynne interjected.

"…Even if we consumed less," Arias continued, "it's unlikely we can support a population this large in the long term. There's just too many of us. And I'm not sure how many will willingly switch over to eating more of the wrigglers without starting a fight, as Brynne mentioned. If Gryphs start fighting over the meat, it'll only deplete what's left faster."

Alissi looked troubled. "I doubt I'd have any luck convincing any of the Strigigryph to try wrigglers. We never had such creatures as those

18

in our desert homeland. There's only one real answer... but I couldn't ask them to fly over the sea a second time. Not after what happened the first time. Our wings aren't made for distances like that. Plus, we don't even know the right direction to head in if we do fly out over the sea again. Maybe we should have Hlaena at this meeting."

"With all due respect," Bala said, his eyes flashing to Arias. "She led us over waters that were infested with a literal monster. I don't know how she chose which direction to go in, but if her magick couldn't help detect or fend off that creature, why should we trust her to lead us again?"

"Because no one else was going to do it," Arias replied with more sharpness than he'd intended. "And she knew it was there; she just didn't know it was hostile. How can you criticize her when none of us could have done better? Besides, she can't be here. She's... unwell." Saying the words reminded him of just how listless Hlaena had become since landing on the island. While everyone else had recovered, she'd progressed in the opposite direction, spending most of her days sleeping.

"Well, we can't just sit here," Brynne said. "It's only a matter of time before this gets out, and once it does, the fighting starts anyway. If that happens, it'll take more than just us to quell it. The whispers are already beginning in the hunting groups."

"You're right," Arias said. "But give me one solution that *doesn't* include crossing the ocean."

Silence followed. Alissi was perhaps the quietest he'd ever seen her. Sympathy crept into Arias's words as he said, "I know the sea is especially frightening for you and the other Strigigryph, but for now it's the only option any of us can think of."

"We won't make it," she whispered, more to the ground than anyone else. "First leaving the desert, then the battle at Arborochre, and now this. There won't be any of us left."

Arias exchanged glances with the others, most of whom diverted their gazes elsewhere. All except for Brynne, who seemed unmoved by the Strigigryph's predicament.

"So, is it settled then? What's it going to be?" she asked.

"Let's take at least a night to think it over," Bala said. "It's a big decision, a life or death one. I'm not sure how best to break the news to everyone that we probably have to leave again. In fact… as much as I want to be in solidarity with everyone, we Ardeigryph have less of a reason to leave. So I may have trouble getting some of mine to accept the news."

"Well, the Pale is happy for you," Brynne cooed mockingly. Arias shot her a look.

"Halada's sake, Brynne. Why are you being so

nasty lately?"

Rolling her eyes, the orange hen stood and shook the sand from her fur. "I'll go tell the Pale that they're eating too much and to prepare to potentially drown again as a result. Let me know when you all decide you're ready." She trotted off, and eyes trailed after her. It was a few murms before Tybrake picked the conversation up where it had dropped off.

"We have as much reason to leave as anyone. This island obviously can't support us all, and no one is going to settle down here without eventually selecting a mate and... well, adding to our numbers. If any of the flock give you trouble, I'll help you sort them out."

Bala nodded, but he was still watching Brynne's departing form.

"That one is trouble," he growled.

"Something must be going on," Arias said. "She's not normally like that. Well, not quite as much, at least. Anyway, I had a thought. Is there any chance that a scout of yours can fly out toward the horizon, just to take a look? Considering this island is here, maybe we're closer to more land that we don't know about. It would do wonders for convincing the others to leave if there's something we can fly toward."

"I can definitely arrange to try that," Bala replied. "I'll let you know what we find as soon as I hear back."

The group slowly broke apart, with the meeting coming to a natural end. He watched Alissi and the other Strigigryph sharing anxious words, and he felt bad for them again. Would there ever be an end to these life or death decisions? Hadn't they deserved some peace and quiet by now? He sighed and loped down the beach, headed to check on Hlaena.

***

The spot Hlaena often rested at was quiet, save for the ever-present slapping of the waves. The mare hadn't changed position from the last time he'd checked on her, and was lying with her legs tucked underneath her body and her long neck snaking over the beach grass. Arias sidled next to her and nibbled at the hair in her forelock.

"Want me to bring you something besides this stringy grass to eat? There's some tastier looking plants near the trees where the Gryphons sleep at night."

Hlaena blew air from her nostrils, causing the sand mingling in the grass to scatter before becoming lost among the blades again. Her maroon eyes were fixed on some distant point on the horizon as she lazily blinked her half-closed eyelids.

"There's some really green, soft grass further inland I could bring you," Arias tried again, scanning across the ocean in case she actually did see something out there in the bright, sparkling water. There was nothing. He looked back at her and scrutinized her, worried. He couldn't be certain, but the crack in her horn seemed deeper than it had been when he'd last looked at it. He peered closer, but she flinched away.

"I can tell you don't feel well, so let me help," he insisted.

Hlaena's eyes finally broke away from the surf. "You can't."

"I can at least try. You're getting worse. There has to be some way to fix whatever is happening."

Hlaena went back to staring at the ocean. For a murm, he thought she wasn't going to respond anymore, but then she said, "I can feel my life source streaming away. Xio knew this would happen if I tried to use my magick to cleanse Naugi. But I couldn't let him try alone. None of us could. This is the consequence of that action, Arias. Brynne told me the prey here is depleting... When you leave with the other Gryphs, I can't come with you. I'm sorry I couldn't take you any further than here."

"You have nothing to apologize for," Arias said. "But you're coming with us when we leave."

"Arias—"

"I just got you back and you're all I have left, Hlaena. We'll carry you if we have to, but I'm sure there's a way to fix whatever is causing this. If you're getting worse, it means the answer isn't on this island. I'm hoping Bala's scouts find land nearby… but if they don't I'll fly off myself to look. We left a mainland, so there has to be another somewhere, right?"

Hlaena gave him a chiding look and snorted, but she didn't speak again. He lay down next to her and used his wing to shield her from the cool wind blowing off the ocean, closing his eyes as worry gnawed into him. He was already worried about how the rest of the Gryphs would react when they were told they inevitably needed to leave the island. If Bala's scouts didn't find land, it would have to be kept secret from the rest. And even if there was land nearby, he wasn't sure where to go first to find help for Hlaena. His knowledge of healing stopped at herbs, and even then it was nowhere near to being comprehensive.

The all-too-familiar weight of hard decisions pressed in on Arias, settling like a cloud in the sky, as if it belonged there in his mind. He could speak to the Ardeigryph to find out which time of the day air thermals were more likely to happen… that would be helpful. He'd also need to find a few Gryphs who would be willing to help him with Hlaena if necessary. Everyone would have time to eat and drink their fill before setting out, so that would help a little. But what of the Strigigryph? He couldn't very well force them to fly out to their deaths. Was there any way that they could survive the journey?

Arias was a spectator to the thoughts that flitted back and forth in his mind, taking up time and energy, but offering no respite. Night fell, and he watched Hlaena wince and mumble to herself in her sleep, the moonlight outlining how prominent her ribs shone through her coat. The mare had lost weight rapidly since coming to the island, and it made him all the more anxious to leave. He tucked his head under his wing, hoping that sleep would sneak in and steal his consciousness away, but it was too much to hope for. Soon dawn tinged the horizon, and he blinked with bleary eyes at the brightening pool of light, staring out until the padding of feet distracted him instead.

Frozen with one paw in the air, Brynne peeked at him from some distance away. She looked between him and Hlaena before asking, "How is she?"

"Not good."

"Is there anything that I can do to help? I know how much she meant to you growing up."

Arias shook his head. "If there is, I don't know and she won't tell me. But I'm going to find a way."

"I didn't know Alicorns could get sick, to be honest. It's a little disconcerting that even she isn't doing well in all of this."

Arias peered at Hlaena from beneath the veil of his wing. "I'm not sure if 'sick' is the right word for what's wrong with her. It seems like she's hurt herself somehow..."

Brynne flicked an ear. "We'll find a way to make her better. I came here to tell you that Bala has some good news for once. I didn't really want to bother you two, but we're all waiting for you in the same place we met yesterday."

"Alright," Arias said, standing carefully so as not to disturb Hlaena. "I could use some good news. Let's go."

***

The circle of Gryphs was in high spirits when Arias and Brynne joined them, and Arias allowed himself to feel cautiously optimistic. Bala, seemingly unable to wait until Arias was within normal earshot, roared, "Another mainland! And within flying distance, too! It'll be tough, but I think we should all be able to make it!"

It was a relief to hear. But it was easy to see a spattering of worry cross the faces of some of the Strigigryph. Alissi stood up, causing eyes to shift over to her.

"What exactly is considered within flying distance to your kind, Ardeigryph?" she asked Bala. "A single beat of your wings easily makes two of ours."

Bala stuttered, apologetic. "You're right. I'm sorry. I even sent one of my bigger scouts out to take a look… He flew for most of the day and part of the night, and he could see the land off in the distance. A great amount of land. There's a good breeze wafting off that much earth, enough to create a very useful air thermal for us to use if we arrive at the right time of day."

"If…" Alissi said, sharing uneasy glances with the other Strigigryph who'd come with her.

"We can leave on a strong updraft," Tybrake suggested. "If we're high enough up, we also don't have to worry about the sea serpent."

Alissi didn't speak, but her expression had a negative response etched into it. The following silence sucked the joviality out of the gathering.

"If we all left," Arias said slowly, "isn't it possible that the island could support a smaller number of Gryphs? Like Alissi and what's left of the Strigigryph flock?

Alissi's eyes sprung to life with hope as the others began to discuss the possibility. "We could ration what's left until the prey has a chance to rebound," she said.

"I know you don't eat from the sea, but maybe I can show you how to catch wrigglers, just in case," Tybrake added.

The Strigigryph all nodded gratefully, and the decision was made. They would all remain on the island, at least until another method that was safer for crossing the watery expanse was found. Arias secretly felt a small weight dissipate from his consciousness; a few more Gryphs would keep their lives after his mistakes back in Naugi's territory.

"That leaves one last matter," Bala announced.

"When shall we depart?"

"As soon as possible," Brynne said. "The sooner we leave, the sooner we can know what we're dealing with and establish a new territory."

Arias saw the wisdom in her words, but also noticed that she left out how the sooner everyone left, the sooner they could stop consuming prey that the Strigigryph would need to survive. She still seemed to hold a dislike for them, one that went far beyond the evils enforced by the Strigigryph's previous leader, Shadowbane. Arias certainly held no love for the Sire who, along with forcing an entire flock to follow his twisted ideals, had also tricked Arias himself into performing cannibalism alongside him. But while Arias's view of Shadowbane stopped with him, Brynne seemed to blame all of Strigigryph kind for his evils.

"If the thermals only blow off the land during the day, we should leave tonight so we can access them," Arias said.

"Ey," Bala and Tybrake both said at the same time, nodding.

It was time to fly into the unknown again.

***

The meeting of Gryphs dispersed with haste, and each headed to break the news to their flockmates. As Tybrake moved off to follow Bala, Arias hurried to catch up to him.

"Tybrake!" he called out, halting the tall

Ardeigryph.

"I'm hoping you'd be willing to help me. Hlaena isn't well, and I think I can find the answer to whatever is wrong with her is on that mainland. I can't leave her here. Would you be willing to carry her if it comes down to it?"

"Of course," Tybrake said without hesitation. "But wouldn't it be easier to leave her here with the Strigigryph, and bring help to her later? You seem to get on well with Alissi, I'm sure she wouldn't mind looking after her till then."

"I trust the Strigigryph, but this is different. I really don't know how much time she has left. I want to be with her."

"You know you can count on me," Tybrake said. "Just let me know what you need, and when."

"Thank you." Arias bowed his thanks, and Tybrake trotted to catch up with Bala and the others.

One thing less to do, Arias thought, then started as he heard a muffled, "Psst!"

He twisted his head to both sides, but there was no one around except himself. He couldn't see anywhere for anyone to hide anywhere, either. Was he going mad? He shook his head and prepared to hurry off after the others. Then he heard his name called out, somewhere from further down the beach, near an inconspicuous mound of seaweed undulating in the shallows. He approached with caution, the cape of feathers around his neck rising with anxiety.

Hiding among the green reeds was a long bill, held well aloft from the waves. A head broke the surface, and he recognized the face belonging to the beak immediately.

"Ratina!" Arias glanced around to ensure that they were alone. "You're alive!" he added, jubilant.

"That's one thing I've always been good at," Ratina said, mirthless but smug. "Is it clear to come out?" she asked, poking her head up a bit more.

"For now. But maybe we should go somewhere else, there's no cover here. Well, besides the seaweed you've somehow managed to use. That water is deeper than it looks."

"I've been hiding around this island ever since the flock arrived here. If you'll speak with me, I know just the place."

"Lead the way," Arias said, falling into the quick lope the Ardeigryph hen set out in. It wasn't a long way to the spot she'd mentioned, a dense little thicket that was lush with tangling vines, well overgrown and tucked away inland. With them lying among the plant life, even Arias's albino coat would be difficult to discern from afar.

"I heard everything," Ratina said, "but you know that my kind—understandably—have no love for me after the things I've done. They won't trust me, and I wouldn't ask them to. By all accounts, they'd be within their rights to hunt me down and end my life."

Arias grimaced. It was easy to see how her past crimes against the Ardeigryph flock would be seen as unforgivable by many of them. "What would you ask of me then, Ratina? I'm not trying to be callous; you've done nothing but help me, and I'd do anything to return the favor. But you can't expect me to keep an entire flock from tearing you apart after everything that's happened."

"I wouldn't expect you to, nor would I ask that of you either," Ratina replied. "All I ask is that you arrange a meeting between Alissi and me. She and the Strigigryph may accept me, and allow me to stay on this island with them. I've never done them any harm, and I think they'll be more accepting of what I did and why I did it. You know me, Quarnar. I know it may sound like the coward's way out, but my goal has always been to survive. I can do that here."

Arias blinked at the name he'd gone by when he'd lived in Shadowbane's flock. The events at Arborochre hadn't happened all that long ago. "I took my old name back," he said, distancing himself from the memory. "I go by Arias. And I'm not judging you for your decisions. I'll do what I can." In Arborochre, he'd seen the side of Ratina that had done terrible things in order to secure her own survival. Her flock, however, only saw a hen who had been willing to kill her own Sire to be accepted by a flock of invaders. His own credibility would be in doubt if he even so much as tried to change their minds regarding her actions. "How did you manage to get here without being caught by anyone on the flight over?" he asked.

Ratina laughed tartly. "It wasn't easy. I tried to catch your attention, but by the time I thought I'd finally caught your eye, others were starting to look a little too hard at me for how long I'd been staring at you. There was more than a little luck involved, and a whole lot of charcoal... which was, for better or worse, in abundant supply after Naugi's death."

Arias didn't like how everything in this conversation reminded him of the unsavory things he associated with Arborochre. "Why don't I go ahead and try to talk to Alissi? I have to be honest by saying that if she isn't receptive to the idea, my ability to help you might end there."

"That's fine," she said. "If I die, I die. It's probably what I deserve."

Arias stared at her for a long time. Then he arched into a steep bow, and the surprise on her face wasn't quickly hidden.

"I don't think I ever properly thanked you for everything you did for me back in Arborochre," he said. "You were the first to tip me off about

Shadowbane. If I hadn't taken things seriously as early as I did, I may have been killed before I ever had a chance to do anything. It's partly thanks to you that he's no longer around to continue doing terrible things to other Gryphs."

"You give me too much credit, but thank you. I thought helping you was one of my dumber decisions, but there's something likeable about you. You should head off now. I'll see you when you get back."

***

Arias wasn't surprised that Larin had already gone ahead of him and spent some time trading goodbyes with the Strigigryph. They'd been close during her time as a Convert in Arborochre, and there was no way she'd leave without farewells. In fact, Alissi was quick to remark on just how late he was in coming by to see her. His serious expression muted her jovial teasing, however, and her eyes grew a little bigger when he told her about Ratina's existence on the island. As Ratina herself had anticipated, she was sympathetic to her plight.

"The dear was just trying to protect herself," Alissi said. "She may not have gone about it in the proper way, but who could blame her at her age when those things happened? It seems that she's never had anyone she felt she could rely upon and trust. We may be different in appearance, but we have the same desires in life. Maybe she'll come to be more trusting if she stays with us."

Similar sentiments bubbled up from the other

Strigigryph who had known her. The slate blue Ardeigryph hen had been an easily recognizable feature in Shadowbane's flock during her time there.

"I'll go now to let her know," Arias said. "Maybe she can also help teach you guys to cast for wrigglers after Tybrake leaves with the rest of us."

"Send her to us; we've made this little strip of coastline here among the beachgrass ours. No one will come looking for her here, and if they do, there are plenty of hiding spots. With a little time, we'll have a decent shelter woven up in no time! It's almost nice, being here... the sand is familiar to us. Reminds us of our desert homeland!"

"I'm glad you're looking forward to your stay here," Arias said with a happy trill. "When I figure things out on the mainland, even if it's just to bring you news, I'll make sure I find a way to reach you."

"You're such a lovely little keythong!" Alissi bubbled. "I'm so pleased you made it out from under Shadowbane's rule. You freed us all. Oh! Come here!"

Arias flinched as the plump hen rushed forward in an unexpected embrace, her short wings wrapping around him. Then he laughed and returned the gesture. Looking into Alissi's bright, sparkling eyes, he felt more at ease with the decision to leave them on the island.

"Thank you, Alissi."

"No, dear! Thank you!" She hooted and bowed so low that the tips of her wings touched the ground. The other Strigigryph did the same. "Too many others were afraid to do what you did. I'm ashamed to say that I was among them." Her voice took on an uncharacteristic note of seriousness as she added, "Never undermine your own achievements, Arias. Because of what you've done, now you truly could be called Glorious One."

Arias let the words sink in, then nodded. "You're right, I'll try not to. I appreciate everything you've done for me, and for Larin and the others." It felt weird knowing that it might be the last time in a long while that he saw the affable Strigigryph hen.

"You know, it's kind of funny," Alissi continued with a wistful glance, "in a way, this has turned out to be our own little paradise. The one that Shadowbane promised us when we left the desert, but never delivered."

"I hope it turns out well for you here," Arias said. "I hope to see you before too long."

The Strigigryph all rose a cacophony of farewell hooting, and he took off back the way he'd come, glad that he had happy news to share with Ratina.

***

Ratina breathed a visible sigh of relief upon

hearing that Alissi would allow her to share the island with her and the other Strigigryph. She gave him a knowing look, and added, "You know, you hate the attention, but you'd actually make a great leader, Arias. You really are one already."

"Nope," he said quickly, "the other Gryphs are doing a great job of keeping order in the flock. I'm happy right where I am."

"I thought you might say that," she said, wagging her tongue at him. "Well, you never know where you'll end up in life—"

"That kind of thing isn't for me, Ratina. Never has been. It's for Gryphs like Brynne, or Sheba, or even Shadowbane, even though his ideals were horrible. Gryphs that are able to get others to listen to what they have to say."

"Are you blind and deaf?" she asked, incredulous. "Half the Gryphs here already see you that way, you know."

"Eh." He ruffled his feathers. "Not for me."

"Fine, whatever. Denial can't be good for you, though."

"Ratina—"

"I'm just picking at you a little," she said, her mood lifted by the news she could stay on the island. "Thanks, Arias… for helping me despite what I've done." She dipped her neck then, solemn. "May our paths cross under more favorable circumstances, white one."

Arias nodded, turning to leave. He was glad Ratina had kept the farewell short; Alissi had laid the parting on so thick that he'd almost felt *himself* on the verge of being overwhelmed with emotion. It was nice to have Gryphs he cared so much about and vice versa. It was hard to leave them behind.

***

The sun was high in the sky as the flock bustled about, making their preparations to depart. There was still an ambient fear of the sea serpent, but most seemed to accept that a death by starvation was far worse and much slower. A few scuffles broke out in the Pale over being forced to leave, with a few Gryphons suggesting that instead they could slay the Strigigryph and take their place on their island. The cruel proposal, along with any other uttered discontent in the Pale, was swiftly put to an end by Brynne. Most of the Ardeigryph were casting for a last meal before leaving, or resting on the beach with their long wings spread out under the sunlight, their gazes anxious despite their relaxed postures. Off in the distance, Tybrake was providing the Strigigryph with an advanced lesson in casting for wrigglers, but his attendees were clumsy in the water with their short statures and even shorter beaks. Their frustrations rose into the air in sharp whistles and hisses.

Arias nibbled at a stray feather on his neck, content that things were going at least as well as they had so far. He'd barely completed the thought before someone tackled him and tried to wrestle him to the ground, and he squawked in surprise before lashing out and resisting. With a hollow chuckle, his assailant tightened their grip, and he immediately knew who it was. He gave a tense laugh.

"I'm not ever complaining to you about being in my head too much again, Larin," he said. "I get your point; I promise I'm not overthinking things." The gryphoness leaped away, eyes twinkling, then waved her tail teasingly at him. He gave her an affectionate bunt of his head, and she returned the gesture, trilling. The language that she, along with the rest of the ex-Converts from Arborochre, communicated with was distinct from those of other Gryphs. It was comprised of a menagerie of clicks, whistles, hisses, and gestures that Arias was still learning. They lacked the ability to speak because Shadowbane had their tongues torn out as a requirement for joining his flock, with the alternative being death. It was just another in a long line of atrocities the Strigigryph Sire had committed during his reign over the defunct Arborochre flock.

"What do you think, Larin? Think another flight over the ocean will go alright for us?" Arias asked. The Gryphon hen puffed her chest out, flapping hard so that her wings snapped against the still air. Then she folded them and tilted her head toward him, clicking three times to direct the question back at him.

What about you?

"I don't think I'll ever be ready for that again,

if I'm honest, but I think it's best if I keep telling myself that I am. Maybe I'll believe it if I say it enough. Did you already eat? I can never bring myself to eat before something big happens... too nervous."

She gave him a concerned look, but her attention was drawn away by a rise of sudden hissing. Her pupils dilated into round, flat disks as she realized it was coming from a group of other ex-Converts—most of the flock had fallen into referring to them as Sentinels due to the way they were always watching things without making a sound—who were being antagonized by some of the Pale warriors. She gave him a fleeting, apologetic look, then dashed off to see what the conflict was about. He was about to follow but saw Brynne there, and it looked like the two hens were already sorting things out before they could escalate. He wanted to head over just in case things looked more peaceful than they really were, but he felt a nagging need to go see Hlaena. He watched for just a few murms more to be sure that things would be fine, then he turned and headed to find the Alicorn.

***

Hlaena was exactly where Arias had expected her to be. When he sat near her, she sent a pointed glance over in his direction, and he pricked his ears up, somehow finding the look to be accusatory.

It was.

"What?"

"Planning to have your Ardeigryph friend haul me off across the sea like a load of preymeat? At least he had the decency to let me know beforehand."

"I can't just leave you here to waste away," Arias said.

"Some things aren't within your control. You're young, but it's a lesson you should have learned by now after everything you've been through," she snapped.

Arias's expression darkened. "You have to know of some place or someone that can at least give us an idea of what's happening to you."

"The bad thing about hundreds of years of knowledge is that it doesn't always stay relevant," she said, her voice turning somber. "All the plants, creatures, even forms of magick, I've watched vanish over time can't help me now. I can't even detect magick anymore. Trying to do so hastens my demise. I can't help you, and you can't help me." She closed her eyes. "I thought it better that you leave me here so that you wouldn't have to witness my end."

"That's enough of that," Arias said, scowling. "We'll think of something."

Hlaena sighed, turning her sad maroon eyes to his. "You don't owe me anything, little one. It's alright."

Arias didn't reply. He didn't want to say that

he still *felt* like he did, regardless of anything she could ever say. He looked away so that she couldn't read it in his eyes. "Are you sure you don't want me to fetch you anything?" he asked, but she shook her head.

"I haven't had a taste for anything since I left Glendale. Everything I try to eat tastes like sand. Bland, tasteless sand that I can hardly bear to swallow."

Arias had assumed that most grass and plants tasted similar to each other, but he didn't ask any more questions, and Hlaena didn't speak. The silence stretched into the night, and they were only roused by the sound of Gryphs lining up along the beach. A few darted to and fro, some going to find a last drink of water before the long flight, while others sought out a particular Gryph they wanted to fly with. Tybrake trotted up with a couple of other huge Ardeigryph, and he gave Arias and Hlaena a questioning look.

"Ready to go?" he asked.

The sooner the better, but Arias figured it would be smart to at least partake of the spring water before setting out. "In a murm," he said. "I should probably drink some of that water."

Tybrake shrugged a narrow pair of shoulders. "Probably not a bad idea, I'll come along for a sip, too."

***

Arias hastened to join those congregating around the small pool of water located at the center of the island, but halted his approach as sharp sounds of dissent began to drift through the greenery. He gave Tybrake a look, but the Ardeigryph was already hastening to see what all the commotion was about. They got close enough to the spring to see a circle of Pale warriors bordering the water. Most were standing around doing nothing, while others were taking long, leisurely sips from the cool liquid, much to the chagrin of others waiting for their chance. Anyone who tried to approach received a swift pecking. Although there weren't many willing to try to hurry them along, it wasn't long before a single, feisty Gryphon hen pressed her way to the front of those waiting. She let out an acidic hiss and leaped onto one of the provocateurs, prompting cries and fluttering wings as Gryphs hurried to move themselves away from the combatants.

Arias and Tybrake both cut their way through the pandemonium, intent on stopping the violence, but before they could get even halfway there, a shadow split away from the frenzied crowd and inserted herself into the fray.

The two scufflers broke apart as they realized they were no longer alone in their battle, and that there was now a wary Larin in between them. The gryphoness who had started the scuffle lowered her head in submission, but the Pale warrior, a young Gryphon hen herself, stepped forward in challenge. She circled with deliberate steps, sizing Larin up, spurred on by the excited cries of others in her flock who were excited to see the fight. The rest of the Gryphs, who'd been hoping to snag a drink, fled to the outer reaches of the trees, far away enough that they couldn't get caught up in the battle, but close enough to watch the spectacle.

Larin didn't move, her stance showing a complete lack of intimidation. Her past was a mystery to most of the flock, including Arias, but her prowess in battle was not. The Pale hen either didn't care, didn't know, or thought she was better. Still, a battle was a battle, and it was the last thing anyone needed before a long trip. Arias snarled, and for the first time the rest of the Pale warriors seemed to notice him and Tybrake standing on the periphery. Two other Pale warriors—both of them young keythongs— separated themselves from the group, with crests and wings raised in challenge. The one facing Tybrake didn't seem too thrilled, but didn't back down, either. Arias twitched what was left of his tail in disbelief.

"Make another move, and the first action you'll see on the mainland is your exile," he said. "That goes for all of you." It wasn't an idle threat, and he heard a number of hateful sneers tear out of the group. He knew that many of the Gryphs who'd just fled wouldn't have any problem standing their ground when they were in the majority. The Pale threw Arias, Larin and Tybrake plenty of cutting gazes as they slowly disbanded, but none spoke. Arias drank from the watering hole as he watched them leave, eyes alert in case any of them decided to try anything. The gryphoness who'd started the fight flicked her ear as she watched them go.

"What do you think that was about?" she asked. "Thanks, by the way. That was ridiculous. I can't believe no one has put those overstuffed *tucas* into their place yet. They've been worse and worse as of late."

"The Pale *has* been acting out of line for quite a bit now," Arias agreed.

Larin's narrowed eyes showed her frustration, her talons digging into the sandy soil as she made a low grating sound deep in the back of her throat.

"They've been bothering the Ardeigryph, but this is honestly the first time I've seen them mess with a Gryphon," Tybrake said. "They tried it on me once, but I guess they weren't used to an Ardeigryph who doesn't back down." He stretched his enormous wings and gave them a quick snap, sending a rush of wind across the ground. "I keep telling my flockmates to stop giving in, but most don't listen. An Ardeigryph would rather run off to snack and sun himself for another day, than to fight and risk injury."

"I'll have to speak to Brynne about it," Arias said. "But, for now, we just need to worry about getting to the mainland. And you," he said, catching the attention of the young Gryphon hen, "it's admirable to do something about a problem, but maybe not so wise to do it against an entire flock. Things could've gone badly for you had no one been around to help you."

The gryphoness gave a sheepish nod, then lowered her head to drink. Arias, Larin, and Tybrake made their way back to the beach, where Hlaena remained exactly as she'd been left. The other two Ardeigryph Tybrake had brought along lounged nearby, but got to their feet when they saw everyone return.

"Nanchu is going to be flying with Bala and Lue," one of the big keythongs said to Tybrake.

"They'll take good care of her," the other added, and Tybrake nodded in agreement.

"That they will. She'll be happy to be flying with more familiar company, I'm sure. No offense to you two, of course," he added with a nod to Arias and Larin. They shrugged in response. Arias tried not to think about how scary it had been to almost lose her to the sea serpent. There had been far too many close calls recently. He reached down and gently nuzzled Hlaena.

"Ready to go?" he asked.

Her only answer was a disagreeable snort. She planted her hooves firmly and gave him an expectant look, and he leaned against her so she could gain her feet without scrambling. He couldn't get over how much thinner she had become in just the little while they'd been at the island.

"I could carry her in my talons the entire way," Tybrake said, "but I don't think that either of us would be too happy about the arrangement after a while."

"You could let her lie across your flank, maybe," one of the two other Ardeigryph keythongs suggested in a low, baritone rumble. Arias blinked at the strangers. They were giant, even by Ardeigryph standards.

"Mm, no, he'd never be able to get off the ground that way," the other said. "The Alicorn doesn't have talons or anything to hang on with."

Arias tilted his head. "What if one of you placed Hlaena on Tybrake's back after he's already airborne? It shouldn't interfere with his wings at all, so long as she doesn't move too much."

The Ardeigryph all considered it, then nodded in agreement. "If it doesn't work well enough, I'll just land right away again," Tybrake said. "Maybe you two can stay close for the first bit of flying, just in case anything goes wrong. Can't say that I've ever tried anything like this before!"

There was more nodding, and then all three Ardeigryph took to the sky, with Tybrake circling overhead while one of his companions dove down to snatch Hlaena up as carefully as he could. After the other keythong had her in his grasp, Tybrake levelled out his flight, gliding with as little movement as possible while the other keythong caught up to him. The implementation of Arias's idea seemed a lot trickier in action. Watching the Ardeigryph dangle Hlaena from his claws as he tried his best to line up squarely with

Tybrake's shoulders made Arias warble nervously. He and Larin flew up to get a closer look, but before they could reach the others, the keythong carrying Hlaena dropped her onto Tybrake's back, eliciting a whoop of excitement from all three Ardeigryph.

"Nice going!" Tybrake cheered, "I'm glad I chose you instead of Seale to do that! He couldn't spear a wriggler if it leapt up and impaled itself on his beak."

"Hey!"

As the Ardeigryph continued to toss well-meaning insults at one another, Arias let out a sigh of relief. "Comfortable enough?" he asked Hlaena when he got close enough to be heard.

"This is fine. Just feels a bit odd," she replied.

"You're going to have quite a time if you get tired of carrying her, Tybrake," one of his companions, the one named Seale, commented.

"Eh, I won't," Tybrake said. "She feels almost as light as a feather to me."

The group quieted as other Gryphs rose to join and follow them. Arias took one final look at the island they were leaving behind, the last bastion to the Strigigryph that had dared to leave their desert home so many seasons ago, and then turned forward to focus his energy on the trip ahead.

***

With the way that things had gone since Naugi's demise, Arias wouldn't have been surprised had a thunderstorm kicked up over the ocean, driving everyone down into the water to drown. Instead, the going was fairly pleasant. The wind wasn't chilly at all, and it guided them along with polite gusts in the direction of the mainland Bala's scout had seen earlier. Even the waves below weren't as monstrous as the ones had been on the way to the island. There was no sign of the sea serpent, but everyone flew high and fast anyway. It wasn't a chance worth taking.

Arias took the time to check on Hlaena often, and after a time he could tell she was starting to get a little annoyed with him. She spent most of the time dozing, her head and wings drooping as the salty air whipped at her mane. As Tybrake had predicted, he didn't have any trouble at all with carrying her.

Though much easier than the journey to the island, the trip was still challenging. Most of the Gryphons were gaping open-mouthed by the morning of the next day, but no one was in any danger of giving up and drowning. The sunlight brought an even warmer day than the last, heralding that either spring was already well underway, or winter was much milder in this region compared with the frigid season they'd experienced in their original territory.

Arias closed his eyes against the bright light glinting off the sea below, trying not to concentrate on how nice a long drink of cold, clear water would be. He hoped that the Gryphs who had been prevented from getting to the spring by the Pale had returned before leaving the island; he couldn't imagine what it would feel like to have started this flight already thirsty. The scout had said that the mainland was only a day and a night away. Arias had flown longer than that before, so he could definitely do this, contrary to what his fatigued wings were telling him. They'd flown all night; now all they needed was to conquer this day.

Most of the group was quiet as they flew. There were no scattered pockets of chatter, or even random calls from Gryphs communicating from different parts of the flock. Everyone, it seemed, had turned their brains off so that they could focus on getting across the distance. Maybe some of them didn't believe that Bala's scout had actually found land, and they were too anxious to see if there was truth to his words to speak about anything else.

The sun reached its height in the sky and then began its descent, its rays dimming to a pale orange. The dull outline of a huge mass of land materialized on the horizon not long after, prompting a hearty cheer from the group. Arias and Larin both looked at one another with relief and excitement, leaning in to catch the last updraft before dusk set in. Even Hlaena raised her head when she heard about the sighting of land, her ears pricked forward as she took her first look.

New land to start over on, with more than enough space for everyone... Arias only wished the Strigigryph had been able to see it with him. After everything they had been through, they especially deserved a new start. Still, he was sure that the island would serve them well.

**

The sun was just slipping below the horizon as the Gryphs angled their wings down to land on the pebble-and-driftwood-strewn coast. There were trees off in the distance, already green with spring, and the area hummed with the chirps, squeaks and grunts of other life. The potential presence of other predators kept the Gryphs on edge despite their numbers, and they decided to send a group out to look for a more protected area before bedding down. Larin was quick to volunteer with a few of her flockmates, and it didn't take long for them to find a nice cove that was protected on one side by the ocean, and surrounded by a high ridge on most of its perimeter. It was perfect.

After checking to see that everyone was safe and resting, Arias jumped at the opportunity to join Larin in some adventuring. Everyone willing to do a bit of poking around had the task of looking for water. It was a beautiful feeling to see that the area seemed not only hospitable, but quite conducive to a comfortable life. There were lots of signs that prey regularly wandered into the area, so water couldn't be too far off. The flora were mostly familiar, but here and there Arias caught sight of a new plant that he'd never seen before. He couldn't help but to wonder whether any of the mysterious plants could help Hlaena somehow.

Arias had never had to scout for water before. Left to his own devices, he probably would've wandered aimlessly, but luckily he had Larin around to point him in the right direction. It was evidently important to head downhill when one was looking for water, which made sense when he thought about it. The hen was also spending a considerable amount of time paying attention to the type of plants they were passing, and he only realized why when he saw they suddenly consisted of mostly reeds and other water-loving plants. Soon, they were standing at the edge of a small peat bog, its water tinted brownish with the leaf matter floating in it. Not caring, Arias and Larin slaked their thirst anyway. The water tasted earthy, but was just as refreshing as they'd hoped. They both lifted their ears as they heard approaching steps, then flattened them in dismay as they realized that two warriors from the Pale were approaching them. Arias tensed in anticipation of another altercation, but it didn't come. The warriors eyed him and Larin, spoke to one another in low voices, and then departed without addressing them. Arias sighed in relief.

"Let's head back," he started to say, but then his eyes trailed down further into the marsh, where a carpet of a particular plant was spreading its soft leaves upward and away from the moist earth. Silver spangle! It had been one of Hlaena's favorite foods when she'd lived in Glendale, and he was surprised to see it here. He figured it had stringent growing requirements, because he'd never seen it outside of Glendale until now. Flanked by Larin, he trotted over to the plant, and jumped as something rustled among the spangle. Larin took a closer look and hissed, but Arias tilted his head.

"Wait," he said, moving closer and squinting. "I've seen these before, I think. They're harmless. You can come out, we won't hurt you. Can you understand the common tongue?"

A tiny pair of fluttering wings appeared above the silver spangle, bearing a small creature that zipped up so that it was at eye level with Arias. It had luminous eyes and tiny hands and feet, as well as small pair of sharp horns that poked above its bright red hair. Those last two were... different. All of the ones Arias had seen around Glendale had been muted, earthen colors, but Arias was pretty sure that this had to be a Fae. It was hard to see them up close on account of how shy they were, but every now and then one was curious enough to stick around. Faes could detect magick, and he hoped that the fact this one was hanging around this silver spangle was a good sign. Maybe the plant had healing properties.

"There you are!" he said, watching the Fae alight neatly on a nearby leaf. It stared at Larin, who had traded her hiss for a low growl, and crossed its arms. Arias gave Larin a look.

"You're scaring it," he said. "Maybe it can help us if we give it a chance."

Larin rolled her eyes, but silenced herself.

"Can you talk?" Arias asked the Fae. It took a few murms to nod, and then giggled into its small hands as if it was shy. It kept its hands cupped over its mouth as it glanced up at him and said, "You... big!"

Arias chuckled. "Well, compared to you, yes, we are. Is this your home?"

The Fae nodded again, and Arias felt a bit hopeful as he asked, "Do you know of anyone who may be able to help my ailing friend? She's sick."

The Fae leaped in a huge bound, nodding with excitement. "Yes!" it said. "Yes, here... come!" It flew back into the air and started off into the forest, and Arias almost followed, but he stopped himself.

"Can you wait here for a bit? I hope that you don't mind, but I'd like to take some of this plant to my friend."

The Fae circled in a lazy spiral and landed on the leaf it had been on originally. It leaned back and moved its feet in little nonchalant kicks, not seeming to mind a wait.

"Thanks," Arias said. "It won't be too long." He turned to Larin, but she was already collecting a hearty beakful of the silver spangle, and he joined her to grab up as much as he could carry. All the while, the Fae watched them with intense interest. Evidently, it was easily entertained.

***

Upon returning to the cove, Arias was happy to see Hlaena perk up and begin eating a few nibbles of the silver spangle. After the first initial taste, she got to her feet and attacked the pile of soft herbs with huge munches, chewing furiously until nothing remained. She gave a happy whicker, seeming to be more herself than she'd been in a while. To Arias, it was just proof that there really was something magickal about the area. He couldn't wait to see what the Fae would show him.

"We'll bring you more later," Arias promised. "But first, I want to check something out."

Hlaena frowned. "Thank you both for bringing me food, but you should really be resting with the others."

"We will soon enough," Arias said. "Right after this."

Larin shot him a worried look and shook her head, and he raised his crest in disbelief.

"What? Why wouldn't you want to take a look? We didn't see anything to be worried about while we were out."

He tried to edge around her, but she sidestepped to block his path. She shook her head again, and Hlaena gave Arias an anxious look.

"Where are you trying to go?" she asked.

"It's nothing," Arias said. "I found a Fae that seems to know of someone that can help you. It was hiding in the silver spangle when we walked up."

"Fae can be helpful," Hlaena said slowly. "Why are you so worried, Larin?"

The hen growled, wriggling her ears and lashing her tail. She shook her head again. Many things were too difficult to explain without words, but sometimes the meaning was clear anyway.

"Maybe we should look for help elsewhere," Hlaena said. "If Larin is worried, it makes me worried, too. She's usually right."

Larin looked over at Arias, smug, and he sighed. "Fine. Maybe you're both right. Let's try to get some sleep, I guess. I'll bring you more silver spangle in the morning."

The trio all nestled in close to sleep, and Arias tried not to feel bad that they'd believed his lie. The murm they slipped off to sleep, which didn't take long after such a journey, Arias rose to his feet in one smooth movement and crept away. Even Larin didn't detect his departure. *Too tired from the flight*, he supposed. Burning to satisfy his curiosity, he backtracked his way to the peat bog.

CHAPTER THREE

The Fae had stayed put just as it had promised. It zoomed around in ecstatic loops upon seeing Arias return, covering its mouth as it giggled.

"Sorry for taking so long," Arias said. "Thanks for waiting."

The Fae nodded, then pointed into the forest. It flew at a pace he could keep up with at a brisk trot, and he was grateful that the creature gave off a luminous glow in the night. The trees above were interlocked into such tight clusters that almost no moonlight reached the ground. He didn't have to follow the Fae too far; soon they came to a round clearing where many other Faes were congregated. He'd never seen so many in one spot before, and they were all the same red color as the one he'd followed. They bathed the packed earth with the glow of their small bodies, and he wondered whether all Faes had secret areas where they lived like these ones did. He turned to ask the Fae who had guided him what they were supposed to do next, but it had already disappeared into the mass of other Faes who were now huddling and peering at the ground.

The feathers at the nape of Arias's neck raised on end. Something didn't feel right. It was a thought he didn't get to dwell on for too long, however. He felt a massive thumping from underground, followed by the earth itself peeling back. Two long, tapered, hairy legs somehow shot out from underneath the dirt. They groped in Arias's direction.

Arias cried out as he scrambled backwards, his speed intensifying as six more legs appeared and braced against the ground. The ground at the center of the clearing peeled back like a lid, revealing a gaping hole inhabited by a fanged creature with far too many eyes for comfort. It made a grab for him, its long legs tapping with muted thudding sounds as it moved. The fangs protruding from its mouth were like backwards claws, dripping with some sort of substance. Arias tore his eyes away from the monster and fled.

Fortunately, the monster itself was not very fast, but its lack of speed didn't help Arias for long. He could hear every single one of the Faes racing to catch up to him. One of them managed to pull up beside him—it may have been the one that guided him—and he half hoped that it would blurt out an explanation that the thing chasing him was in fact some form of terrifying healer. Instead, it caught his eye and opened a mouth that was home to thousands of tiny, needle-sharp teeth. At the same time, he felt a number of petite bites sting his pelt, accompanied by screeches of, "Left overs! Left overs!" from the Faes. Arias opened his wings, his fatigue forgotten, and flapped them to buffet the brunt of the Faes away, but the action seemed to anger their monstrous companion. It screeched, spitting a glinting web of something that landed just off-center from Arias. Whatever it was, it was clearly very sticky, because it had trapped a number of the Faes as it had flown through the air. They cried and shrieked, biting at it with their nightmarish teeth, and Arias threw himself sideways as he heard another glob of the stuff being launched from somewhere behind him. He skidded, tumbled, and was on his feet sprinting again without thinking twice.

What to do? Think! Instinct told Arias that there was safety in numbers, but some wiser part of himself overrode the thought that he'd be protected if he took shelter with the other Gryphs. He couldn't lead this eight-legged carnivore and its meat-eating posse of Faes back to them. His snapped to an upcoming clearing among the treetops, the first he'd seen since entering this dense area of forest. He spread his wings, and every Fae within reach of him seemed to sense his thoughts, because they all raced to settle on his face. He closed his eyes, screaming and tossing his head, as they tried to chew out his eyes, and then everything abruptly went intensely quiet, wet, and sticky, as something heavy landed on top of him.

With a jolt of panic, he realized that he'd been snared. Heavy footfalls announced the slow approach of the true danger he'd been fleeing from, and the Faes all seemed to know to give way to it. Their cries of "leftovers" made much more sense as Arias pieced together the sort of twisted relationship they must have with the large beast.

Arias was caught so securely that he couldn't even flex his talons. Taking a bite at the webbing proved to be a mistake. An acrid, salty taste invaded his senses, and he spat and gagged. So, this was it, then. He remembered Larin's smug expression when Hlaena had agreed with her before he'd left the cove, and he wished that he had just listened to them. What if they were next to fall victim to these creatures? The eight-legged beast's thumping footsteps drew closer, coupled with the moist sound of it twiddling its mandibles in anticipation, and Arias squeezed his eyes even more tightly shut. As he did so, however, something warm and flickering burst to life around him, and his lids sprang open in surprise. He was on fire. And not just any fire, but *purple* fire.

"I'd be very still if I were you," a musical voice called out from somewhere close by. "Wouldn't want to accidentally burn more than web, if I can help it."

The Faes and their monstrous ward froze at the sight, then drew away as the flame raced across the ground toward them. The frightened chattering of the Faes faded into the distance, and Arias felt primal fear course through his heart as he returned to the fact he was on fire… but somehow he wasn't being burned alive. The voice had said not to move, but flying for his life sounded like a decent idea once again. He took a deep, steadying breath.

The flames died down all at once, then gathered together and manifested into a form not too different from Arias's own. Piercing eyes gazed down at him from the flames that had collected next to him, complete with huge wings and a spiked crest. With a hiss, the flames extinguished, leaving a brilliant creature with radiant red and gold plumage, eyes that shone like jewels, and a set of powerful talons. Its tail was so long that the elegant quills reached well past the distance between them, twisting around Arias in a delicate curl.

"It's been a long time since I've seen one like you in this region," it said.

Arias blinked. "I've never seen one like you," he replied in awe. He felt a general sense of amusement emanate from the creature, and he jumped away at the oddity of it, prompting an audible chuckle from his savior.

"We are somewhat kin, you and me. There was a time when the Phoenix and the Gryphon shared the same territory. As for Anansi, the beast who tried to eat you… well, his kinship is only with the Pixies and his stomach."

Arias glanced into the darkness, where tiny pricks of light suggested that he and the Phoenix were still being watched with interest. "I thought they were Faes," he said, grimacing.

"Definitely not," the Phoenix said. "From the looks of you, they got in a couple of good nibbles, though. You must taste pretty good for them still to be hanging around."

"I've never heard of anything called a Phoenix before. Thank you for saving me. I wish I had something to offer you."

"I don't need much these days."

Arias looked one way, then the other. "Where did the fire go?" he asked.

"Ah. That was just me making my grand entrance. You made quite a bit of noise trying to escape. You're lucky that I'm both nosy and have a sense of moral justice." With a brilliant flash of light, an inferno tore across the ground, engulfing Arias in the purple fire once more. He resisted the urge to cry out, though the flame was so bright, he had to close his eyes against it.

"We Phoenix *are* fire," the dancing flames said. "I'm usually pretty good natured. But when I want to, I can bite pretty hard."

The fire singed the tip of one of Arias's wings, and he yelped and swatted at them; they vanished in response and reformed. The Phoenix reappeared in their midst, and Arias watched him in wonder as he sat and preened at a few feathers in the same way that Arias would preen himself.

"Do you have a name?" he asked. "And how do you do that?"

The Phoenix tilted his head. "My name…? It's been a while since I've been asked that. Uhh… a few hundred years ago I went by Aaga. You can call me that. And how do I do what, exactly?"

"Turn into fire. Is it something you learned? Or is it magick?"

Aaga cocked his head one way, then the other. "Well, I've always been able to do this. My kind are as old as time itself. Our very lives begin and end with flame; I've never really known anything different. I'm surprised you know what magick is, Gryphon! Anyway… I was very close to a nice nap when you drew my attention with all that screaming. Travelling across a whole region is hard work, you know. If you ever get the chance to become a guardian, I'd advise you not to. All these creatures constantly asking for your advice gets old after a century or three. It's why I keep to myself these days." He winked. "They can't ask for anything if they can't find me."

With that, he disappeared into a swath of fire, then slowly dwindled down to the size of a single ember. "Farewell!" he said.

"Wait!" Arias called out, prompting the ember to grow a little bigger.

"Yes?"

"Uhh... I know you said you hate to be asked for help all the time, but I was wondering if you knew of something or someone who can heal my friend. She's an Alicorn."

The Phoenix reformed. "An Alicorn, you say?"

A general wave of interest washed over Arias, and he nodded. "Her name is Hlaena."

"I haven't seen an Alicorn in forever! And forever is a long time, even by Phoenix standards! Wait... why would a healer need a healer? How do you know an Alicorn, anyway?"

It was becoming strangely difficult to listen to Aaga's words. Arias shook his head, and refocused his attention. "Well, it would be a long story to answer all of those questions. But I can if you want—"

"It doesn't matter," Aaga interjected, sending a sensation of dismissal across to Arias. "Believe it or not, I've never seen a real Alicorn before. I've seen Pegasi, but they just lack the same regality Alicorns are said to have. You know what I mean? Where is this 'Hlaena?' I'd like to see her. There may be someone who can help you far, far north of here, but I don't know if they're still around or not. I haven't bothered to check in a long while. Now, let's go see this Alicorn! You should probably head to somewhere safe anyways… I mean, you know that Pixie bites are venomous, don't you?"

"What?"

"We'd better hurry if you're going to get out of range of Anansi and the Pixies. I may save you from being eaten alive, but I'm not going to carry you. I'll keep them from following you; that sounds fair. I get to see an Alicorn, you get to not be eaten alive. Deal? Deal."

Arias watched the mass of Pixies twinkling in the distance, aware of a creeping numbness that was beginning at the nape of his neck. He started to run in the direction he'd originally come from, but stumbled so much that he had to settle for a speedy trot. Whenever he glanced over his shoulder, he noted that Aaga was following as a bright ember.

Anansi and the Pixies didn't follow.

***

By the time Arias made it back to the peat bog, his trot had devolved into a limping hop. Those Pixie bites were no joke. Aaga hadn't said anything since they'd set off, and Arias was too tired to bother with unnecessary conversation anyway, which left him with plenty of time to think about how stupid his journey past the peat bog had been. He'd nearly been eaten by a giant eight-legged beast and was now covered in tiny stinging bites, but at least he was alive, he supposed. And if he thought he felt stupid now, he could only imagine how he'd feel once Larin and Hlaena realized what he'd done.

Dumb, dumb, dumb.

He sneaked as well as he could to the outskirts of the cove where he knew there wouldn't be quite as many Gryphs present, hoping not to be noticed despite his glowing Phoenix companion. Whoever was posted as guard was doing a terrible job, because he succeeded in escaping notice, and collapsed with a grateful sigh into a tuft of overgrown grass.

"You made it!" Aaga said, his ember growing and shrinking with emphasis. "Look how many of you there are! I didn't know you guys mixed with Ardeigryph. The Gryphons I used to know were very exclusive. Now then, you promised me an Alicorn! Where is she?"

"We had... Strigigryph, too," Arias said, struggling to formulate words. When did thinking become harder than speaking? Sleep sounded amazing.

"Hey, not before you point out the Alicorn!" Aaga chastised. "I can still burn you alive, you know."

Arias let his eyes drift over to where Hlaena and Larin had last been sleeping. "There," he said. "The cove..."

Aaga's spark shot off into the darkness to investigate. He returned just as Arias was closing his eyes.

"What an exquisite creature!" he gushed, circling around. "Magnificent!" His spark stopped. "You know, I just remembered something! The group north of here that I mentioned could maybe help you with that nasty crack forming in her horn. They're called—"

Arias clawed at his consciousness to stay awake. What was that last word that Aaga had said?

Kirin. That's what he'd said. "They're called Kirin." It was the last thing he heard.

***

Waking up was a difficult process. Not because Arias wasn't ready to wake up, but more because he couldn't quite open his eyes and access his motor skills. The Pixie bites burned like ten thousand stings. And that incessant jabbing sensation... what was that? It took an enormous effort, but he forced one eye open a sliver. "Mmm," he groaned.

A dark blur faded into view. It pecked at him again.

"Ow," he mumbled. The jabbing sensation stopped, and he closed his eye again to slip back to sleep. He felt a hard yank at his crest.

"Ow! Stop, stop, I'm up." He peeled his eyes open and peered up, waiting for his vision to stabilize. Larin, Lue and Tybrake all stared down at him with worried expressions.

"What in the brine happened to you?"

Tybrake asked, standing back a safe distance. "Come down with some sort of pox, or what?"

"You look like you got into a fight with a thorn bush," Lue added, peering down her long bill at the myriad of nibbles peppering his body.

"I'm fine," Arias said, to the immediate disbelief of everyone surrounding him.

Larin narrowed her eyes and hissed.

"Yeah, I'm sorry. I shouldn't have gone out. You and Hlaena were right." Arias arranged his feet to stand and hoped his legs would comply, however unwillingly, with bearing his weight. They trembled dangerously as he stood, and he lurched sideways before he could catch himself. Larin rushed forward to break his fall, and he decided to stay where he was for a while.

Larin clicked at him, cross.

"They're Pixie bites. They are their parting gift to me since I left before the horrifying monster they live with could eat me."

Larin gave an exasperated huff, and Tybrake shook his head.

"Wait," he said. "What? I haven't seen any Pixies around. Where did you find enough Pixies to do *that* to you?"

"There's a peat bog that Larin and I found not too far from here, and there was a Pixie there that claimed it knew someone who could help Hlaena. I thought it was a Fae, and Larin told me not to follow it, but I had to know. Well, I learned that Pixies aren't the only thing out here that we need to be careful of. There's a huge, predatory thing named Anansi that lives a little way past the peat bog. It almost succeeded in eating me, and if it weren't for Aaga the Phoenix, I wouldn't be here right now. Everyone needs to be aware that it isn't safe to go near that place."

"I'll be sure to tell everyone," Tybrake said, incredulous. "Are you sure you're alright?"

"I'll be fine," Arias replied. He supposed that he felt as well as one could possibly feel after being attacked by Pixies, running for his life, getting captured in a sticky substance, and then being set aflame with magick fire. "Where's Hlaena?" he asked.

"Still asleep," Lue said. "Also, there's something that you should probably know... a gryphoness challenged Brynne last night. She ended up getting ousted out of her position as Matriarch of the Pale. Some hen named Hilda is leading them now."

"What! When?" Arias asked, incredulous.

"Late last night," Tybrake said. "They were a clawing, snarling whirlwind that woke everyone out of a dead sleep. Brynne put up a good fight, but that other hen..."

Larin clicked in sad agreement.

"Is Brynne okay?" Arias asked, finding his legs more successfully this time.

"I think her pride is hurt more than anything," Lue said. "No one has seen her since then. I'm sure she'll be alright."

"Can we really say that, considering how aggressively the rest of the Pale has been acting as of late?" Arias asked. The other three shuffled with unease, and then Lue said,

"They haven't really done anything alarming since then. But we've still been watching them just in case."

"Fair enough." Arias knew that if Brynne didn't want to be found, she wouldn't be. He wondered what sort of Gryphon this 'Hilda' must be to have bested a hen like Brynne. The idea of anyone gaining victory over the orange warrior seemed surreal. He took a few experimental steps and, feeling in no danger of collapsing, said, "I know it sounds crazy after what happened last night, but I promised Hlaena I'd bring her some more silver spangle this morning. Will you guys go with me to get some? If we see any Pixies around, we can turn back."

"Maybe we'll go get the plant," Tybrake said slowly, "and you can stay here and rest."

"Yeah," Lue added, "you look pretty scrappy. What does the plant look like?"

Larin gave a small hop and pointed to herself with her tail, and Arias said, "Yeah, Larin can show you. I guess that does sound better. But be careful. I don't know if the Pixies will be around."

"We will," Lue said, heading off with Larin and Tybrake in tow. Arias picked his way deeper into the cove to lay down next to Hlaena. More sleep didn't sound too bad.

It wasn't hard to find.

***

Hlaena was busy chomping her way through an absolute mountain of silver spangle when Arias awoke. She had her eyes closed, muzzle pushed deep into the pile of greenery, jaws working from side to side as she pulled the leaves into her mouth. She flicked an ear his way when she heard him stirring.

"I thought I'd never taste silver spangle again," she said after swallowing a wad of the stuff. "Thank you for finding it. I already thanked your friends for bringing more back for me." She took another huge bite.

"Did you see what happened to Brynne?" he asked, and she shook her head.

"I didn't even hear it. I was sleeping too hard. I've never slept so much in my life… I haven't been awake much longer than you. What happened?"

"Some gryphoness named Hilda challenged her for leadership and won. I knew there'd been some unrest in the Pale lately, and I meant to talk to Brynne about it before it got too bad, but I didn't think it would ever actually amount to anything. I should've asked her about it sooner."

Hlaena stopped chewing and trained her huge, maroon eyes on him. "It's possible the outcome would've been the same, Arias."

"Maybe." He waved his nub of tail. "I'm glad to see you're eating again, though. Are you feeling better?"

"Much better than I felt back on the island, at least. This silver spangle doesn't taste like sand, either. There must be more mana here than there was there..." she trailed off, squinting. "Come closer, Arias."

"Why?"

"You didn't head off into the darkness after you promised Larin and I you wouldn't, did you?"

He stiffened. So the others hadn't told her. "Well, yeah. But it's alright. Look, the bites are already starting to heal. They don't even really hurt anymore."

Hlaena flicked her ears. "Are those Pixie bites?"

"Yeah, but—"

"We need to leave," Hlaena said, tail swishing anxiously. "Right now."

"Why? What's going on?"

"Pixies track their prey, Arias. If not immediately, then the next night. And it's already a little too late in the day to wonder when they might start."

Arias's eyes darted to the light of early evening that was already threatening the sky. "I'll let everyone know right away," he said, dashing off.

The time of day meant that most Gryphs would be gathered in preparation to sleep for the night, and he hoped it also meant that his announcement would be easier to get out. It ended up being much less challenging than he could ever have anticipated. All he had to do was to mention "meat-eating Pixies" and "giant killer beast" in the same sentence, to garner the attention of almost everyone present. It was just as well. As everyone took to the air, he noticed a few specks of red dotted behind leaves and inside dark crevices… but it could have just been his imagination.

***

After putting some distance between them and the threat of being devoured by Anansi and the Pixies, the Gryphs relaxed their pace. Some chose to remain sky bound, but the great majority trekked along by claw, getting a feel for the land. Arias walked next to Hlaena, happy that, while she was nowhere near first in the group, she was keeping up well enough to be far from dead last.

"Hlaena, have you ever heard of a Phoenix

before?"

She tilted her head a bit to the side as she thought. After a brief pause, she said, "No, actually. Why?"

"One named Aaga saved me from the Pixies. He mentioned that there's a group of something called Kirin, and that maybe they can help you."

"Kirin? I've never heard of them before, either. Then again, I've never left the mainland in all my years of living, until now. Still... I'm not sure I'd trust anything anyone says in this strange land just yet."

"I trust him. He helped me. And it's better than nothing, isn't it?"

"I suppose it can't hurt to look."

Happy that she'd at least agreed to checking the claim, Arias added, "He also said that there are creatures that look like you called Pegasi."

Hlaena snorted. "Now, I *do* know what those are. And I think I can go the rest of my life without meeting another herd of them."

Arias waited, hoping that she'd tell a story, but she drifted back into silence. He wondered who was leading the group from further up ahead; they were headed north more or less, but he supposed the direction really didn't matter much to most of the flock. They would travel until they found another suitable spot for an eyrie, or at least a good place to settle down.

When the group came to a valley of immense proportions, morning had come. Everyone started to scout for water again; and they found it, in the form of a great lake that stretched all the way out to the edge of the valley. The body of water was so large that it reminded Arias of the sea. It must have reminded the Ardeigryph of it, too, because they took no time at all to begin flying over and casting for wrigglers. The Gryphons took their cue and headed off into the surrounding forest to explore and hunt, and Arias decided to get a drink of water before looking around a bit more. He found a number of curious objects strewn around the shore: there were rocks with bits of reed tied to them, lengths of aquatic grass that were wrapped around driftwood, and other mysterious configurations, all stranded far above the tide line.

Gulping water, still eyeing the strange items, it took Arias a while to realize that he was also being watched from deeper underwater. The creature was large enough that he took a hurried leap backwards, crest raised in alarm. It didn't move any closer. The hair on its head undulated with the movement of the water, and its dark eyes, set in a flat face, peered at him with an intensity that made him take yet another few steps back. It had a streamlined body, smooth-looking and yet covered in tiny scales that sparkled in the light. The lower part of its body was like that of a wriggler, covered in larger scales of an amber color, and ended in a sharp, forked tail fin. Arias almost thought that the creature had wings, but as it swam a little closer, he could see that they were an additional set of fins, ones that fanned out from its shoulders as it poked his head above the surface. It raised an arm above the water and seemed to beckon to him with webbed fingers, but he didn't trust it. Predation and curiosity weren't so far away from one another, after all. He stared back at it, however, thinking that it seemed as inquisitive about him as he was of it. He was still secretly grateful for the land separating them, however. He probably would have stared at it for a lot longer had he not heard,

"Hey. Arias, right? I'm Hilda."

Arias wheeled around to find the gryphoness that had beaten Brynne in a duel. She was a rather plain looking hen, flaxen in color with dark speckles across her face, and she had a strong build and determined eyes. Arias was immediately on his guard upon hearing her name, but she appeared to have come alone and was sitting a respectful distance away from him. She eyed him with disinterest, as if he both wasn't a threat and wasn't much to look at.

"See something in there?" she asked with a sense of interest that bordered on the sarcastic. If Arias already didn't like her before, he figured his opinion of her was no longer in danger of dragging any lower.

"What do you want, Hilda?" he asked.

"I'm just letting you know that I'm not here to make enemies, that's all," she said. "I see that many Gryphs here seem to respect you for whatever reason, and I have no plan to deviate from that courtesy. Since we're pretty equally matched as far as numbers go, maybe we'd better start negotiations now."

Arias lashed his stubby tail, and for once was glad that it was too short to express his emotions openly. "We have double your numbers," he said. "And what negotiations are you talking about?"

"Oh, you're counting the Ardeigryph?" she laughed. "Sorry, they just don't seem to be much in the way of fighting, so I didn't add them in. Anyway…" she gestured in a wide arc with her tail. "Negotiate when it comes to this land, obviously. You seem like the diplomatic type, so why don't we split up our territories now? No fighting, no bloodshed… sounds pretty good, doesn't it? The Pale will take the lake area, and you and yours can have your choice of any of the surrounding area."

Arias laughed before he could stop himself. "Assuming I'd agree to this ludicrous allotment— and I won't be agreeing to anything without the input of the others anyway—why do you think you get first pick? Like it or not, we all came here as one flock, and we're going to keep it that way when we decide on territory. If you don't like it, you're free to leave."

Hilda's eyes flashed, but her words came out in a purr. "The Pale doesn't respect cowards, and thus we don't see the Ardeigryph as part of anything. Maybe Tybrake, but even then… he's still one of them and stands with them. If you had an Alicorn that wasn't broken, maybe I'd be more inclined to take you seriously. As things are, I'm trying to be reasonable with you. If you don't agree… well, we can always settle things the ancestral way."

Arias felt the fur along his back beginning to bristle. "I'll be reasonable with you as well, then, in telling you that this conversation is over."

Hilda hissed, lowering on her forequarters as if to pounce, but sneered and kicked dirt in his general direction instead. Perhaps she realized that he outweighed her by a good amount, or maybe the story of his fight against Shadowbane had reached her at some point. He couldn't guarantee that he could do it again, or to any Gryph he chose, but it had certainly bolstered his reputation as a fighter in the flock. He watched Hilda saunter off, then after a few murms, he glanced down into the waves again.

The strange creature had vanished.

CHAPTER FOUR

Arias couldn't find Larin, Tybrake, Bala, Brynne, or even Lue. Hlaena was resting after the long trip over to the lake, and he didn't want to bother her. He decided to save his worries until they could be addressed properly... and for the murm, Hilda and the Pale were behaving.

That night, Arias watched as Bala and all the other Ardeigryph gathered around the lake. The silence was eerie as their tall forms paced up and down the shore, long necks bowed as they rustled their wings in unison. With each pass, a few darted out of formation and took a sip from the water, and then they resumed the solemn processional. He'd never seen anything like it.

"What are they doing?" he asked Hlaena, who was watching nearby him.

"Honoring their dead," the mare replied.

No one disturbed the sacred rite. Arias didn't

ask for further explanation of the event. He could just make out Tybrake near the front of the group, close to where Bala must have been. The Ardeigryph marched around the lake until the light of day touched the sky, and then, with a cacophony of calling, they all rose into the air and flew off into the east. By the time the sun fully crested the horizon, the lake was mostly serene again. Their long homage to the fallen complete at last, the seafaring Ardeigryph returned to the valley, content that they had carried the souls of their comrades up to the highest realm of the afterlife.

***

Arias crept through underbrush, looking for any signs of prey. He hadn't eaten since leaving the island, and he suddenly missed having communal food. There didn't seem to be anything nearby worth tracking and, by the end of his hunt, all he'd captured were two longear. They were enough to stave off his hunger, and better than nothing, but it didn't help that they were quite scrawny after the winter.

Returning to the flock, Arias found Tybrake and Lue side by side, fast asleep. He hadn't really noticed at the time how close the two had become over the last few moons, but the two seemed inseparable these days. He also realized he hadn't seen Larin since they'd arrived in the valley, which was worrisome. He tried to tell himself that Larin was quite capable of looking after herself—much better than he was at taking care of himself, for sure—but it still nagged him that he hadn't at least heard from her. He asked a few nearby Gryphs if they'd seen her, and received only head shakes. Even the other Sentinels hadn't seen her, and a few indicated similar levels of anxiety over her disappearance. Worry flared in his gut as he took off to look for her in earnest, beginning at the lake.

Arias had almost forgotten about the strange half-wriggler creature he'd seen in the waters there, but now it jumped out of the water the murm he drew near, gesturing wildly. He froze, startled, and then it pointed. Following the direction indicated, he made out a white blur down the shoreline. He squinted harder, cursing the dazzle of the sparkles dancing on the waves, until he realized it was Hlaena. And circling her was a creature of some sort. It slowly backed into the depths, and without another murm's hesitation, Hlaena splashed after it, disappearing under the deep water.

"Hlaena!" Arias yelled, flying above the dark depths of the lake. There wasn't even a ripple to suggest that there had just been two creatures in the shallows mere murms before. He called out again, and a trickle of movement attracted his attention; something was writhing below the reeds, tangled and fluid, accented by flashes of white. Arias took a deep breath. He had swum plenty of times before, but diving was an entirely different experience, and one he'd never had any interest in. He tucked his wings to his sides and dove in.

***

Even lit by the sunshine above, the water in the lake had a greenish pallor to it. The bottom was indiscernible, only a drop off into a black

80

abyss. Arias trained his eyes on the half-wriggler creature who was trying to wrest Hlaena free from the hideous monstrosity that had fastened its hold on her. The beast had an equine shape, but with hazy white eyes, a mane and tail made of tattered reeds, and a face that was skeletal and half rotted away. Hlaena didn't seem to be aware that she was being pulled in two different directions. Her eyes were closed as if she were asleep and totally unbothered.

The half-wriggler gave Arias a pleading look, and he hurried to help. He was clumsy underwater, however, and couldn't put any strength into helping to pull Hlaena to safety. Instead, he swam over and bit deep into the bony neck of his new enemy. The foulest taste he'd ever tasted filled his mouth and drove him to retch but, being underwater and hungering for oxygen as he was, he resisted the urge. His action was successful though. The hideous creature let go of Hlaena—and grabbed onto him, instead.

The light of the surface dwindled to nothing. All Arias was conscious of was a reed-like tail wrapped around him, and two white eyes that glowed despite the surrounding dark. The more he stared into those eyes, the more accepting he was of being in the depths. Exhaling the rest of the air he had in his lungs felt like a welcome relief for some reason. He couldn't see much past the eyes of the creature, but he was aware that what little else he could see was blurring. Fantastic images danced through his mind— images of a summer paradise, green and lush and warm. Larin was running toward him in happy bounds, and he settled into the bliss. Was this what it meant to drown? If so, it wasn't so bad. It meant he could rest here forever.

A rippling sound cut through the water, and Arias felt a pair of talons wrap around his chest, dragging at him. The beast with the white eyes blinked, and its hiss cut through the water as clearly as if it had made the sound on land. It opened its fetid mouth to take a bite at whatever new entity had joined it in the depths. However, it received a swift jousting from a long bill in response. Squealing, it slackened its grasp on Arias. The darkness gave way to its former greenish hue, and Arias was aware of two great, feathered wings flapping on either side of him, propelling him and his savior gracefully upward with sweeping strides. When they finally broke the surface, Arias gulped air as if he would never have a chance to breathe it again. Lue dragged him the rest of the distance to the shore, and then a few lengths further, giving the edge of the lake a paranoid clearance.

"That was a lot creepier than diving in the ocean," she said, shaking water from her feathers. "What were those things? And Hlaena," she said, turning to stare at the mare, "why in the brine did you go into the lake?"

Hlaena lay trembling on the shore, her sodden ears drooping. "I didn't—I mean, I don't remember going in after it. It looked so inviting when I saw it on the shore."

"Inviting?" Lue exclaimed. "How could

anything about that thing have looked inviting? I barely saw Arias dive under. You're lucky that wriggler-looking thing dragged you out, Hlaena. I could only choose one of you to save."

The mare drooped her ears further. "I should've known it was dark magick. I can't see anything in the ether anymore... it looked like another Alicorn when I first saw it."

The trio jumped as they saw movement in the lake again. It was the half-wriggler, though, swimming into the shallows to gesture again. It held something up, waving, and this time Arias eased closer to see what it was, cocking his head at the ring of shells it extended to him.

"Are you giving it to me?" he asked. The creature held the shells up higher, insistent. Lue warbled in warning.

"Maybe it's not such a good idea to—"

Arias shrieked as the half-wriggler grabbed him by the neck and shoved the seashells over his head, yelling, "Stop making this so hard! Can you hear me?"

The voice was distinctly female. He paused. "Is that you? You can talk?"

"Finally!" The half-wriggler fell dramatically back into the water, floating on her back. "Yes! Hello, strange creature! My name is Naia, and I'm a Mermaid! I'm guessing you've never seen one of us before, and you wouldn't have, either, had I not been placed in this stupid lake! Anyway, what are you? I'm guessing those are your friends?"

Arias turned to see where Lue and Hlaena were watching the exchange with curiosity. "Yes, they're my friends. My name is Arias, I'm a Gryphon. Thank you for your help."

"My pleasure!" Naia said. "You really should be careful of the Kelpie. This lake may be huge, but I've spent enough time here to be tired of sharing the water with that disgusting thing. It isn't interested in other aquatic creatures, but it'll take whatever it can get from the land. It really wanted your friend with the horn, more than anything I've ever seen it want before. I think your long-necked companion surprised it, though. Nice fly-swimming, by the way!" she called to Lue.

Lue cocked her head. "Umm, Arias? How can you understand that thing?"

"Those shells it placed around his neck must have special properties," Hlaena murmured. She added a tentative, "Be careful, Arias."

He nodded and turned back to the Mermaid. "You said you were placed here? Why?"

Naia lowered her mouth below water and blew bubbles. "I don't really want to talk about it, but it's a punishment. An unfair one. I can't leave this lake, and I have to bear witness to the terrible way the Kelpie steals the essence from every land creature that wanders too near to the lake. And there's no one to talk to! That necklace you're wearing is a joke, I've tried convincing a few of the woodland creatures to wear it, but they all either ran or tried to eat me. I've tried to leave this cursed place so many times. None of my plans ever work." She pointed to the menagerie of contraptions scattering the shore. "I figured I could hook one of the lower branches of one of the trees up there, and—I don't know—hoist myself up high enough to make out which direction the ocean is. We Mermaids can't be out of the water too long," she said, stroking her neck. "Gills and all. It doesn't matter anyway, I never got that far." She swam in a circle, splashing the water with her tail. "I'm okay with being straight forward, you know. I only helped you because you looked like you could maybe help *me*."

"You want to be taken back to the ocean, which is way further than you probably think," Arias said.

Naia nodded eagerly.

"Wait a murm," Arias said. "How will you go back if you were brought here as a punishment? Won't whoever imprisoned you here just bring you back?"

"I'll be fine. There was a huge uproar over me being brought here. I know a few of the Mer who will keep me safe."

"Well, you did help us in a big way," Arias said. "There isn't much water along the way, though, so are you sure you'll be alright?"

"I'll make it work!" Naia said, eyes glowing with excitement. "You promise you'll help me, though? You're not going to leave me here, are you?"

"I won't leave. But someone else may be a better choice to take you that far. I could probably find an Ardeigryph willing to do it."

"A what?"

Arias nodded toward Lue, who was still watching from the shore. Naia made a face.

"Not to be rude, but I've been watching those things snap creatures out of this lake to eat for a while now, and..." She held up her scaled tail and splayed the fin. "I'm not saying I don't trust them, but I'm not exactly in love with the idea, either."

"I see. All right, I guess."

"Okay, I'll be right back! I can't wait to leave this bland freshwater behind! Ocean, here I come!" She bared her teeth—which Arias had never seen before as a gesture of happiness, and found intimidating as her teeth were all quite sharp—and then dived underwater with a small splash. Arias returned to Hlaena and Lue.

From the murm Arias started explaining what he was planning to do, Hlaena and Lue were against it.

"What if she's working with the Kelpie and this is some sort of trap?" Lue asked. "You can never be too careful in a new territory."

"She saved both Hlaena and me. I really don't think it's a trap. I wouldn't ever have known what happened to Hlaena had she not gotten my attention. Besides, it's only a day there and back." His eyes darkened with worry. "Have either of you seen Larin?"

The two paused. "Now that you mention it," Hlaena said, "I haven't seen her since we got here. I assumed she was off with her Sentinels, exploring."

"She would never have gone for this long without letting at least Arias know," Lue said. "I'll go look for her right away. I'm sure she's fine, though. Do you want me to send Tybrake along with you, Arias?"

"I'll be fine, thanks; he's done more than enough for me these past few days."

"We should let the others know not to drink from this lake alone," Hlaena said. "Just in case the Kelpie returns. And I'll let Larin know where you've gone the murm we find her."

Arias nodded gratefully, and then noted that the seriousness had left Lue's eyes.

She snickered. "Ey, Arias... you're going to smell like wriggler! Ha!"

He narrowed his eyes. He'd never really thought about it. "Whatever," he said.

***

Naia had a small satchel of woven aquatic grass, which Arias supposed contained whatever belongings a Mermaid kept. He ended up having to wade into the shallows so that she could climb on, and just feeling the cool water sent a shiver down his spine. The murm he hefted out onto land with her clinging securely to his back, regret seized him.

"You're a lot heavier than you look," he grunted.

"I should pluck a feather for that comment!" she said, huffing with indignation.

"Only if you like the idea of being dropped off my back once we're airborne," Arias replied. He looked for a good place to take off from, then called out, "Hang on tight!"

Naia reached down and immediately placed a choke hold around his neck, and he reacted with a swift peck between her eyes.

"Ow!"

Halada's sake, not that tight! Are you trying to kill me?"

She gave a nervous chuckle and wrung her hands apologetically. "Sorry. I've never been flying before."

Reason dawned on Arias. "Are you scared?"

She fiddled with her satchel. "Maybe a bit."

"Oh, you'll probably like it. I know I do. I can remember my first time flying, though, so I can see how it might be a little scary for you. But don't worry, I won't let you fall. I was kidding about that."

Naia nodded, though her expression was displeased. He didn't have to look to know that her eyes were squeezed shut as he started running, calling out, "Here we go!" He dug in, straining with the added weight, and clawed at the air with his wings. All his flying over the past couple of months was probably the only reason he was capable of climbing upward, and while his shoulders weren't particularly happy with the extra weight he was asking them to carry, he wasn't too worried. He started to look for an air thermal, aware that Naia was pressing her face deeper and deeper into the feathers at the base of his neck.

"This is way worse than I thought it would be! I think I'm going to be sick. I can't even make out the lake we just left anymore! How high up are we? This is horrifying!" she whimpered. "If we fall, we're *dead*. You do realize that, don't you?" She reinstated her death grip, but Arias was so busy stifling a chuckle at her alarm that he didn't immediately reprimand her.

"Well, it's a good thing we're not going to

fall." Naia let out a squeal of dismay as he angled over to an air thermal, and settled into an updraft that would push them west.

"What would make you feel better? You said you've been waiting a long time to talk, so let's talk."

"Umm," she said in a shaky voice, still hiding in his feathers. "What happened to your tail?"

"It got ripped off."

"By the blue," Naia breathed. "I'm sorry!"

"Me too."

Naia shifted with a grunt. "My tail is falling asleep. Mind if I move?"

"Just don't move fast and it should be okay. Thanks for the warning." Arias focused on holding steady while the Mermaid swung her tail sideways so that it hung over his side. It was odd to compensate for the extra weight on one side, but he got used to it fairly quickly. He could hear Naia taking swigs from something she'd pull out of her satchel every now and then, and he eventually turned to scrutinize her out of curiosity. It was a hollow bulb of some sort, and she stopped mid-sip to stare back at him, her sparkling eyes wide.

"It's creepy that you can turn your neck that far."

Arias rolled his eyes and went back to looking ahead. "It's creepy to me that you *can't.*"

"And you guys sound terrifying," she went on, as if he hadn't said anything. "You're much more civilized with that necklace on."

"This thing is called a necklace? How does it work? Are all shells special like this when strung together?"

Naia laughed. "No, I'm afraid that's not how it works. This one is special—enchanted by a sea witch. But you can use it to speak to intelligent water creatures. You can keep it if you'd like. Maybe one day it will help you, the way it has for me."

Arias flapped his wings harder as the thermal he'd been riding petered out, and he dipped a little as he looked for another one. "Thanks. I'm still a little surprised that you decided to ask me for help if I'm so scary."

"I don't know," Naia replied. "The way you were staring out over the water intrigued me. I could tell you were thinking about something. Most of the other woodland creatures don't do that."

Arias snorted. "Yeah. Well, I wish I did that a little less, to be honest."

"Don't say that! Then we would never have met. No one is going to believe that I was rescued by a flying bird-monster."

"You have an interesting way with words, especially with you still on the back of said monster."

"I don't mean it in a bad way! I just mean that you look big and powerful, that's all."

"Hmm."

Naia gripped a tuft of feathers and leaned forward to take a careful peek over his shoulder, then sat straight again, letting out a small squeak. "No!" she whimpered. "Still too high."

Arias laughed. "It's fine if you don't like it. I didn't like diving into that lake. I guess if you'd asked me to go down there with you, I'd probably be pretty scared, too."

"That lake is scuzzy and gross," Naia said with disgust. "You should come to experience the ocean sometime! It's way prettier, and we keep Kelpies out of our homeland. Just don't come asking about me for some time. I'd better let things settle down."

Arias thought of the sea serpent, unfathomably huge and hidden somewhere in the ocean depths. "Nothing bothers you in the ocean?"

"We're good at defending ourselves. Most creatures learn quickly that the Mer aren't to be interfered with."

"I see."

Arias bantered back and forth with the Mermaid all the way back to the rocky shore of the ocean. The sun was still high in the sky, but would be starting on its descent before long. As Arias waded into the shallows so Naia could climb down, she noted its position.

"You'll be okay on the way back?"

"Yes. I think if I hurry I can make it back to the others before nightfall. There isn't much to be wary of in the sky at night, but being on the ground is a different story."

Naia shimmied off his back and splashed into the sea, resurfacing immediately to screech with joy, arms outstretched. Then she pressed her hands to her mouth to cut the sound off, casting a cautious eye out over the waves. When all remained quiet, she turned back to Arias with her teeth happily bared.

"I can't thank you enough!" she enthused. "I wouldn't ever have made it back here without you!" She splashed water at him and twirled, sighing. "You have no idea how good this feels on my scales!"

"I can't say that I do," Arias said, amused. "And I'm happy to help. Thanks again for what you did earlier." He started to head back to shore, but Naia called out after him, cross.

"And where do you think you're going? Come

93

get a hug, at least!"

Arias paused, head tilted. "A what?" he asked. He waited for her to give him something, but instead, she flung her arms around his shoulders and squeezed him as hard as she could. It was like being choked again, but this time it was out of adoration instead of fear. It was a little confusing, but she seemed happy.

"If you ever need any help with anything sea-related, know that you can call on me. It might take me a little while to get to you, though. The ocean is a big place. And..." she wrung her hands. "There's something you need to know. I'm sorry for telling you this now, but you have to understand. I was afraid that if I told you earlier, you wouldn't have brought me here."

Arias frowned. "What is it?"

"The Kelpie isn't the only cursed thing about the area around the lake. You should take your friends and leave when you get back. There's something that lives in the woods... the only thing I know is that it has a long, scaled tail, and it walks on two legs. It can freeze whatever it looks at, and I don't think the spell can be broken."

"What! How could you leave that out? My missing friend could have been frozen by that thing! I—" He paused. She was right that he wouldn't have brought her here had she told him. She looked down into the waves, guiltily, and he sighed. He also wouldn't have known about whatever creature this was without her help. Not until it was too late, possibly. "Thank you for telling me, Naia. Take care of yourself. I need to go."

She continued wringing her hands as she watched him take off from the shore, his pale wings taking him higher and higher until he was just a speck in the sky.

***

It was well after nightfall when Arias made it back to the Gryph encampment by the lake. An anxious Bala was waiting for him with bad news. The tall Ardeigryph was pacing among a group of other concerned Gryphs, most of whom were speaking of the horrors that might have befallen their flockmates. The murm Bala saw Arias, he dashed over, his crest raised.

"The number of the missing Gryphs keeps rising," Bala said. "No one can account for them, and now everyone is too afraid to even consider searching. I know it sounds bad, but maybe we should cut our losses and move on. This new mainland seems much more dangerous than we could ever have imagined. Do you think those meat-eating Pixie things followed us here?"

"No, it's not the Pixies. We would have seen them," Arias said. "There's a creature that lives in this forest with the ability to freeze others. And from the sounds of it, it's not a basilisk… it walks on two legs. Maybe it can be slain, if we're careful. Or dealt with in some other way. If our flockmates are just frozen, we have to find them and see if we can undo the freezing. We can't just leave them behind."

Bala squirmed. "I mean, it would be horrible, but we *could* do that. Flying to another location is possibly our safest option."

"We don't know that," Arias replied, trying to keep his voice calm. "We have no idea whether this thing can fly, or whether there's more than one of them here. We could fly off someplace else and end up in a whole nest of the beasts, then we'll not only be frozen or dead, but we'll be cowards on top of it."

"I know that Larin is among the missing," Bala said. "Lue went looking for her, and now she's vanished, too. What if you go out searching and don't return, as well? We can't risk losing anyone else."

"Just stay here and keep everyone together," Arias said. "It'll be alright. I'm going to see if I can learn anything else before I head out." He had no idea whether everything would be alright or not, but he knew Bala was the type of Gryph who thrived on that type of encouragement. The Ardeigryph Sire nodded with hesitation, and Arias went to seek out Hlaena. She wasn't hard to find, standing in the company of the Sentinels. The mute Gryphons all dipped their heads in a shallow bow of respect when they saw him.

"Larin's group decided to try to find her with a search party of their own, despite the fact that almost every Gryph who has tried the same plan hasn't returned," Hlaena said, her tone scolding. "I was able to talk these few out of it, but it's interesting how no one listens to an Alicorn with no magick." She flattened her ears as she said the last bit, and Arias was too stunned at the bitterness in her voice to reply for a murm.

"I'm sure everyone is just worried about the missing Gryphs," he said. "You did well to stop even these few, and it's more than anyone else has done so far. That Mermaid told me what might be causing the disappearances, and I'm hoping you might know what the beast is. The gist of it is that it has a long, scaled tail, walks on two legs, and can freeze creatures somehow. I probably should have asked her for more information, but I was in too much of a hurry to get back here. Does it bring anything to mind?"

Hlaena lifted her ears, and her expression was grim. "It sounds like a Cockatrice," she said. "I've only seen one once, and I wish I hadn't. It ambushed another mare, and before I realized what was happening, it chased me down. The instant I looked at it, it froze me, too. It's a horrible feeling... you're conscious the whole time, just unable to move. The Cockatrice was violent if encountered, but uninterested in eating any of its victims. It merely continued to wander about the forest after subduing its prey."

"Did Xio unfreeze you?" Arias asked. Hlaena shook her head.

"He and many others certainly tried. Xio even tried using his magick on the Cockatrice itself, to no avail. He nearly got himself frozen in the process! No, it was Naugi who freed us. He heard about the situation and came to investigate. When he realized what was going on, he killed the beast, but not before it froze two of his heads. Anything the Cockatrice froze was freed when it died. But Arias, no one here can kill a Cockatrice. Their magick is too powerful, and they're fast. They aren't small creatures."

"How big?" Arias asked, and Hlaena gave him a withering glance.

"Too big for anyone here to take on, Arias. It would make even Tybrake look like a cub."

"I'd like at least to know for sure that this is what happened to my friends," Arias said, prompting another warning look from Hlaena. She couldn't stop him, though, and she knew it. She sighed.

"Who would've known that you'd grow into such a stubborn keythong," she said. His eyes must have twinkled at the comment, because she narrowed hers in response. "I can already tell that there's nothing I can say to stop you."

"What do you expect me to do, Hlaena? They're my friends."

There was a long pause before the mare said, "Tell me you didn't bring me this far just so I can lose you, too."

Arias couldn't hold her gaze at that. "That's not fair, Hlaena."

"Life isn't fair." She flared her nostrils in a huff.

"I promise I'll be careful."

"Fine," she snapped, then lowered her eyes. "I hate being like this. I can't stop you, and I can't help you either."

"It'll be okay. We're going to find a way to fix you."

She gave him a long look, like she was drinking in what may be the last sight she ever saw of him, and then she turned away. "Be safe," she said.

"I will." He took a step into the darkness and then looked back at the sad form of Hlaena, brooding alone. The Sentinels edged closed to her with reassuring clicks, and he felt a little better. They'd look after her until he could get back.

***

Arias had hardly set off before a young Ardeigryph ran up to him, a nervous tremor in his voice.

"Some of the Pale warriors found a few of the missing!" he said. "You were looking for them, weren't you?"

"Yes," Arias said, noticing that he hadn't seen many Gryphs from the Pale. "Is Hilda keeping most of the Pale safe with the other Gryphs?"

"No," the young keythong said as if it was

obvious. "She charged off into the trees with most of her warriors, yelling that whatever was taking her flock couldn't take on all of them at once."

Of course. How did someone so rash take charge of an entire flock? Bala was a coward, but at least he had a good heart. It was a shame that Hilda, for what she was worth, was such a skilled warrior. Maybe the Cockatrice would do more than just freeze her, fixing one problem for everyone.

"Will you show me where they went?" he asked, and the Ardeigryph gave a hesitant nod.

"You can just describe where to go if you don't want to risk it," Arias added, seeing the apprehension playing on the youngster's face.

"No, no! This way!" The keythong dashed off, and Arias almost had to struggle to keep up with him, until they got a good distance away from the rest of the Gryphs. His pace flagged as he pricked his small ears, staring hard at every moonlit shadow and jumping at every movement. Arias didn't blame him. He was just as on edge himself, straining his eyes to look for any unfamiliar shapes in the darkness After a bit, the keythong crouched low beside some brambles and jerked his head.

"There," he whispered. "Do you see them?"

Arias crouched beside his guide and cast his eyes in the direction indicated, his gaze settling on a lone figure in the middle of the woods. It stood motionless, and after hearing nothing and looking around for a long murm, Arias broke cover and eased his way over to it, ignoring both the knots in his stomach and the Ardeigryph's muted cry of alarm. The youngster sprinted back the way he'd come after seeing that his warning wasn't heeded, and Arias forced himself to press on, determined to get a closer look.

It would have been easy to dismiss the object as anything from afar: a boulder, a large stump, or even the raised roots of a fallen tree. Stark, still, and smooth in texture, the details engraved in the statuesque figure were undoubtedly those of a Gryphon. Even as solid and immovable as she was, Arias could recognize the gryphoness. Larin was locked in a state of permanent escape, her beak open in a vicious hiss that was directed at something no longer there.

"Larin?" Arias pecked the figure gently. No reply issued forth.

A scream of sheer panic echoed through the forest from the direction the young Ardeigryph had run in, and Arias's fur stood on end. He wanted to scramble back to the cover of the brambles, but he could already see something shifting in that direction. Without even gazing into the eyes of the Cockatrice, he found himself already rooted to the ground in fear. *Fly!* he yelled to himself in his head, but his wings remained frozen at his sides.

A macabre beast melted into view, its wrinkled

head covered in patches of feathers of a curious green color, the same color as its small, tattered wings. Despite walking upright on two legs, the remainder of its body was serpentine, right down to its long, pointed tail. In the low light, its scales sparkled like jewels, each vertebra of its back accentuated by a dark, blood red spine. It was strangely vertical, with the bulk of its length being its tail, but even then it was perhaps as big as three Ardeigryph keythongs. Its eyes were—

Arias automatically looked down after his first initial glance at the Cockatrice, and its screech upon seeing him finally unlocked his wings. He shot through the first patch of open sky he could find in the treetops, grateful that, despite being winged, the creature didn't fly after him. He resisted the urge to look back to see if it was following him, afraid that it could freeze him even from a distance.

The murm Arias touched down in the flock, he was bombarded by questions.

"Have you seen the beast?" a Gryphon hen asked.

"Did you find the others?" another asked.

"Were you followed?" an older Ardeigryph keythong asked with a frightened glance around.

The questions piled on so high that the din became unimaginable, and Arias shrieked for order. Silence fell as shocked eyes rested on him.

"I know things have been… less than hoped for ever since leaving the mainland," Arias started. "But we have to survive, or everything would have been for nothing. Yes, I have seen the Cockatrice. We don't know its range or whether it is alone, so I recommend we stay together until we can find a way to deal with this one and get our flockmates back. I suspect that it is alone and that its territory is this immediate area, but I could be wrong. Everyone must remain calm while a way to kill the beast is found. If anyone has any ideas—"

Excited murmurs rose up.

"— besides ganging up and killing it with our eyes closed, then I'd like to hear them."

Silence fell again. Arias sighed. "We should be safe here for the night, but let's double our sentries. No patrols, that's too risky. And stay away from the lake…" he trailed off. The lake! An idea sprang into his mind. He ran off to find Hlaena again, leaving his announcement to the flock half finished.

"Hlaena!" Arias cried, hating that he was about to ruin the hope in her eyes with his next proposition. "I have an idea. You'll have to let me know if it might work."

Hlaena set her jaw, but lay down to listen as he described his hasty plan. The Sentinels similarly listened, excited to hear that anyone had an idea at all.

"You said when you saw the Kelpie, you didn't see it as what it was, right? You saw something you wanted to see—another Alicorn. You said it was dark magick. Is there any reason the Cockatrice would be immune to it?"

Hlaena tilted her head, perplexed by the proposition. "The Cockatrice I encountered in Glendale was quite powerful. I have no way of knowing how strong the Kelpie is, because I can't sense its magick in the ether. The Cockatrice might just freeze it and continue on its rampage."

"Is it worth a try to lead the Cockatrice to the Kelpie? Naia said I could talk to water creatures with these shells around my neck."

Hlaena wrinkled her muzzle, flicking her ears. "Can't you find someone else who can run faster?"

The Sentinels all pressed in heroically, but Arias shook his head.

"Why? I'm not slow. I've had my fair share of running for my life, too. I'm experienced at it, even." He should have known that Hlaena wouldn't find the last bit funny. She didn't.

"You can't see that well, though. What if you trip, or get snagged in something, and manage to get yourself caught?"

"Hlaena, I can see just fine. My vision is only bad when it's bright. Besides that, I wouldn't feel right asking anyone else to do this. I already escaped from the Cockatrice once, but when you first encounter it, it's hard not to freeze up. All any of us have to do is to fly. Just don't let it sneak up on anyone. When I saw it in the forest, I only knew it was there because someone screamed, and I saw it moving in that direction. It was almost completely silent." He thought a little longer. "You know, I'd feel a lot better if you were helping to keep watch, too."

Hlaena gave him a flat stare. "You'd feel a lot better if the mare who was already frozen once by a Cockatrice kept watch for another one?"

"Well, you know what to look out for. Most of the others don't."

She deliberated, and then nodded. "Alright then. But you'll come back if you don't think it will work?"

"Yes. This is the only idea I can think of that might be worth trying; you were right when you said that none of us can go up against that thing. As hard as it is to think of leaving Larin, Lue, and the others behind, it would be the right thing to do if this fails. At least, until I can think of another way to help them later on. I'd never just leave them here."

"I know," Hlaena said. "We should make sure there's no way you can come under the Kelpie's spell, though. There's no Mermaid to help us this time. We should bind your eyes."

"With what? The grass around here is short. I

haven't seen any vines or anything like that since we've landed." Arias opened a wing and poked at the longer flight feathers at its tip, but they were too rigid to bend without breaking. "Have any of you seen anything around here that I can use to tie around my eyes?" he asked the Sentinels, but they gave reluctant shakes of their heads.

"Use my tail," Hlaena said, swishing the long, silver hair. "It's long enough."

"But you need it," Arias said.

"It's not close to summer yet, and I won't need it until then, anyway. It'll have grown back by then."

"Are you sure?"

She waved her tail again and chuckled. "Now we can be two of a kind, Arias. At least, until mine grows long again."

He wiggled the stump of his tail, happy that she was able to find a touch of humor in the situation.

Hlaena's tail was a lot tougher than it looked. The silken threads resisted being severed by biting, and when one of the Sentinels tried to simply pluck the long threads, she almost took a hoof to the face.

"Enough!" Hlaena said, prancing sideways and away from the group of Gryphons and their avid attempts to remove her tail. "Your beaks aren't sharp enough. I'll cut it."

Before Arias could warn her against using her magick, she'd sliced her tail cleanly across. She winced as it fell in a heap to the ground, but seemed alright after using so little of her energy. She brushed Arias away before he could investigate further.

"You have Gryphs to save," she said, turning him the other way. "Can one of you tie my tail around his eyes?"

The Sentinels were eager to comply, and followed him out to the lake. The rest of the flock watched from afar as his eyes were bound, and he walked to the edge of the shore by sound alone. He waited, heart racing, listening to the lapping of the water. It was a while before he picked out a sound that wasn't the natural movement of the waves, a deep rippling sound that indicated something much bigger than a simple wriggler was present. The gasps of the others further up the shore confirmed his suspicion, and it wasn't long before he heard sputtering curses.

"Wretched land scum! The Mermaid has been up to her tricks again, I see."

"I've come to barter with you," Arias said, and he could feel the Kelpie move closer, so close that he could feel its fetid breath on his neck as it responded with a hoarse chuckle. He wondered what form the creature had taken as it stood next to him on the shore.

"A trick, no doubt," it said.

"Not a trick," Arias replied. "We could use your help. And you could stand to gain, if you're interested."

"What could you possibly have that a creature such as I may be interested? I'm sure this is simply a way to exact your revenge after I nearly took you and the Alicorn mare." The Kelpie returned to the water with a splash.

"Wait!" Arias cried, and the Kelpie laughed again. "I'm listening," it said in its distorted voice. "Speak, land-walker."

"Do you have any interest in the Cockatrice at all?" Arias asked. He felt the Kelpie return to his side.

"Ah, I see. So the Cockatrice is preying upon your kind… What a lucky individual. What are you proposing, weak one?"

"I'm guessing that if you were interested in that Alicorn, you're interested in the Cockatrice, as well," Arias replied. The Kelpie seemed to deliberate.

"Surely you lack the strength required to deliver such a creature. I nearly had you in my clutches by mere chance. One look, and the Cockatrice would have you. Go away, daft fool. You waste my time."

"The Cockatrice will deliver itself, if all goes according to plan," Arias said. "Besides, what do you have to lose?"

The Kelpie circled him, its footsteps sounding crisp and dainty, unlike those of a being who dwelled in the water. Arias resisted the urge to peek at whatever the monster had become, but suddenly it tore the blindfold from his face. He clenched in surprise, eyes still closed. The Kelpie snorted, returning to the water.

"You are… unusual. It isn't often that I meet any who are bold enough to face one such as myself. This shore is a prison that holds the delights of the land only a few tantalizing lengths away from me. How sweet the essence of you land-dwellers is! Bring me the Cockatrice, that I may feast upon it. Though it knows of my wiles, maybe you can make it forget for a time…"

The Kelpie slipped back underwater, and Arias didn't open his eyes until he'd turned and walked a good distance from the shore. Those in the flocks who had been watching his exchange with the Kelpie stared with wide eyes and open bills.

"You should all move further inland and away from the shore until we see how this ends," Arias called to them. "I don't know which part of the lake I'll reach first, and I don't want anyone getting in the way when I get here."

The flock obligingly shuffled further into the tree line without complaining, and Arias took a deep breath. He'd never used himself as bait before, but it was the only way he could think to get the Cockatrice to follow him to the water's edge. It was the only way he'd probably ever get his friends back.

***

The woods were ominous as Arias stalked toward where he'd last seen the Cockatrice. Even the moon seemed to want nothing to do with the situation, having hidden itself being a thick bank of clouds. A few brave Gryphs had offered to help him, the bulk of them from the Sentinels, but he'd instructed them to keep watch with the others. Too much help could result in confusion, and all it would take was one more frozen Gryph to start a panic in the flock. He crept a talon's length at a time, ears pricked as high as he could get them, until he got to the spot where Larin was frozen. The Cockatrice didn't keep him waiting long.

When the horrendous screech started up *behind* him, Arias almost jumped out of his own skin. He took off, recalling only how Hlaena had told him that Cockatrices weren't only large, but they were fast. This Cockatrice was indeed fast, and Arias could feel every instance that the beast nipped his heels. The Cockatrice was no longer concerned with being stealthy, and its two legs sent it forward faster than Arias's four. Some part of Arias's brain overrode his conscious actions. He was flying before he realized it, eyes trained ahead as he tore for the lake.

It couldn't have been more than a murm to fly to the lake, but for Arias, it felt like an eternity. His heart was in his throat as the lake veered into view, and to his horror the Kelpie was at the edge of the water, staring not at the Cockatrice, but at him instead. Its rotted face contorted, shifting into something else familiar, something he couldn't look away from... but before he could look too long, the Kelpie turned its gaze onto the Cockatrice, and fixated there.

The Cockatrice stopped dead in it tracks, and Arias made a swift landing further upshore to watch the interaction. The silence was deafening as neither creature moved, their eyes locked onto one another. With a sudden snarl, the Kelpie squealed and backed away, its tattered tail splashing water, and Arias realized with a sinking feeling that its boney nose was no longer bone, but stone. He looked between the two, watching the Kelpie back further and further into the water, it's glowing eyes blazing like fire in the murky water.

The Cockatrice crowed as if victorious, but to Arias's surprise, it took one wooden step after the other into the lake. Its halting movements were unwilling, but it seemed unable to resist whatever visage the Kelpie had conjured up for it. Arias wondered what illusion could be so powerful that even a creature like the Cockatrice couldn't resist, but he felt only relief as the dreadful beast waded into the lake, so far that only its head was visible. There it stopped with its wattled beak halfway agape, and with wicked speed the Kelpie rushed up and snatched it into the depths, vanishing again in the blink of an eye. Only a series of bubbles indicated that there had ever been anything other than Arias near the shore. Before long, there was just the calm lake, deceptively peaceful for what lay beneath its waves.

***

It took Arias a while to come to terms with the fact that his plan had worked. He kept waiting for either the Cockatrice or the Kelpie to emerge from the lake, but neither did. It was only the frightened blubbering of formerly-frozen Gryphs that broke him away from staring at the water. Their cries that there was something horrid in the forest drew hurried reassurances from the rest of the flock. Arias joined them, happy to have everyone back, but he was only truly satisfied when he saw Larin at the fringe of the group, reuniting with the other Sentinels. He ran over to her, but before he could reach her, Lue nearly bowled him over in her zeal to describe the Cockatrice. It wasn't until he got out the words, "It's been taken care of," that she paused, questions in her eyes.

"How? When?" Lue asked, confused.

"It's a story for later on, while we're getting away from this place," Arias said. He cast a look over the group, noting that Hilda and most of the other Pale warriors were once again within their ranks. He also caught sight of the Ardeigryph that had led him to the Cockatrice, and he breathed a sigh of relief upon seeing that the keythong was safe. The glass-like reflection of the lake offered no movement and, with a last backward glance, Arias rose into the air. Like leaves blown on the wind, the rest of the flock—plus one Alicorn— rose to follow, leaving the eerie patch of forest behind.

CHAPTER FIVE

With the cursed forest left behind, Arias drank
in the praise of his flockmates. They mostly
travelled on claw, stopping intermittently to feed
and drink as they inspected the land, and in that
time, the thought of hunting never crossed
Arias's mind. The others offered him enough
preymeat that he hadn't felt the pangs of hunger
since leaving the lake. Even some of the Pale
warriors seemed to be warming to him, much to
Hilda's chagrin. The peace didn't last long,
however.

Bala and the rest of the Ardeigryph were
beginning to become fractious, as they hadn't
come across a suitable body of water in the days
since leaving the lake. While most would eat
whatever meat they could fit into their bills, they
preferred wrigglers, and the normally amicable
seafarers began to become uncharacteristically
irritable. It was the perfect arrangement for an
altercation to take place, and it finally came to
pass on one sunny afternoon.

"We will continue north. There's no reason to change course now that we're this far in," Hilda announced. "We're bound to run into more good territory eventually. That is, if you longnecks can keep up. I'm tired of hearing your whining day and night. We'll be going in circles before you know it, if we decide to change direction based on the silly wishes of your kind."

Tybrake scoffed, drowning out Bala's much milder response. "And who made you leader all of a sudden?" he asked, bristling.

"One doesn't need to explain what is already clear," Hilda said, sneering.

Bala narrowed his eyes. "Not over me and mine, you aren't."

Hilda's smirk disappeared. "Is that a challenge?"

Tybrake hissed, spreading his wings. "I'll show you a thing or two. Just give me the word, Bala, and I'll shred this overgrown runt down to size."

Bala didn't reply, but he was already lashing his tail, sizing Hilda up. Other warriors from the Pale noticed, and they edged closer to the ruckus, their hackles rising. The Ardeigryph were similarly gathering. Lue bounded up to stand next to Tybrake, her eyes flitting from Gryph to Gryph as she waited to see who would make the first move. Arias barely had time to run in between the groups, hoping to defuse them.

"Now everyone, I realize we're all pent up and—" he was cut off as Tybrake shoved him aside as easily as if he were a mouthy cub, not even looking at him as he said,

"Stay out of this one, Arias. "We'll take care of it. You've done more than enough for us."

"Count me in."

Arias hadn't heard the voice in so long, he turned to look, flabbergasted. Brynne squeezed her way to the front of the group, and Hilda's ears flattened against her skull the murm she caught sight of her. Brynne gave no warning as she leapt onto the other hen, and Arias danced sideways as the battle began in earnest without him. He scowled, crouching to avoid the groping beaks, talons and claws that tried to include him in the fight. Finally, he crept away to stand in the company of more sensible Gryphs.

"We don't have the time or the energy for this!" he called out once he was a safe distance away, but they were too busy tearing one another apart to care. The Sentinels looked between him and the fighting, but in the end they followed Larin's example and didn't join in. Arias sighed, irritated, and stalked off to find Hlaena. He understood why everyone was frustrated and wanted to fight, but he didn't have to be around while it happened.

"We're not going to get anywhere like this," Arias huffed, exasperated. Hlaena looked up from the greenery she was picking at with half-hearted nibbles, dull eyes slowly blinking. Arias frowned.

"Are you alright?" he asked.

"I don't feel so well right now," she said. "That's all."

"Is there anything I can get you?"

The Alicorn mare gave a slight, almost imperceptible shake of her head. Arias noticed that the crack in her horn had edged deeper, working its way closer to the base where it connected to her head. His eyes flicked back to the flock, embroiled in turmoil. He'd set out originally to find help for Hlaena, not to watch senseless fighting over who was leader. He watched Hilda moving through the flock, slashing at one Gryph's hindquarters, sinking her talons into the flank of another, her eyes alight. She liked destruction, that much was clear. And she liked power. It reminded him a little too much of Shadowbane. What would it take to wrest that power from her?

Arias singled Hilda out and trotted in her direction, avoiding the attempts of others to engage him. When he was close enough to close in on her, he started running, and the fast movement caused her to wheel around, pupils dilated like flat discs in her blood-streaked face. She met him with talons outstretched, and he was overcome with surprise. Hilda was *strong*, much stronger than she looked, and he grunted as she tried to drive him backwards. The instant other

Gryphs realized he'd joined the fray, their own battles died out, their curiosity to see the outcome of the struggle garnering more interest than their own squabbles.

Unable to compensate for the differences in their weight, Hilda ducked away from Arias and came at him from his side. She was a blur that appeared to come in from one way, and then flashed to the other instead. He hissed as he realized that she'd put him into a defensive position so easily. Unlike Shadowbane, who was easily blinded by his own frustration, Hilda remained level-headed despite the frenzy of battle. Meanwhile, she was learning his weaknesses rapidly, including just how badly his vision was impaired by light. She kept her back to the sun, and Arias found himself willing his eyes to focus, as he had countless times in the past, but Hilda remained an obscure phantom that danced before him, silhouetted by rays of light. Arias pricked his ears, but it was hard to hear her over the shrieking of the surrounding Gryphs. She slammed her shoulder into him, knocking him off balance, and used the moment to wrench him sideways off his feet. Arias found it even more difficult to accurately see her from his new vantage point on the ground, but he could make out her eyes, bloodthirsty and savage, and her crest rising as she reared up. Only one thing occurred to him in that murm. Hilda didn't want to win this spat.

She wanted him dead.

Hilda's beak contacted Arias's throat just

117

enough to draw blood before she was hauled off her feet and thrown to the ground. She scrambled back up, looking for the culprit who had disturbed her victory. "Who would deny me my right?" she snarled. Larin bore down on her, and Hilda was quick to arch her back in challenge, her tail bristling.

"A spar in the flock never goes to the death," Tybrake said. "Any leader knows that. You know that. It's why you let Brynne live when you bested her."

Hilda's warriors gave conflicted calls, and the hen herself didn't reply. Her eyes flashed to Arias instead, as if gauging whether she could still finish him.

"It's one thing to claim victory in an unfair fight," Lue said, "and another to try to kill your opponent. Leave now, while you still have some grace to your name."

"Maybe you won't face the price for what you just tried to do if you get out of here fast enough," Tybrake added, snaking forward.

Hilda's eyes darted to Arias once again, her talon still planted firmly on his chest. His proximity seemed to enrage her, but, as Larin, Lue, and Tybrake edged closer, she stepped away, tongue lolling in exertion. After a few murms, she said,

"He's not worth it anyway. Let's go." She didn't say it to anyone in particular, and as she trotted into the forest, she didn't look back to see how many of her followers came after her. Whatever the number, it was enough. Those that stayed behind lowered their tails and ears apologetically.

"I didn't know she was like that."

"I can't follow a leader who would kill in a spar."

"Forgive me. Your leader fought with honor despite not being whole."

Arias collected himself from the ground, reassuring his friends that he was fine. Just a few cuts and bruises. But the last comment from the unnamed Pale warrior haunted him. *Despite not being whole*. Was that how other Gryphs saw him? As a cripple who overcame his deficiencies and needed to be treated like a cub when he failed?

Bala was disheveled after his run in with the Pale warriors, but he looked satisfied enough after seeing Hilda depart. "It was about time that someone faced that *tuca* head on," he said. "I never expected to see you enter the fight. Are you all right?"

"I'm fine," Arias said quietly. Bala and Tybrake shared a glance, and Arias added, "Someone needed to do something about her. You weren't, so I did. Let's go."

Arias set off at a walk, and the others moved to follow him. Hilda had fought many Gryphs, but she hadn't tried to kill any until she'd defeated him. She hadn't tried to kill Bala even though he'd been right there, ripe for the taking. Not that the feeling of someone wanting him dead was new to Arias... but why him?

"I'm glad to see Hilda gone," Bala said, falling into step alongside Arias. "It couldn't have happened a murm later. There was something wrong about that hen."

"I doubt it's the last we'll see of her," Arias said, casting a look back to make sure that Hlaena was keeping up alright. The Alicorn mare's eyes were closed as she walked, trailing in the general direction of the flock. She stumbled every now and then, and Arias decided they wouldn't walk too far today. Thank Halada that she probably hadn't seen him nearly get his throat ripped out just now.

"Bala," he said, slowing. "We need to call a meeting."

"I agree," the Ardeigryph Sire said. "Let's find a place to stop for the day."

"No," Arias said. "Right now."

Latching onto the seriousness in his voice, Bala passed the word to have everyone halt and gather. They did so. Arias cleared his throat.

"There wasn't going to be any peace until Hilda was ousted, whether by her death or otherwise. I don't know if any of you object to her departure, and frankly I don't want to hear about it. The Alicorn travelling in our group is important to me. The Ardeigryph gathered here object to our travelling, and I can understand it their frustration. Their kind thrives on the water. I can't ask you all to follow blindly after me when there's a huge and abundant ocean just a few days away from here. Travel so that you avoid the Pixies, and I'm sure you'll be just fine. That goes for anyone who is tired of this endless quest for something that I'm not even sure exists. But I have to go on. I have to try. And I wanted to make this clear to all of you."

Bala opened his mouth to retort, but Arias went on, "Bala, your flock needs you. Tybrake, Lue, and many others are happy to help you in making the harder decisions. Don't leave them to follow after me. The same applies to the Sentinels. And for those of you that have abandoned Hilda's company, you'll find no better flock to be a part of. There's safety in numbers, and with a flock this big, you won't have to worry about Hilda seeking retribution for your departure. I can't promise the same if you decide to travel in smaller numbers, but you're free to do what you want. With all of this said, I'd like to be left alone for a while. I'll come to say goodbye to all of you in a while."

***

Hlaena was already snoring softly when he walked over to lie next to her. She looked strange with her long mane and short tail, even stranger than she looked with her fragmented horn. Arias closed his eyes; not to sleep, but to think. The fact that Hilda was gone brought him only a small

121

measure of relief. He realized that he was travelling in an unknown land on the poorly founded hope that a Phoenix he'd met once was right about a group of healers who may or may not exist. He hadn't asked Aaga when he'd last seen the mysterious beings. Afterall, the Phoenix had said himself that he'd lived for centuries. Arias had no plan for what would happen if there was nothing to be found in the north. But somehow, chasing after a "maybe" seemed better than doing nothing.

Soft pawfalls heralded the presence of other Gryphs, and he turned to see Larin, Lue and Tybrake, all with guilty expressions for invading his privacy.

"It's fine," he said, and they all visibly relaxed.

"I know it's dumb to ask whether you're okay, but we want to help!" Lue said. Tybrake nodded and said,

"It's hard to believe that the ones who went off with Hilda are the same ones who helped us to take down Shadowbane and his followers back in Arborochre. It's especially hard to believe that Hilda was originally among them."

Larin shimmied forward to nestle in next to Arias, poking him with a wingtip and then pointing to Hlaena with a tilt of her head.

"She hasn't eaten for a while," he said, worried. "And she sleeps a lot. She told me she didn't feel well earlier, and it's the first time I've really ever heard her say that. I can tell that the crack in her horn is getting worse; it has ever since she used her magick to cut her tail back at the lake. I wish I could have stopped her from doing that. I don't know how all of these things are interconnected; all I know is that it means I have less time to find a way to help her. When Xio and the other Alicorns' horns shattered, it killed them. I can't lose Hlaena like that, too. I got so angry when I saw everyone fighting over stupid things, I..."

He trailed off, and Tybrake and Lue seemed embarrassed for having participated in the fighting at all.

"We want to come with you," Lue said.

"No, the flock needs you," Arias said. "Especially now, with so many changes happening. They'll need someone reliable to lead them back to a safe territory near the sea. Bala is a great leader when he has someone confident to back him up. That's you two. And Larin, the Sentinels need you, whether or not your group thinks you have a leader at all," he said.

Larin hummed and shrugged, indicating that she wasn't too worried about the stability of the Sentinels in her absence.

"No," Arias said. "You can't just abandon your roles like that."

"Like you're trying to do?" Tybrake said. "The leader of the Pale literally just tried to kill you, and you're trying to convince us that you'll be safe travelling alone alongside a sick Alicorn. You should at least have someone around for guard duty while you sleep." He puffed out his chest. "Guess I'll take the job."

"It's not leaving my post if I never had one, and no," Arias retorted, "I don't need you to travel with us."

"I wouldn't expect Hlaena to be able to follow you around however far you need to go if she's this weak," Lue said. "You'll need an Ardeigryph around to help carry her whether you like it or not. Besides, the extra company can't be too bad. An extra set of eyes is never a horrible thing, either."

Larin nodded in agreement. Everyone knew she was the keenest in the group.

Arias hated to admit it, but they all did have good points.

"You're the only thing that kept us together when we were under Shadowbane's rule," Lue said. "You have to at least allow us to see to it that you'll be safe if you go on without the flock."

Arias sighed. "You are right. But a big group of us will only attract attention. And there's no way I'm leaving Bala to manage this group by himself. He needs your council. I'd like to have Gryphs I can trust to stay here. Larin, you have a level head and the ability to help keep order with the rest of the Sentinels, and Bala is familiar with and trusts your judgement, Lue. The fact that you all get along and would all be here means I'd worry a lot less about what's going on here while I'm gone."

Tybrake rearranged his wings with a smug look on his face, then added a hasty, "I'll be back before you know it, Lue!" when he saw the way the gryphoness was staring at him.

The Ardeigryph hen didn't look happy, but she nodded as she said, "It's the right choice. We'll keep a sharp eye out for Hilda, in case she tries to return. Everything's going to be fine. You should just concentrate on helping Hlaena to get better."

The others agreed, and Arias finally felt vindicated for his choices. He bowed so low that his beak touched the ground. "Thank you. For everything."

***

Leaving the flock was harder than Arias had expected. He crossed necks with more Gryphs than he ever had before in his life; some were even hens and keythongs that he didn't know, but that knew him. They all thanked him for the things he'd done for them, and wished him well on his quest to help Hlaena. Regardless of the heavy atmosphere, the Ardeigryph were ready to head back to the sea, and the Sentinels were just as eager to stake out a new home. They ended up departing that night, leaving Larin, Lue, Tybrake, Hlaena, and Arias behind.

Arias had tried unsuccessfully to get Larin and

Lue to leave with the others, but they'd refused, preferring to stay with him until he set out. He had already known that Larin would be too stubborn to head off at his word, and so he sat with her in the darkness, their heads resting on the other's back, waiting for the murm Hlaena awakened and ended their time together. Tybrake and Lue sat together a distance away, speaking to one another in low voices, their words muffled by the wings they'd tucked their heads under.

Arias was incredibly comfortable in silence around Larin, and not just because she was mute. There was a shared understanding that didn't often require words, and it was something he hadn't encountered with many other Gryphs that he'd known. He busied himself with preening her feathers, pulling the glossy black feathers through his beak until every single one lay flat. The gryphoness clucked happily and closed her eyes, and he was glad to see her in higher spirits despite his imminent departure. His own feathers were bedraggled after his brief spat with Hilda, and he was just about to start in on them when he heard Lue say,

"Hey, not to interrupt, but is that... normal?"

Arias followed the Ardeigryph hen's gaze, over to where Hlaena was lying. The cracks in her horn glowed maroon, like burning embers that leeched magick into the surrounding air. The mare shuddered and whimpered to herself, and Arias walked over to rouse her, placing a concerned claw on her shoulder. The murm he touched her, her eyes shot open, and arcane magick arced from her horn in a blinding burst. Arias felt it sizzle through the plumage on his chest, but by the time he jumped back, the crackling energy had already dissipated with a snap. The other Gryphs were already on their feet and backing away, eyes wide. Hlaena blinked at them through bleary eyes, shaking her head.

"I didn't mean to startle you," Arias said. "You were somehow using your magick while you were asleep... I've never seen you do that before."

"I'm sorry. Are you hurt at all?"

"Between you and Hilda, I'm not going to have many feathers left, but I'm alright."

"What do you mean, 'between me and Hilda?' And where has everyone else gone?" she asked. "It's too quiet."

"Everyone headed back to the coast, without Hilda and those who followed her. She caused some trouble and we banished her, but it's hard to really enforce something like that in a new land where we haven't even claimed territory yet. She took half of the Pale with her, but I'm hoping it's the last we see of her."

Hlaena looked him over, her eyes lingering on the cuts and gashes she didn't remember him having the last time she'd seen him. "What kind of trouble did she cause?"

"It's nothing to worry about, Hlaena. It's

taken care of now. Can you stand?"

The worry didn't leave her expression, but she heaved herself to her feet and took a few hesitant, unsteady steps. She flashed her audience an embarrassed look.

"I'm sure I'll be fine once I get going. Is everyone here coming?"

"Not us!" Lue bounded over to Larin and draped her wing over the other hen's back. "We're going to help watch things back at the coast. The Sentinels all listen to Larin, and Bala is still pretty new at leadership; he trusts Tybrake and me, so it'll help to have at least one of us stay behind. We want to make sure that you have a home to return to!"

Larin nodded her agreement, and they dashed over to exchange a final goodbye with Arias. He realized he didn't know how long he'd be gone for, and it made the last crossing of their necks particularly bittersweet. Still, determination fueled him as he called goodbye to the two hens and watched them disappear into the night sky. He faced the mystery of the north without fear, falling in behind Tybrake and walking beside Hlaena, ready for whatever challenges the strange land had in store for them.

***

Tybrake stayed at the head of the group, having found his bearings, and set them on a path northward. They didn't get far before Arias felt that they were being watched. After Arborochre, he never disregarded such gut feelings, but before he could address his suspicions, the watcher revealed herself. A dejected-looking Brynne limped out into the path behind them, her amber eyes averted.

"I'd like to come along, too. I don't want to return to the ocean with the others."

Arias was planning to dismiss her, but there was a desperate quality to her words that stopped him. He looked her over. It was clear that she was the worse for wear after her tussle with Hilda, though he didn't really have a leg to stand on when it came to that.

"I don't know what lies to the north, Brynne. Flying is one thing, but hunting is another. You're limping pretty badly. It might be safer if you fly off after the others and rest at the coast. You're a fast flier; you can catch up with Larin and Lue."

Brynne snorted. "It's not the first time in my life I've had a limp, Arias. I'll be fine. You barely heard me following you with a bad leg; it's not that serious."

"I won't tell you no," he said slowly. "But I'll ask you one more time—are you sure you're up for it? You look pretty ragged."

"Speak for yourself," she snapped. "I said I'm fine."

Arias shared a long look with Tybrake, but no one said anything as the orange hen scowled and fell into line behind them. The silence persisted, and Arias wasn't in the mood to try to start conversation, anyway. Tybrake adjusted his speed so that Hlaena and Brynne could keep up more easily, and Arias recounted everything Aaga the Phoenix had told him, to keep his mind from wandering into memories of Arborochre. It seemed that, whenever he was idle, he remembered his experiences in that forsaken place, and they were memories that were better left forgotten. Aaga really hadn't told him much, and, thanks to the Pixies, he hadn't had a chance to ask more from him He went over the information again and again in his head, trying to find extra meaning in the few words Aaga had spoken, but he found nothing new.

The sun was beginning to lighten on the horizon when Tybrake halted and looked back. "I haven't eaten anything in a few days, so I'm going to go off and do a little hunting. I think a rest wouldn't be a bad thing right now, either. Will you all be fine here?"

"We'll be alright," Arias said. Brynne and Hlaena wasted no time in settling down down near one another to rest, and Arias figured that the break couldn't have come soon enough for them. He lay down as well, beak tucked under a wing, but eyes and ears alert for anything alarming. Tybrake started off into the forest, calling back, "I'll try to bring enough for you and Brynne if I catch anything."

"Thank you." Arias watched the wind rattle through the new, green leaves on the trees above, bringing the fresh scent of thawed earth from somewhere far away. Hlaena stirred and reached out to strip the foliage from a nearby bush, chewing with a look of disdain before spitting the wad of greenery back out. She looked longingly at the tenderer leaves growing higher up, but she settled back down with a quiet snort. Arias stood and stretched, leaping up to scale the tree with ease. He selected a smaller branch to rip free, and dropped it within Hlaena's reach before clambering back down. The Alicorn nibbled at the small, bright leaves halfheartedly, but swallowed them this time. Arias couldn't help but notice that the longer he looked at her, the more she seemed different. *Older*, somehow.

"Hlaena, how old are you?" It was something he'd never thought to ask before.

The mare took so long to answer, he almost thought she wasn't going to. Finally, she said,

"I'm not sure. I've lost count." She swallowed another mouthful of leaves.

"Really?"

"Mhmm. Arias, I don't think I've ever explained to you how magick works, have I?"

Arias leaned in. Indeed, she had not.

"Well, you know what magick is, but you probably don't understand how it's based on mana. You can't see mana. It's basically the same as energy, but instead of fueling life, it fuels magick."

Arias nodded. That made sense.

"Most creatures don't know how to manipulate mana. We Alicorns have an innate ability to do so. Some are better at using magick than others, of course, but it's a skill we all have at some base level, particularly when it comes to healing. It's more of a feeling than a conscious thought or action. Or at least, it was." She sighed, using a hoof to scrape a line in the earth. "Whenever I'd heal something—" she erased half of the line using her nose "— the cost would be the expenditure of my own energy and health. A little rest, maybe some food, and I'd recover just fine. However..." She erased the line entirely, then said,

"Naugi was already far past mending when I tried to heal him anyway. In doing so, I offered more than I had access to. Speaking to others, I've learned that you and the other Gryphs took measures to somehow gift me enough of your own mana to survive, but I'd already given up such a large amount that even now I still owe mana that I don't have. The world exists in a balance, and until I give back what I offered, my decline will continue. I have no knowledge of anywhere or any way I could acquire that much mana. I assume that my eventual death is the only way harmony can be restored in the ether."

Arias grimaced. So he hadn't imagined that it looked like she'd aged. "If you were able to offer that much mana in the first place, the inverse is probably true as well, right?"

"I admire your stubbornness." Instead of answering further, Hlaena continued to stare at him, then finally said, "You have changed, Arias. I never really asked you what happened to you after you left our forest. Xio told me how you were doing in Skyhaven of course, but everything after that is unknown to me."

"Xio lied to you about Skyhaven," Arias said. "I mean, he didn't mean to. I lied to him. I only did it because I didn't want you all to worry about me. It wasn't long after I had that meeting with Xio that things fell apart." Arias wasn't happy to recount the experiences he'd had leading up to his time in Arborochre, but he felt like Hlaena deserved the truth. After he fell silent, she dropped her eyes, troubled.

"I should have gone to check on you," she said. "I allowed Xio to convince me otherwise, but it was in the same way that we should have investigated further when we started finding dead and dying creatures in the forests surrounding Glendale. We placed too much faith in Naugi. Perhaps we might've found Shadowbane long before events unfolded as they did, and saved both you and many other creatures from such a terrible fate. I feel that we all stayed in Glendale for so long, safe from the effects of the outside world, that we forgot the weight that actions can carry. Keeping to ourselves was the wrong choice."

"Wishing things in the past could've happened differently is one thing," Arias said, "but the only option we have is to continue moving forward, to whatever lies ahead. Why don't we both promise each other not to dwell on it?"

Hlaena looked up at him, her expression unreadable. "It would seem that in the time we've been separated, you've become the master, and I the apprentice."

"I don't think that could happen even if I lived forever, Hlaena."

"I doubt that," she replied, but her eyes were merrier somehow. The two drifted into silence, and, after a while, Arias's thoughts turned back to the journey, and to Tybrake. Was he having any success with his hunt? And as if reading his thoughts, Hlaena spoke up, saying,

"Tybrake's been gone for a little while, hasn't he?"

"Yeah. You think I should go to check on him?" He didn't want to leave Brynne and Hlaena alone, but he also wanted to go to see if Tybrake needed an extra set of eyes and talons for anything. His eyes fell on Brynne, lying with her eyes closed, ears flicking lazily as she took in the sounds of the surrounding forest. She opened an eye a sliver and said, "If you're so worried, go track him down. I'll keep watch."

He must have stared at her for a little longer than he should have, because she added, "I'm injured, not dead. If anything attacks that I can't handle, there's probably not much you could've done, anyway."

"It'll be fine," Hlaena said. "I'll help keep watch, too."

Arias was hesitant, but he turned to take the path Tybrake had taken. Tracking was never his best ability, and he probably wouldn't have known which way to go had he not been watching the big Ardeigryph start off in this direction to begin with. With a pang, he realized he missed Larin already. She would have made short work out of this. He hoped he'd been right to ask her to help watch over the flock back at the coast, but he knew Bala would need the additional leadership. As noble as Bala's attempts were, he had a severe lack of foresight. Hopefully Hilda would never be a problem again, but Bala was no match for a Gryphon like her. Not even close.

Tybrake was standing so still that Arias almost missed him. He looked something like a tall tree in the forest himself, with his long legs slanting up into his even taller chest and neck. He had his eyes glued on something that Arias couldn't see, and so Arias crept with as much stealth as he could manage, taking soft steps, until he was right next to the keythong. He still couldn't see what the Ardeigryph was looking at, however, and he was about to open his beak to ask when an entire section of tree limb swung out in an arc. He had to brace himself to hold in a cry of shock as he made out the form of the creature the limb was attached to.

The beast was like a giant peryton, but with antlers so huge and moss-covered that Arias hadn't thought there was any way they could be attached to a living creature. It didn't have the wings of a peryton, though, and it was huge; bigger than Tybrake, even. Despite its shaggy fur, it was easy to see how well muscled the beast was. It bellowed and thrust the magnificent crown of bone on its head forward again, jabbing and wrestling with an unseen foe, its sharp antlers leaving deep gouges in the surrounding trunks it scoured. Arias held his breath as the creature threw a casual glance in his and Tybrake's direction, then started to browse on a small bush.

Arias glanced at Tybrake. "Did it see us?" he asked so quietly that his tongue barely moved.

Tybrake shook his head, unbelieving. "I don't know," he whispered. "Should we go for it?"

Arias looked from Tybrake to the giant, his eyes lingering on its enormous antlers again. Like bone branching from its head, he thought. *Bonebrancher.* "I don't know…" he started.

"We might not find anything else today," Tybrake cut in. "These woods are strangely empty."

"Do you even know how to track?"

"No. I eat wrigglers, Arias. Anything else is just a lucky find."

Arias debated as the creature turned and

started to amble away. "We all could use a little something to eat right now. Let's just treat the bonebrancher like a giant peryton."

"Bonebrancher, eh? I like it. Maybe I can kill it the way we killed Shadowbane's warriors?"

Arias grimaced. "I don't think you want to be anywhere near those weapons on its head."

Arias started forward, and Tybrake fell into line as they stalked as close as they could to the beast. It was somehow more gigantic up close. Arias felt a sudden urge to flee, but pressed it back. He burst into a run, with Tybrake on his heels. Their quarry bolted for a few feet, then swung its hindquarters around, putting its antlers in the space between it and them.

Arias dug in to change course, trying to avoid impaling himself on the sharp points, and he heard Tybrake scramble sideways. The Ardeigryph circled off to one side, and the bonebrancher turned its body so it could keep both of them in its field of vision. Arias feinted toward it a couple of times, trying to attract its attention so that Tybrake could move in, but it didn't flinch. In fact, the creature didn't seem afraid at all. This uncomfortable suspicion was confirmed as it bellowed and charged toward him, head lowered. Arias yelped and darted back, hurrying up the nearest tree that looked big enough to both support his weight and keep him away from the ferocious prey. The bonebrancher didn't change its trajectory, and instead rammed its bony crown into the trunk, rattling the entire tree. Arias's eyes widened. The creature didn't just look intimidating. It *was*. With Arias out of reach, the bonebrancher snorted and pawed at the ground, its attention drifting back to Tybrake.

"Climb!" Arias yelled, which proved to be unhelpful. Tybrake jumped and immediately slipped, his narrow talons being unsuited for the task. The trees were too close together to allow for any flying, either. Arias silently cursed to himself. The thought had never occurred to him that Ardeigryph may be poor climbers. The bonebrancher charged toward Tybrake, and Arias gave an exasperated hiss as he leapt down from his branch and shrieked for the creature's attention. It wheeled around, snuffling, and bore down on him with relentless intent, its sharp hooves thundering against the ground. Arias and Tybrake's screaming rose to the same pitch as they scrambled to escape, both running in the same direction with haste. Arias struggled to think rationally as he fled, but the only thing that flitted through his mind was how foolish he and Tybrake had been to try to eat such a formidable looking beast in the first place. It was huge, fast, well-armed, and had all the muscle any creature could ever want. Did it even have a weakness?

"What's going on here?"

Arias's head whipped around, and he caught sight of a splotch of orange melting from the trees. Brynne froze as she saw the behemoth in their midst. Hlaena wasn't far behind her. The bonebrancher considered its two new targets, lowering its antlers as it took aim, grunting.

Brynne, her injuries forgotten as she watched the fearsome creature start to barrel towards her, disappeared up a nearby tree in a blink, leaving Hlaena alone in the corner of forest. The mare took an uncertain step backwards, and Arias dug in, hoping to cut in and distract it, but he was nowhere near fast enough.

Hlaena turned as if to run as the beast closed in on her, but instead of fleeing, she shifted all her weight to her forelegs and lashed out with her hind end, sending the force of the impact into a well-aimed kick. With a tremendous sound like the breaking of thick ice, one of the bonebrancher's antlers severed, landing with a heavy thud. The beast itself staggered backwards, shaking its head and blinking rapidly before collecting itself and tearing away into the forest. Arias stared in disbelief.

"Sky's end, Hlaena! I had no idea you could aim like that!"

"And thank goodness you can," Tybrake exclaimed. "That thing wasn't going to stop until it had us trampled into the ground. Thank you."

Brynne crept down from her tree, embarrassed. "Sorry for leaving you down there, Hlaena. I wasn't expecting a giant, murderous peryton when I caught up to these two."

"It's no one's fault," Hlaena said. "But we should get out of here. I don't know if I have another kick like that left in me, and it might return later for whatever reason. It seems awfully territorial."

"I am very in favor of getting out of this forest," Tybrake said, already turning to begin continuing the journey north. The rest of the group followed, and over time Brynne's embarrassment faded until it gave way to a sliver of amusement. Arias only just heard her mutter,

"Send a couple of keythongs to find prey, and they end up getting attacked by it instead."

He and Tybrake both pretended not to hear the comment, choosing to focus on the path ahead instead, but Hlaena whickered softly upon hearing it. The trip out of the forest was blessedly uneventful, and when the first patch of open sky appeared, Arias almost leapt for joy. It was early enough for more travel, but after recent events, and with a thunderstorm rumbling from afar, they decided to stop for the day. They chose a cluster of boulders as their preferred spot to gather and rest. Hlaena selected a spot next to Brynne, and the two spoke in quiet voices while Arias tucked his head under his wing a little distance away. Tybrake was already asleep and snoring practically from the instant of lying down, and Arias envied how easily he fell into slumbering.

Arias stared at a particularly round boulder resting at the top of the rock pile, and he found himself thinking of the tale Brynne's mother, Iba, had told him about the origin of the Spirit Walker, the very first albino Gryphon. She'd told him that they'd obtained their mysterious color by accidentally eating the moon, and even though he couldn't see the pale disc amid the thick clouds, he wondered what it would taste like if he could ever fly as high as the Gryphon in the story had. However, his fond memory of the affable Iba dissolved into sourness the murm he recalled he'd never see her again. Shadowbane had already paid for his terrible deeds with his life, but it didn't undo the terrible things the Sire had done. Arias's ears rose as snippets of Hlaena's conversation with Brynne drifted over to him, and he was surprised to feel a spear of jealousy at how easily they spoke with one another. When was the last time he'd talked so freely with Hlaena? Not since...

Arias stood up abruptly, garnering curious looks from Brynne and Hlaena.

"I'm too hungry to sleep," he said. "I'm going to see if there's anything close by."

"You know that's a bad idea," Brynne warned. "We've already come across our fair share of dangers in this land. Wait until tomorrow."

"I'll stay close," Arias said, twitching his stub of tail. He loped away before she could get out another retort.

***

The silent night was a welcome refuge as Arias stalked across the dry, shrubby grassland. Shadowbane's words echoed in his mind as a sliver of the moon finally peeked down from its hiding place in the sky, sending down a single, feeble cast of silver light.

There are many names for what you are, but unlucky is far from true.

Arias had trusted Shadowbane, and it had been the most regrettable thing he'd ever done. However, if he'd never been caught and brought to Arborochre in the first place, it was possible that things would have played out the same way regardless. He would have been safe in Glendale with the Alicorns, while the Gryphons of Skyhaven were murdered in their sleep by Shadowbane and his followers. But even so, he was the one who brought the knowledge of poison to Shadowbane. Naugi would have lived, and the rest of the Alicorns, and—"

He tensed, looking back, but relaxed when he saw that it was only Brynne trailing him. She was far too good at that. She waved her tail amicably and said,

"Told you that a little limp wouldn't slow me down."

"How long have you been following me?"

"Long enough to figure out that something is bothering you." She didn't say anything else, just fell into step with him under the moonlight that was beginning to wax dim. After a while he said,

"You know what I miss? Our old hunting outings."

"Those were some good times" Brynne replied with fondness. "And even though I gave you a hard time, you were still the best flusher I've ever hunted alongside. I've hunted with a lot of Gryphons, and you were still better than them, even as a cub."

"Really?" It was the only job Arias could reliably do as part of a hunting party, since his coat color tended to reveal him to prey long before he got close enough to pounce. As an adult he'd learned to mitigate it, as well as becoming a better hunter in general. His best stalking was done during the winter, when he could use the whiteness of the snow as camouflage.

"We shouldn't go too far," Brynne said, "but maybe we could go on a quick hunt right now, for old time's sake. Just think of how excited Tybrake would be to wake up to food!"

Arias gave a bit of a chuckle, though the mirth didn't touch his eyes. "No, you were right earlier. We've already been gone long enough; we can't leave those two asleep unguarded. Let's head back. We could both use some rest."

"Not as hungry as you thought, then?"

Arias didn't reply, but he could feel Brynne's amber eyes on him as she added, "Hlaena's worried about you, you know."

"Yeah. I know."

"Things aren't hard just for you, Arias. You should try to remember that."

143

He finally looked back at her. "Why did Hilda take the Pale away from you?"

Brynne's eyes flashed, but her voice was only somber as she said, "She blamed me for the loss of our old homeland, and for the loss of part of our flock to that sea serpent. She was always ready to raze Arborochre, but I believed we weren't ready. Coming across you and the Ardeigryph was a lucky break for us that changed things, but I have to wonder… had we done things her way and been successful, it's possible Naugi would never have been poisoned, and we would never have had to cross the sea in the first place. At first, she was an outspoken voice all by herself… Then I watched as she slowly convinced more and more Gryphons to join her side. I knew I'd lose eventually." She sighed. "It was like watching you and Kayane all over again."

Arias thought back to the bitter elder hen. She'd divided Skyhaven flock over him, and punished others until they joined her way of thinking. It came down to either him leaving and giving Sheba, the Matriarch, a chance to regain peace in the flock, or him remaining and seeing just how far the flock was willing to destroy itself over him. In a twisted way, Kayane running him out of Skyhaven had saved his life. Only a few moons later, Shadowbane and his warriors had visited the flock and destroyed it.

"I don't blame those who stayed in the Pale for supporting Hilda after my defeat. I slowly lost favor with the others, and they always put their weight behind supporting whoever was the strongest. I was the one who originally instilled that value in them, so how could I go back on it now?" She narrowed her eyes. "It just angers me that she finally won a match against me, and there's nothing I can do about it."

"Could you find her and challenge her again?" Arias asked. Even as he said it, he knew it wasn't a good idea. "I know how much the Pale meant to you. And if they followed you this far, it must have meant you were a pretty good leader. Hilda will take those with her down a dark path if she has her way, and I don't like the idea of it, but I'm not sure what we could do about it. I'm nowhere near as good as you are in a battle. I could hardly keep up with her. That you held out against her as long as you did is amazing to me... and I'm sorry I didn't ask whether you needed my help earlier. Maybe I could have done something to keep her from challenging you in the first place."

Brynne shrugged. "If Gryphons wanted to leave, it wasn't my place to try to stop them. We have the few who joined Larin's group, so at least some of them still have a brain between their ears. Besides, I think leading the Pale was just some sort of dream I wanted to fulfill. I formed them from a scattered group of survivors, and I was the one who made them into a real flock. None of them knew I used to be lowborn. It was all snatched away from me so fast, I guess my first reaction was anger. But I don't think I'm that hen anymore. I'm not even sure I want to go back to being her. I thought that if I joined you and busied myself with trying to do something good

145

by helping Hlaena, then maybe then I could decide what to do by the time I got back to the rest of the flock. Not much of a plan, I guess, but better than nothing."

"It is," Arias said. "I remember how it felt to become Quarnar. I finally had respect and acceptance from other Gryphs, but it came at a cost that I wasn't comfortable with. Some things are better left behind."

"Since when are you the one giving me advice?" Brynne cuffed him playfully behind the ears, and he snapped at her, missing on purpose.

"Let's go hunting tomorrow," he said. "For old time's sake."

"I'll take you up on that," Brynne replied, her tail lashing in anticipation. "Let's do it."

The two returned quietly to the pile of boulders where Hlaena and Tybrake were still resting, and Arias settled next to Hlaena and closed his eyes. Finally, sleep found him.

CHAPTER SIX

Dawn came with a welcome warmth; it was one of the first mornings Arias didn't notice his breath puffing in the air when he awoke. In the daylight, it was easier to see that the thunderstorm threatening the horizon the night before was still present, and was huge enough to stretch across the entirety of the plain they'd have to cross. Brynne wiped sleep from her eyes as she regarded it.

"That'll have every bit of prey worth eating sheltered in," she said. "We might want to put off hunting until after it passes over."

Arias nodded, watching streaks of lightning leap within the dense cloud cover. He'd never seen a thunderhead quite so big before.

Tybrake tilted his head, squinting. "It's weird how it's not moving any closer or further away, isn't it? I could have sworn it was in about the same place before I fell asleep last night."

Three sets of eyes examined the storm for a bit, then agreed with him.

"Maybe it'll clear up before we reach that point," Arias offered.

Hlaena looked up from where she was still nestled in among the boulders and said, "Either way, a flat grassland isn't where we want to be if there's lightning about. Also, I don't see any way past it that doesn't involve a lot of time wasted in trying to go around. There's something unnatural about that storm."

Arias tried to focus his eyes on something in the mist of the storm, but he couldn't be sure it was really there. Was it a simple boulder? A lone tree? Something alive? He blinked. "Is there something in the middle of that tempest?" he asked aloud. Again, three sets of eyes examined the storm.

"Not just one," Tybrake said. "There's three of… whatever that is."

"Looks like a bunch of skinny cliffs," Brynne said. They all stared for a bit longer, until Tybrake's rumbling stomach broke the silence again.

"Well, we aren't going to learn anything or find any food by sitting around here," the Ardeigryph said. "Can we at least start moving, and make a decision on the way?"

Agreement with the plan was uneasy, but there really was no alternative. The group made their way toward the storm, and the landscape became more foreboding as they went. The grass dwindled until it gave way to bare earth, and Arias made out massive dark marks in the dirt that swirled outward like giant black webs. Everyone's pace slowed with uncertainty as they walked on ground that was soggy with the amount of rain pelting down, their eyes narrowed against the stinging droplets. It only took a single lightning bolt striking once, much too close for comfort, to halt their advance.

"There's something causing this storm," Hlaena said, her mane already matted to her neck by rainwater. "Look!"

The Gryphs followed her gaze, noticing that while scattered bolts of lightning were striking randomly, the three strange objects that they'd noticed before were being struck at regular intervals. They seemed to be made of some sort of rock.

"Watch out!" Brynne hissed, ducking as something swooped low enough to become visible in the swirling cloud cover. It was huge and feathered, and changed course to circle before landing some distance away from them. With wings folded, the Aquila wasn't nearly as big as it had seemed on the wing, but it was still a formidable creature. Its storm gray plumage crackled with electricity as Arias, Tybrake and Brynne regarded it with suspicion.

"Don't try to intimidate it," Hlaena called out. "It's not a battle we'd win."

Arias froze into place, still untrusting, but eager to avoid a conflict. The Aquila watched as he, Tybrake, and Brynne obediently sat near Hlaena, and then it turned to look at the Alicorn instead.

"What strange company you keep, mare," he said, electricity still coursing through his dark feathers. "I would have rid my territory of those three, had I not seen you among them. As I'm sure you know, our kind have always shared the sky as allies."

"I'm well aware, and thank you for not attacking," Hlaena replied. "I assume this maelstrom is your doing?"

"Indeed. My mate and I have chicks on the way, and they will not hatch without the constant touch of our electricity." He nodded skyward, to where the barest outline of another Aquila flashed among the clouds. "My mate can maintain the storm on her own for a time, but I won't leave her for long. What is your business here?"

"We must continue our journey north," Hlaena replied. "We don't wish to take up more of your time, or to disrupt your nesting, but may we pass?"

The Aquila took a step closer, his sharp talons squelching in the moist earth. "Ordinarily, I'd say no," he said. His piercing yellow eyes stared at

Hlaena with an intensity that drew Arias and the others to their feet again. The Aquila shot them a glance, electricity popping as if in reminder, and continued to move closer. "But I sense that something… isn't quite right." He traced the outline of the crack in her horn, then closed his eyes. "I've known very few of your kind, Alicorn. In less than a moon, spring will be well upon us, and our young will be hatched and no longer dependent upon our storm to survive. But I don't think you can wait that long, can you?"

Hlaena hesitated. She shook her head.

The Aquila ruffled his feathers, then nodded. "I'll speak with my mate," he said, "though she may be hesitant to halt this storm for even the time it would take for you to cross. Wait here."

He disappeared into the swirling abyss of thick clouds above with a mighty whooshing of his wings, and Arias moved slightly closer to Hlaena. She looked miserable standing there, shivering as rainwater dripped off her long eyelashes, and he wished there was more he could do. Presently, the Aquila's mate landed to speak with them; she was distinctive with her larger size and pale, smoke colored plumage. She glanced over Arias and the other Gryphs before addressing Hlaena by saying, "I am sorry for your plight, but we cannot break this storm. We've dutifully tended to it all winter awaiting the hatching of our young ones. However, I can see your safe passage through it. If we fly quickly, my absence from maintaining the storm won't harm our chicks."

"I've been too weak to fly for a while now. Even if I could, it wouldn't be fast by any means," Hlaena said, crestfallen. The Aquila hen blinked.

"Very well. Then with your permission, I'll carry you across. The rest of your... companions are flighted, I assume?"

Arias and Brynne nodded, but Tybrake was staring upward with wide eyes. "We're flying into *that?*"

The thunderhead rumbled as if in acknowledgement, and the Ardeigryph gulped.

"Stay close to me, and the lightning won't touch you," the Aquila said, growing impatient. "If everyone is in agreement, we'll be going now. Maintaining a storm of this size is a challenge for two Aquilas, let alone just one. If you are unsure, turn back and be done with it."

"It's the only way," Arias said, hoping to encourage Tybrake. "It'll be okay. You can fly in the middle if it makes you feel safer. I'll take up the rear."

The keythong gave a slow nod, eyes still trained above.

"Let's go!" the Aquila boomed, throwing herself into the wind. "Stay close!" She snatched up Hlaena, and her huge wings carried them aloft with incredible speed. With nervous glances at one another, Arias and the other two Gryphs rose to hurry into the black thunderhead after her.

***

It wasn't impossible to see the Aquila hen in
the storm, but it might as well have been. Arias
and the others followed her brief outline
whenever the lightning flashed to reveal her,
knowing that, while not expressly said, getting
lost in the storm promised a bleak fate. Arias
blinked constantly as the rain spattered his face.
Forcing his eyes open past a squint was a
challenge in itself; rainwater blurred his vision the
murm he tried to get a look at anything, and he
found himself shaking his head incessantly. Naia's
seashell pendant whipped against his neck so hard
that it stung. It was difficult to believe that the
Aquila was taking the brunt of the turbulence,
with Brynne and Tybrake lessening the effect
even more by flying ahead of him. Arias
constantly felt as if he was on the verge of being
ripped asunder. It took focus and luck to even
stay in the vicinity of the Aquila.

Static crackled through Arias's fur, and he
gave a cry as a lightning bolt lanced past his right
wing, disappearing into the squall below. The
thunder that followed was so loud that Arias
could no longer hear the pattering of the rain or
the howling of the wind, just a hitch pitched
whining that permeated his ears. The dark form
of the Aquila male became visible in a flash of
light off to their left, and he called out to her as
she passed by. She returned his call, and Arias
watched as the male busied himself fanning the
clouds with his colossal wings, keeping the clouds
charged with electricity. Then Arias got his first
look at the mysterious towers that the pair were

so meticulously watching over.

The three towers everyone had glimpsed from afar were pillars of shiny, dark stones. At the top, and presumably also at the top of the other two, was a single, luminous egg, red hot from repeated lightning strikes. At the same time as Arias marveled at the sight, his crest was yanked upward without his input. He looked ahead to see what was going on, and saw that Brynne's fur and feathers were also standing on end. Hlaena yelled something that he couldn't hear over the gale, but his confusion was interrupted by the brightest flash he'd ever seen in his life, followed by a deafening thunderclap. He was momentarily blinded and deafened, but the first sight he saw when he regained his vision was a maroon glow. The Aquila dipped sideways, her gaze chastising as she screamed,

"Fly closer, all of you! You're too far out, I can't protect you if you're too far away!"

The trio of Gryphs hurried to comply, crowding in so close around the Aquila that they may as well have been carried in her claws alongside Hlaena. The only sign they had that it was safe to begin to relax was the reduction of the wind's howling, and the thinning of the sheets of rain. Soon it was just a soft patter, and then nothing at all. The sun reached down with a tentative ray, offering precious little warmth as the Aquila hen banked to land, depositing Hlaena carefully on the ground below. The Alicorn mare took a single step and then collapsed into a heap. The Aquila gave a sad cluck and shook her head.

"You diverted that last bolt of lightning as it slipped by me, but it seems to have been too much for you. I'm sorry, but I can't leave my mate to tend the storm alone any longer. If you don't reach whatever it is you are looking for, I wish a peaceful passing to you. Let no one say that the Aquilas haven't been hospitable to your kind on this day." She addressed only Hlaena, but Arias, Tybrake and Brynne bowed low in thanks, regardless. Hlaena managed a small dip of her head and said in a weak voice,

"Indeed, none will say such a thing. Thank you."

The Aquila stepped carefully over Hlaena, opening her stormy wings, and the Gryphs used their own wings to shield themselves and Hlaena from the buffets of wind that followed her departure.

"A little rest, and I'll be fine," Hlaena said, closing her eyes as her head sank lower and lower. "Just a few murms of sleep…"

She was asleep before she could finish the sentence, and so Arias and his companions gathered in close around her, damp and isolated at the edge of the storm, and tried to find some rest for their own aching muscles. Arias was beginning to forget what normal life felt like. A long flight across the ocean, followed by a brief rest, and then another long flight across the ocean, followed by a brief rest, and then an intense flight through a thunderstorm… he hoped this wasn't a pattern that would continue. If he thought he was hungry before, he had no idea how bad it would be after such a flight. The gnawing in his stomach never ceased, and was a constant reminder that it had been far too long since he'd eaten a good meal. But between the two persistent agonies of hunger and exhaustion, the latter overcame him. Once he lay down, the idea of rising again didn't cross his mind. No one spoke, aside from the occasional groan as someone stretched out a limb, or, in Brynne's case, a muttered curse. Tybrake's expression was dark as he lay with his feathers ruffled against the residual wind, and Brynne looked as surly as ever as she tucked her head under a wing to sleep. Arias followed her example, and drifted off before he was even aware he was slipping away from the world of the conscious.

***

Arias was the first to wake before any of the others. It was midday. He didn't exactly wake of his own volition; the terrible reminder of how foodless his belly was drove him to his feet, however unwillingly. He didn't wake anyone—they definitely needed the rest—and he doubted he'd find anything to eat anyway. He hadn't seen anything alive since leaving the bonebrancher, so he figured it was safe enough. He felt nothing close to capable enough to hunt successfully. Despite his best attempt, he'd hardly made it away from the others before Brynne stirred and rose to trail him.

"Halada's tail!" she grumbled. "And I thought I was sore before. Let's agree to never do anything like that again, why don't we?"

"I'm just going to look for anything to eat," Arias said. "I can't remember ever wanting food this so much."

Brynne snorted. "Well, maybe I can double your chances of catching something. Let's try to stay close, though."

"Yeah. Are you sure you wouldn't rather stay here? You're still favoring that leg."

She snorted. "I told you, no need to worry about me. Let's go."

"The winds forbid if someone cares to ask whether you're alright, huh? Why don't you take the right? I'll take the left, and drive anything I find toward you."

Brynne slipped off to comply, adopting the best stalking pose she could maintain, and Arias mimicked her low, creeping crouch. It wasn't easy to see in the tall grass, which was high enough to brush against his chest, and rustled at even the slightest touch. Every so many steps, he popped his head up to scan the area, making sure he was keeping Brynne within sight. They swept the area tightly, ensuring there was no chance they missed any sign of any creature whatsoever. Their careful advance paid off when Arias heard an obvious rustling among the tall grass directly ahead. He went rigid, hoping Brynne was paying attention, and thankfully she was. They both sank into the grass, so low that only the tips of their ears and crests were visible, locking onto the same point of focus. Brynne would stay put; she was far enough ahead to take whatever it was if it ran either straight or toward her. All Arias needed to do was to make sure it chose one of those two directions to flee in.

It was hard to see the creature clearly as it browsed among the grass, ignoring the taller blades to pull at the small, tender shoots that were just beginning to peek up from the soil. Its body was mostly shades of brown and green, a perfect color to vanish into the similarly-colored foliage. Arias took a tentative step, then another. If he wasn't so focused on capturing and killing the thing, he might've drooled down his chest in anticipation. He took in as much detail as he could, excited to see that there was enough meat for all three of them to eat from. The creature was a bit smaller than he was, but it would still probably take both him and Brynne to bring it down. He willed himself not to blink as the beast stopped picking at vegetation and cast a cautious glance across the plains, somehow sensing that it wasn't quite alone. The two thick, serrated horns on its head caught Arias's eye, and he mentally noted that he'd have to look out for those. They forked at the ends, forming sharp points that arched forward in a way that almost gave him pause. Almost.

The closer Arias got to his quarry, the more interesting the creature became. Oddly enough, it almost seemed to shimmer when it moved, and Arias realized that it had green scales that ran all along its body, creating a strange contrast against the abundant tawny fur that grew from its mane, tail, and lower legs. The creature pranced nervously on its dainty cloven hooves, and Arias held his breath with each small movement he took toward it, not wanting to startle it too early.

Arias was close enough now that he could see the eyes of the beast; the large orbs were almost serpentine in appearance with their sharp, vertical pupils. The creature returned to plucking at grass again, and he noted that it was gathering them up in its mouth instead of eating them, almost like it was saving them for later. That was a bit unusual, but he supposed that creatures made nests and such out of grass all the time. He was close enough that it would notice him at any murm. He hoped that Brynne was ready. His tongue seemed to guide him forward, prodding him to advance toward the source of delicious and unaware meat browsing just in front of him. He swallowed hard.

The creature stopped browsing for the second time. Its strange eyes swung toward Arias, and he tensed, feeling that it must have seen his white pelt among the waving brown blades of grass. But instead of bolting away, which would have immediately spurred him into pursuit, it turned and simply started to walk away. He stalked it a bit further before springing into motion, and the creature looked over its shoulder, trading its walk for a trot, still holding the grass shoots in its mouth. When Arias started to gain on it, it sprang into long, effortless leaps, and he had to put everything he had into sprinting just to keep up with it. Brynne joined the chase early, realizing she'd have no chance of catching up to the speedy beast if she waited even a murm longer.

She was keeping up with Arias despite her bad leg, but their quarry remained just out of reach. Snarling, Brynne opened her wings and propelled herself forward with a mighty leap, talons outstretched. Arias's heart soared; Brynne was directly lined up to take the beast down! But then the creature shifted to running *on top* of the grass, leaving Brynne to tumble to the hard ground.

Intent on not letting their food escape, Arias held his surprise in check as he hurtled past Brynne and leapt skyward, hoping to cut off any possible escape route the creature chose. The beast turned to look at him with its strange eyes. It wasn't even panting! How?

It doesn't matter, he thought. He'd gained the tiny distance that he needed to capture it, and that was all he needed. He closed his wings with a snap and dropped toward the earth, talons grappling for whatever meaty parts he could sink his claws into. The creature dropped its mouthful of grass as it let out a single cry, tumbling to the ground. Arias didn't have a chance to do much else, however, because it drew in a sharp intake of air, eyes briefly flashing an iridescent gold as it exhaled not air, but a tongue of fire.

Arias withdrew with a yelp and scrambled backwards as the flame singed his fur and feathers, and Brynne, having rejoined the chase, skidded to an abrupt halt somewhere behind him.

"Did it burn you?" she asked, alarmed. "Open your eyes! Can you see?"

"I'm fine," Arias panted, brushing her away. It took him a murm to check to confirm that was actually true, and to his relief, it was. *Thank Halada for that at least*, he thought sinking to the ground to catch his breath. He tried to determine where the beast had run to, but it had seemingly vanished into thin air. Was there no end to the odd, dangerous creatures of this land?

Brynne was already tracking ahead to try to find the whereabouts of their prey, and she fluttered her wings with a yip of surprise not too far away. Arias followed after her, and soon saw why. The plains ended in a sudden drop off, and the abrupt edge was well hidden by thick grass. The path down the cliff face was covered in loose rocks, none of which looked disturbed by anything having passed by recently. Down below, in a gorge, was a patch of forest and a glimmering river.

"Unless it went under the ground, it had to have gone this way," Brynne said, still trying to catch her breath. "Unless it's hiding somewhere out here... but I don't see how. Did you see it running on the top of the grass like that? I don't even know what to think anymore.. I hate this place."

"I saw," Arias said, flopping down next to her. "I'm pretty sure that my stomach is just going to digest itself at this point."

Brynne stretched her good leg forward to scratch at her hide. "I think mine already did."

Arias traced the outline of the gorge, trying to see past the trees that gave cover to whatever secrets it held. "I know we nearly drowned in that storm back there, but I could use a proper drink. Maybe Tybrake can catch some wrigglers in that river down there. I know that I'd eat anything right now."

Brynne made a gagging imitation upon hearing that. "I think I'll just starve to death; those things are disgusting."

"Suit yourself." Arias stood and started to head back the way they'd come, and Brynne reluctantly fell into line behind him.

"I hate it when prey escapes," she said, peering back at the gorge. "Even weird prey that can breathe fire. Did you see how plump and juicy that thing looked?"

"Please don't talk about it. Thinking about it only makes it worse. I can't believe it escaped. Maybe we'll have another chance. Let's just focus on getting back for now."

***

Tybrake didn't hide his look of dissatisfaction upon seeing Arias and Brynne return with empty claws. He perked up, however, when they told him about the gorge.

"Where there's water there's bound to be wrigglers! Let's go!" he roared, jumping to his feet.

Arias would've chuckled at the Ardeigryph's

plucky reaction, but instead he found his eyes drawn beyond Tybrake, to a suspiciously still Hlaena. He frowned, leaning down to nudge the Alicorn. "Hlaena. Wake up."

Brynne and Tybrake fell silent as they, too, eyed the mare. Her eyes were still behind their lids, her nostrils no longer flaring as she breathed. Whereas before it was clear when she was asleep, it no longer seemed to be the case.

"That Aquila said she used her magick back there in the storm," Brynne said quietly. "You don't think that doing that...?"

Tybrake averted his eyes, looking somber. "Ah. I'm sorry, Arias. You really did try. I thought she'd make it. At least she went peacefully, in her sleep. We'll dig her a nice spot. You'll see."

Arias didn't respond. He kept watching the mare for any sign of life, any flicker at all that suggested she was still alive. There were sounds, but not from Hlaena. They were coming from the grasslands, from behind. Tybrake and Brynne wheeled around, immediately alert, but the creatures weren't trying to hide. It was the same prey they were chasing before, but with another, much larger member of its kind alongside it. This one was distinct with a long beard, shaggy mane, and horns that contorted into many tines. Tybrake's eyes lit up upon seeing it.

"I never thought food would deliver itself," he said, snaking toward the smaller creature. Brynne hissed for him to stop.

"Never take the offspring while the parent
draws near," she warned. "Prey on land doesn't
willingly approach, Tybrake. This is the same
morsel that evaded Arias and me just now. It can
breathe fire and run on top of the grass; it's no
simple prey. We should be wary that it sought us
out. These things could be intelligent. Arias! I
know now's not the time, but you need to pay
attention. *Please!*"

"Looks like one of you has some sense," the
larger of the two creatures said, amused. "It looks
like you were right, Ly-ra. They are savages."

Tybrake's long bill dropped open. "You can
talk?"

"I feel it would be more appropriate for us to
relay surprise that *you* can talk, especially
considering the fact you tried to eat my
apprentice earlier. It looks like you have plenty of
food here already! Anyhow, seeing as you can
understand the common tongue, I suppose you
must be of some measure of intelligence, which
makes this much easier. You're in Kirin territory,
and you are not welcome. I have no idea how you
got past the guardian of the southern forest, or
the nesting Aquilas, or how you were stealthy
enough to bring down this Alicorn, but
regardless, while I commend your evident
tenacity, I now request that you leave
immediately. Leave the poor Alicorn. She'll be
given a proper burial. Such a divine beast is
worthy of more than being consumed by

savages."

"Hlaena isn't food." Arias flattened his ears, but his voice remained level. "And I'm sorry that we thought you were. A word from your apprentice, and we would've stopped our pursuit. We were just headed north to try to find some help for Hlaena. Please, do you know of anyone or anything to help save her?"

Brynne shot him a withering glance. "Arias…"

Ly-ra sniffed delicately in Arias's direction, wrinkling her nose. "It is hard to believe a story like that from a lying scavenger," she said. "Master Mati-jai gave you an order, not a suggestion. Depart, and leave the Alicorn behind."

"He already said she isn't prey," Brynne growled. "And we aren't following any commands from a runt like you. I decide where I am and am not welcome, and you may have your little fire trick, but I've a few of my own. Why don't you just take your high and mighty attitude and leave us?"

Ly-ra laughed. "You don't actually think you could've caught me back there, do you? I let you get that close, just for fun, and to laugh at how you looked with your tongue lolling out of your head. I bet you thought you caught me by surprise, but the tactics you flesh eaters use is old news to me. I could give you all the time from the beginning of your life to the end of it to catch me, and I'd still rest easy with the knowledge that you'd never be able to."

Brynne hissed, tail bristling. "Let's see if you're right, then."

"Enough!" Mati-jai snapped. "Ly-ra, don't argue with such low-ranking beasts. Take the Alicorn, and let's be on our way."

Ly-ra winced at the rebuke, then trotted forward, but Brynne and Tybrake sprang forward to block her path. The young Kirin looked over her shoulder at her master, and Mati-jai let out a frustrated sigh. He dipped his head sideways, his horns giving off the slightest aura of gold, and Brynne and Tybrake both let out a cry as they were lifted off the ground. Mati-jai looked them over, head still held sideways.

"Just remember that I gave you the option for a peaceful resolution. Goodbye, now."

Brynne and Tybrake struggled, but, before they could do anything, Mati-jai whipped his head in the other direction, and the two Gryphs were flung skyward. It wasn't a gentle toss. They were hurled as easily as though they were pebbles, and they flipped head over heels as their screaming faded into the distance. For the first time since the appearance of the Kirin, Arias raised his crest in alarm.

"Now, wait a murm—" he started, but the invisible force grabbed hold of him, levitating him ever so slightly off the ground.

The amount of force it took to send Arias so high and so far was inconceivable. The air was rushing by so fast that he couldn't spread his wings to slow himself, let alone get in half a breath of air. He only regained control of his wits after the magick fueling his momentum fizzled out, and his descent took on some semblance of normalcy. It was a dizzying spiral to the ground below, and after landing, he had to lie down for a few murms, eyes closed so that he couldn't see the lurching of his surroundings. He wasn't sure how long he lay there, with his innards still feeling like they were twirling without him, but eventually he heard Tybrake calling out from some distance away. As he called back, Brynne stumbled up to sit next to him.

"Halada's sake," he growled, feeling sick. Brynne just flattened her ears and squeezed her eyes shut. Tybrake eventually appeared a while later, his feathers in a wild disarray.

"Why is everything in this new land a dumb *tuca?*" he groaned. "What happened to normal prey? Normal water, without sea serpents and such in them? Is that asking too much?" He lay down and buried his head under a wing, still moaning.

The horizon finally stopped shifting enough for Arias to focus on the distant sight of two figures moving across the plain, a white object floating through the air alongside them. Indignant anger rose in his gut.

"I'm going back," he said. "I didn't come all

this way just to let some preymeat steal my mother. If anyone is burying Hlaena, it's going to be me."

"Don't think I'm afraid to go back just because they're cheating magick users," Brynne spat. "Winds above! When I get my talons on that little one…" She dug her claws into the earth, eyes hard. "When I get my talons on her," she said again, tail lashing.

"Ey," Tybrake agreed, "What annoying creatures! We said we didn't mean to try to eat them. Great waves, I never want to experience this again. We need to be careful while we find out where they're staying in that valley. Everything has a weakness. Just… ugh. Give me a murm." He buried his head under his wing again.

"If their magick is anything like Alicorn magick, they can only use it in a certain radius," Arias said. "We have to split up; staying together will only make it easier for them to overcome us again." He paused. "And I have to say, if I get my claws on either of those Kirin, I can't promise that I'll be entirely peaceable this time."

Tybrake and Brynne snorted their agreement.

"First we should try to find some food and water. We won't be any use against those dumb gizzards in our current state," Brynne said.

"Yes," Arias said. "No use wasting time. Let's go."

It didn't take Arias long to come to the edge of the gorge again. He, Tybrake and Brynne had all taken different paths across the grassland, just in case the Kirin were on the lookout for them. It was tempting to glide down the sheer face of the slope to the shining ribbon that he could make out below; it was almost certainly a sizeable stream or river. He couldn't risk the exposure, however, and opted to clamber carefully down the incline, keeping to the cover offered by oversized rocks and awkward sprigs of brush. His progress was probably faster than he should have let it be, but it was hard to force himself to slow his pace when he got close enough to hear tell-tale trickling nearby.

Cutting through the surrounding dense greenery to find the dark green water glinting in the sunlight was enough to urge Arias into a cautious trot. With a final glance around, he drank from the water, sure that Tybrake would be ecstatic to come across it. He felt hollow even after drinking the water, feeling neither quenched thirst nor sated hunger. With Hlaena gone, it felt like everything else he cherished was subject to being yanked away. What if Hilda had already returned to take revenge on the flock, and Larin and Lue's presence hadn't been enough of a deterrent? And Alissi and the rest of the Strigigryph may already be starving to death. There was no guarantee that the prey on the island could sustain them after being decimated by all the Gryphs before their departure.

Arias stared into the silt at the bottom of the

river. What did a Gryphon do when he had nothing left at all? Brynne and Tybrake had agreed to help him get Hlaena's body back, but what good would that do?

The Kirin could kill my friends, leaving me as the only one alive.

He shook his head at the thought. Could he really turn back and just leave Hlaena behind? He felt like he'd already failed her and the other Alicorns too many times. He owed her at least this one thing. And if he couldn't accomplish it, maybe he deserved to die. He didn't have time to stop Brynne and Tybrake—he had no idea where they were—but he could make sure he was the first one to reach the Kirin. If he could do that, maybe he could save Hlaena before they put themselves in danger.

Arias set to work picking at the fine silt along the edge of the river. His Ardeigryph friend Ratina had taught him a trick back in Arborochre, a camouflaging method that would involve the still-chilly mud along the riverbank. Ratina had rubbed ash and charred bark into her brilliant blue plumage to dull the color, and he did the same thing now with the wet, clay-like earth, making sure to cover every bit of himself. With a final roll to make sure he had a thorough coat of it caked onto him, he crept away from the river, shivering. His disguise was every bit as heavy and as frigid as he'd imagined it would be, but it was better than announcing his presence to the Kirin. He cut away from the river, wanting to find out whether the Kirin lived in distinct groups. Most intelligent creatures did, after all.

Always keeping close to cover, Arias headed
downstream. It wasn't long before he reached a
rocky outcropping that came right up to the edge
of the river. He wouldn't usually have thought
anything of it, except that now he'd have to either
swim around it, climb it, or fly over it. While he
considered his options, a pair of Kirin casually
meandered *into* the solid rock. Arias stiffened,
wondering whether his eyes were deceiving him.
He ducked into some reeds. Two different Kirin
walked out from the stone, laughing and speaking
with one another in an interesting language as
they disappeared into the forest. He waited to see
if the two original Kirin would reappear after
they'd gone inside the rock. They didn't.

Arias crept through the greenery to get a
better look at the outcropping, but the new view
of it didn't deepen his understanding of what he'd
just witnessed. Another Kirin, this one a small
buck, emerged from the rock, yawning, and
cocked his rear leg as he waited just outside the
odd entrance. It took a murm for Arias to realize
that he must be standing guard. He was the laziest
guard Arias had ever seen, but still. He was
around the same size as Ly-ra, and it wasn't long
before he lay down, forelegs crossed, and
dropped his head. A wriggler flipped out of the
river, and the resulting splash roused the guard,
but it wasn't long before he'd settled down again.
Arias watched with forced patience. Would
another Kirin join him? Was he actually even a
guard? How did he walk out from solid rock?
And what other abilities did these creatures have?

He watched as the Kirin's head weaved lower and lower, until finally he was flat against the ground, his breathing slow and even.

Arias stared at the guard with a critical eye. It was *too* easy. But what else could he do? He ran from where he was hiding, and easily covered the distance to the guard, slowing to a soft walk as he drew near. He listened, and was surprised to hear sounds of talking and laughter coming from the rock behind the prostrate Kirin. He poked experimentally at the rock with his beak, jerking back with a muted cry as, instead of resistance, he passed through the stone. He'd made enough noise to wake his sleeping companion, however, and there was a brief murm of Arias staring into the eyes of the shocked Kirin before he sprang into action.

Hopping on to sit squarely on the back of the stunned guard was easy for Arias, but holding the Kirin's muzzle shut with his claws and hanging on at the same time was much more difficult. Amazingly, the guard was able to struggle to his feet, and alarm coursed through Arias as the Kirin took a lurching step toward the stone. Arias placed his razor-sharp, hooked bill to the buck's throat, and he froze.

"This is what sleeping on guard duty gets you," Arias growled. "Tell me where that Alicorn is. Don't raise your voice above a whisper when I release you!"

He remained seated on the slick scales covering the guard's back, and received a spiteful glare as the Kirin looked backward at him, eyes sparkling gold. The murm Arias released his mouth, a deluge of the strange language he'd heard the other Kirin speaking from afar came out. Arias cuffed him between the eyes, hissing. "You speak the common tongue, I already know you do. No more nonsense!" The guard's eyes were hard, but he sighed, and his eyes paled to a flat green.

"Alright, I'm not going to do anything. My master is going to kill me... You're one of the flesh eaters, aren't you? You're not going to try to hurt anyone, are you?"

"I'd rather not. Let's go."

"I can't walk with you on my back," the guard complained, exasperated. "It's a miracle I'm even standing."

"I don't believe you. Let's go."

"Please! I promise I won't try anything, on my word."

Arias snorted. "Words aren't worth much. You do, however, look like you might taste pretty good to my friends and me. I could always just kill you and hide you in those bushes for later. I never thought I'd get this close to one of you, but now that I have, you're not so scary after all. What's it going to be?"

The Kirin gave him another glare, but took a step forward.

"Not so fast," Arias said. "We're going to check to see if the way is clear first, aren't we? And one more thing. If I die, you'd better bet your weird little horns that I'm taking you with me." And to emphasize his point, he placed his head right alongside the Kirin's neck, so that he could see everything and make good on his promise, if needed. The Kirin swallowed as he poked his head into the strange rock-entrance—it looked like solid rock, even though it obviously wasn't—and into the bright world beyond.

***

It was hard for Arias to make sense of what he was seeing at first. He didn't understand how there could be light in a place away from the sun, and yet there was. There were huge spheres of it, swirling above stone pillars in the corners of the gigantic space—a space filled with plants, intricate patterns inlaid into the solid ground, and flowing water that began and ended somewhere he couldn't make out.

"This way," the guard whispered, even though Arias was still firmly seated on his back. Arias expected a trap, but the spaces they entered and left were empty of Kirin as they proceeded on their way. Through the walls, he could hear murmuring, always soft and reserved, and the clicking of cloven hooves tapping against the hard stone floor, but he never saw the makers of the noises. He became aware almost immediately that the paths the guard was taking him on were on a downward slant, leading him into the bowels of the earth. He felt a lurching in his gut as he recalled the entrance to Arborochre, similar in its entryway of twisted cave systems deep beneath the forest. That horrible place, hidden under the guise of a sweet paradise... he shook his head. He was here to collect Hlaena, nothing else. He tried not to let his eyes wander as he took in entire walls of stone that cascaded to the ground as ornately as a waterfall, small globes of light revolving in alcoves, and interesting mushrooms and mosses that grew as cheerfully as if they were above ground in the soil. He focused on the guard instead, who seemed genuinely terrified to have him on his back, as Arias had hoped he would. The guard's fear must mean he didn't have the magickal prowess of the Kirin he'd faced with his friends on the plain.

"Everyone's at Peace right now," the guard spluttered. "We should be fairly alone. You won't hurt me, will you? I promise I won't do anything."

Arias didn't reply. He was attempting to memorize the way out, just in case something did happen and he needed to make a quick exit. The Kirin stopped in a small space that had a single hole cut into the high ceiling, just large enough to light the area. All manner of plant life had been crammed in here, enough that they were bunched up against the walls: bright flowers, fragrant boughs, ferns, grasses, leaves, and bundles of twigs. All had been tied into neat bundles according to their kind. And at their center, lying on a pile of beautiful purple flowers of some sort, was Hlaena, solitary and pale against the vibrant color. Arias resisted the urge to cross the space over to her. He noted with dismay that the hole in the ceiling was much too small to fly through, and that there wasn't enough space to take off from, anyway. He gave his prisoner a meaningful jab.

"Why do you have her here?" he asked.

"I-I don't know! It's not me! I'm just an apprentice. I thought they were going to revive her."

Arias blinked. "Revive her? You can do that?"

"Well, she's not dead. Not yet, anyway. But you're just going to eat her anyway, so why do you care?"

Arias froze. Hlaena was still alive! How? It didn't matter. It was only a matter of time before Peace, whatever that was, ended. The Kirin guard was looking at him over his shoulder, eyes nervous. Arias said,

"I don't want to eat her. She's very important to me, contrary to what you all seem to think. You have the ability to use magick, don't you?"

The guard swallowed hard, nodding.

"You're going to help me take her. And then you're going to tell me how exactly you'd revive her."

"Okay, okay! But listen! She's really not in any shape to travel. I wouldn't try to move her, especially not with my clumsy magick. She's barely alive, you know? Wait! Please, believe me! If I move her and she dies, I don't want you killing me for thinking I was lying or something."

Arias opened his beak to reply, but before he could, his eyes were drawn to the shadow of shapes falling across the entrance of the space. In a flash, he pressed the guard to the ground and stood over him, the hook of his bill pressed against the Kirin's neck.

Mati-jai pressed through the entry way, looking entirely unsurprised. He gave a frustrated sigh when he saw Arias, and dismissed his two companions, both of whom were giving shocked cries of alarm. They scampered away obediently.

"I was hoping you wouldn't come, and yet, here you are," the Kirin said. He dropped his eyes to Arias's prisoner. "I'm not surprised you got past that one. I told them not to use him for guard duty. No one ever listens to me, though. You'd think being an elder would command more respect."

The guard Arias had in his claws had become a limp, trembling heap of fur and scales. He almost felt bad for him. He was sure it wasn't possible to feign fear *that* well.

"Let the apprentice go," Mati-jai said. "He was minding his own business. I'm the one who took you for an impromptu flight, remember?"

Arias didn't slacken his grip. "Hlaena is one of us," he said. "I'm not leaving without her."

"Not that again," the elder snapped. "Your kind should not be keeping the company of a creature like her. Let him go, or you won't be seeing your friends again. I'll release you together—peacefully—and without repercussions, but only if you release him, and leave without the Alicorn."

Arias didn't move. "No."

"Yes," Mati-jai said, not hiding his annoyance. Or I'll fling you again, whether you're holding that fawn or not, only this time there won't be a sky to catch you. He'll understand that his death will be for the greater good… but you, how will you justify your wasted life? I can guarantee you won't survive. I'll make sure of that."

Arias studied Mati-jai. It was impossible to tell whether he was lying or not, but, considering the strength he'd shown before, Arias decided to believe him. His captive's quaking and whimpering also seemed to verify the validity of the threat. Nevertheless, he wouldn't back down. "I'm not leaving without her," he said again.

Mati-jai snarled, but the ugly expression was almost immediately replaced by one of conniving. "You're smarter than I thought, flesh eater. Fine then. Why don't we come to a compromise? Let the apprentice go, and I'll let you live, perhaps even leave with the Alicorn, if you let me Witness your memories."

Well, that doesn't sound dangerous at all. Arias had

no idea what Mati-jai meant by "Witnessing" his memories, but he didn't like it. "If I'm such a foul creature to you, what value could my memories possibly have to you?"

The elder Kirin chuckled. "Ah yes, you are much smarter than you look. However, you've already placed yourself in a position to be killed by me, so why does this matter? It's humorous that you think you have some power here. Admittedly, you're right, I don't want that apprentice to die, but he isn't *my* apprentice by any means. His master will find another pupil, and may hate me for a while, but all things pass with time. And I have lots of that left." He lifted his ears as the unmistakable shrieking of an Ardeigryph echoed from somewhere up above. "Well, I'm getting tired of watching you try to reason your way out of this. Blu-shi, I'm sorry for this. Die knowing that you served your master well, wherever he or she is."

Arias felt the Kirin tense in his grasp. In a shaky voice, the guard whispered, "For the glory of the Everspring!"

Something about the finality of the statement unnerved Arias. The elder Kirin's magick started to take hold of him, slipping through his fur and feathers like tingling rivulets of dew. He threw his hostage away from him.

"All right, you're right. You win. Please don't punish my friends, though. They were only following me." He retreated back a few steps, and Mati-jai signaled for Blu-shi to retreat. The young guard did so with haste, casting not a single look back as he scrambled out of the space. Arias watched him go, feeling surprisingly little. He'd come here without a plan, and had accepted that getting caught was a possibility. He was, however, disappointed that he was letting this all end without a fight. He couldn't pretend that he wanted Blu-shi to die, though. It didn't feel right to punish someone who was involved by chance, however well it might have spited Mati-jai and the other Kirin.

Mati-jai stepped closer, and Arias held the Kirin's strange, vertical gaze. He wondered whether the elder would snap his neck like a twig and be done with it, but something chaotic in the creature's eyes let him know it wouldn't be quite so quick as that.

"You're a bold one, I'll give you that," Mati-jai said. Arias, once again, didn't reply. It was interesting how this old Kirin, despite his grizzled features, managed not to look feeble at all.

"Close your eyes," Mati-jai barked. "Or, if you'd rather, I can gouge them out for you."

Arias complied, trying not to let his hatred of the creature show. The transition into "Witnessing" was immediate. He was vaguely aware of his legs folding, and then it was as if his physical body had faded away, as if he were dreaming, caught in a *fuhkrata*. And then came the greatest intrusion of his privacy that he'd ever experienced in his life.

While Arias's innermost dialogue had always been only accessible to him, Mati-jai's malevolent presence revealed that was no longer the case. The Kirin perused his mind as if it were an object of supreme interest, delving through various memories and looking at them this way and that; even Arias's emotions weren't safe from his parasitic examination. Mati-jai looked through the experiences of Arias's cubhood, taking extra care combing through the times he'd spent hunting with Brynne.

The process of trying to resist Mati-jai was inexplicably uncomfortable. It was almost painful, though not in the physical sense. Arias could sense the elder's engrossment growing as he pored through his memories of Naugi, of his past interactions, of Skyhaven. He was forced to recollect his altercation with Kayane three times, and then Mati-jai spent some time examining his relationship with Shadowbane. He skimmed through most of Arborochre, disinterested, until he reached the point of Naugi's visit to the Strigigryph—the visit that would ultimately result in Naugi's poisoning and demise, in Hlaena's injury, and in the deaths of dozens of Gryphs and Alicorns.

Arias dug in, not willing to share the events, and he felt Mati-jai do the same. The mental anguish was blinding as the Kirin tried to force the timeline of events to continue, but Arias refused to furnish the visual tale any longer. For every violation that Arias resisted, Mati-jai strengthened his own grip on Arias's mind, and the invading presence transformed into a blinding agony that compelled Arias to comply. Arias cried out as his mind's eye became a blazing sunburst behind his eyelids, and Mati-jai prodded one last time before relinquishing his control with a grunt of annoyance.

Body trembling, Arias realized he couldn't see Mati-jai for all the tiny, bright dots swimming in his field of vision. Taking deep breaths only seemed to exacerbate the high-pitched ringing in his ears. Above it all, he heard Mati-jai, still obviously displeased, say,

"You really are a fool."

***

Arias opened his eyes to darkness. There was no color from plants, no opening in the ceiling to let in light, and no Hlaena. There was the residual sound of the nauseating ringing he'd heard before, but it was now at a bearable level. He flopped over onto his side, and started as he heard,

"So, you're not a simpleton, I take it? We could have avoided all of this had you just kept your word, you know."

Arias made out the dim outline of Mati-jai sitting across from him.

"What did you do to me?" Arias accused, his voice barely a whisper.

"You mean what did *you* do. I hope you know that you were nigh unto breaking your own mind. Resisting a Witnessing is a guaranteed way to end up permanently stupefied. The Kirin doing the Witnessing has all of the power, you see; I only stopped because I want to know the rest of that story. It's been at least one hundred years since I've Witnessed something so interesting. What could be so important that you'd sacrifice yourself to keep me from knowing it?"

"Not... going to tell you," Arias managed to rasp.

Mati-jai snorted. "Why don't you sit here for a while and... collect yourself. I have to decide what I'd like to do with you. Of course, that choice might be much more favorable if you'd let me see the rest of that story."

"My life isn't for your amusement."

"Well, you've clearly never been interrupted in the middle of a good tale," Mati-jai said. "And you could be hiding something dangerous from me. At the very least, I'll have to keep your friends captive until I find out what it is."

"I'll never let you in my head again," Arias snapped. The creature was much too interested to have pure intentions.

"Your kind are much more complex than I thought possible. Here I thought that you were just mindless flesh eaters, too busy slaking your bloodlust by murdering innocents to bother with civilized thoughts. Perhaps I've judged you too harshly—although you do have a horrid stench about you."

Arias narrowed his eyes. "I do not stink."

"No, no, not stink in the physical sense," Mati-jai replied, waving a hoof. "Although you are positively covered in muck for some reason; why is that? I mean that you stink in an *incorporeal* sense. We creatures who have access to the ether are attuned to these things. The deaths of all the creatures you've killed hang in the air about you like a fetid cloud. I presume you've even eaten off rotting carcasses at some point." He made a gagging motion, adding, "It's positively repulsive."

Arias ignored him. He was just becoming cognizant of the fact that he didn't know where he was—just that he was trapped in a dark space with Mati-jai. The Kirin seemed to sense his thoughts, and said,

"We're currently below ground, but I'll show you the way to the surface and to your friends if you wish. I'd like to let you leave here without further conflict, but I'm hoping you'll hear me out on an offer. Now that I've Witnessed some of your life, I'm hoping that you'll stay and help me if I help you. I may know of a way to help Hlaena."

Arias's ears raised. "You do?"

"Maybe," Mati-jai said suggestively, getting to his hooves. "Is that a yes?"

Arias paused. This Kirin had the power to kill

him immediately if he so wished, but was instead feigning negotiation with him. Still, what choice did he have? And what if Mati-jai was serious, and he really did know of a way to help Hlaena?

"I'll add in that if you agree, there are some rules," Mati-jai said. "While you were slumped on the floor deciding whether to be a cripple for the rest of your life or not, your two companions were listening to and agreeing to my plan so that they could be released."

Arias chose to ignore his very deliberate choice of wording as he waited for him to continue.

"First, you are not to disturb the other Kirin here under any circumstances. Most of them already object to your presence for various reasons; no need to give them more. Second, you are not to hunt, by any means, within the confines of our territory. It may offend the others. The last is only for you to hear, and that is that you must keep your word if you agree to assist me. If you don't, I will track you down and take my retribution. We Kirin take contracts very seriously."

"First tell me what you need me to do," Arias said.

Mati-jai seemed pleased. "Very well. Let us go back to the higher levels of the temple where we can get some light, though. I can see that you're feeling better. It's dreary down here."

Arias was happy to agree to that. He didn't like being below ground... not after Arborochre.

The Kirin's temple was much bigger than it appeared to be from the outside, due in large part to all the levels they'd bored through the ground. Arias followed Mati-jai up a series of steps cut into the solid rock, which lead to an interesting passageway that spiraled upward and was lit sparsely by small orbs of light set into the ground itself. Every now and then, another passageway branched off into a different direction, but Mati-jai never deviated from the main path. Arias noticed interested looks from the Kirin he passed. The creatures ranged from tiny fawns who barely had manes and horns to shaggy beasts more akin to Mati-jai himself. He remembered the elder Kirin's words about his acceptance by the others of his kind, and kept his eyes cast downward.

"Am I allowed to talk to other Kirin besides you?" he asked Mati-jai.

"Only if they speak to you first. Turn here. This will take us to the garden."

Arias obeyed his instruction, following the gradual slant in the passage upward until the strange spheres of light gave way to natural sun. As before, the opening was disguised as natural stone, that was only revealed to be false when Mati-jai casually passed through it. Arias stopped to poke at the exit the same way he'd done at the very first entrance, still untrusting of the illusion.

"Why are all of your entrances and exits like

this?" he asked. "I get it's some magick trickery, but... why?"

Mati-jai smirked a little as he replied, "A joke, let's call it, of one of the founding members of our community here." He offered no further explanation. Instead, he said, "That is quite an interesting piece of jewelry you have there, friend. Where did you get it?"

"I found it," Arias lied, understanding that he meant Naia's necklace. He wished he could hide it away. Mati-jai snorted, but didn't bother to ask anything more about it.

Arias entered the garden through the wall, and was taken aback by the wide variety of plants growing there. A small forest was enclosed by a stone wall, although some of the trees reached up to the very top of it. There was even a small brook bubbling through the garden, though he once again couldn't see where it began or ended.

"I suppose that you haven't seen intentionally planted vegetation before," Mati-jai said, plucking at a gnarled vine that had overtaken the branch it had been climbing on. "Most of these were brought in as saplings or seeds. I planted this one myself. Can you believe it's nearly two hundred years old?"

Arias pulled his attention back to Mati-jai, almost not catching the implication of the words. "What? You're *that* old?"

Mati-jai plucked a green sour-looking fruit

with his magick, looking offended. "You don't have to make me sound so ancient. After all, I didn't grow this fabulous beard and mane by being a young buck like you." He dangled the fruit in front of Arias.

"If you eat this, it may make you feel a bit better."

"What kind of plant is it?" Arias asked, not moving to reach for it.

The smirk returned to play across Mati-jai's face.

"What?" Arias asked.

"The irony of a murderous beast being interested in herbs and the art of healing is… kind of funny, is it not? Although I suppose that you are perhaps a bit less inclined to the slaying of others than many of your kind. I can't fathom what could have possessed an Alicorn stallion to rescue and raise a creature like you. Where is he, by the way? Xio?"

The fate of Xio and the other Alicorns lay tucked away in the portion of Arias's memories that he'd managed to protect from Mati-jai, and he wasn't about to give away any other information. Mati-jai eventually dropped the fruit to the ground, his smirk vanishing.

"Straight to the point then, eh? That's fine. Why don't you sit, at least?"

Arias did so, his eyes darting to watch the movement of other Kirin deeper within the forest. Most were adults, but there were two small fawns whooping and chasing one another. When the adults saw Arias, they all stopped and watched him with wide eyes, and called for the young ones.

"What's this creature doing here?" one of the adults, a doe, asked. "I heard there were flesh eaters here, but I thought that you'd sent them away!"

Mati-jai shrugged before turning and saying, "All is well. Let the rest of the elder council know that I may be setting up an agreement with this Gryphon."

Gasps of shock rippled through those gathered. "Why? These types of beasts do not belong within the confines of our temple, Mati-jai. You've always tended to be outrageous, but this is unheard of. I'll be letting the elder council hear of this immediately!"

"Oh, go and tell them whatever you wish to, like the many other times you've reported me to the council for trying to advance this stars-forsaken place! How can you expect Kirin to continue learning and growing if we never leave this territory, never form new alliances, and never test the limits of magick?"

The doe scoffed, "You're always going too far. I won't have the young ones around to hear this level of rebellion. The old ways are the correct ways, and if you can't accept the customs of your own kind, perhaps you should consider that you are free to leave."

"The old ways weren't 'the old ways' until we decided that they were. There are new ways, just waiting to be discovered—"

"I've allowed you to speak freely this long because you' are my superior and you are part of the elder council, but I've heard enough. All of you, let us depart. You'll hear of this later, Mati-jai." The doe pushed past, followed by the others, who didn't bother to contain their looks of incredulity. Mati-jai pressed his ears against his head, clenched his jaw, and didn't say anything. When he noticed Arias tilting his head, he sighed, looking annoyed.

"I'm old enough to remember a time when we Kirin didn't hide behind the walls of this temple, learning and teaching the same lessons over and over," Mati-jai said. "Our knowledge of herbs, of life, and of magick will never improve if we don't take chances. This society experienced an amazing period of discovery in its past. I was part of the founding of a spectacular group that started to explore the limits of our capabilities. The attack I used on you and your friends was developed by me! No other Kirin even knows how to grasp the ability, because they're all too busy studying what they've always studied, and teaching what they've always taught. Ehh… I would apologize for doing that to you, by the way, but… well, you didn't give me much of a choice, did you?"

Arias flattened his own ears at that last comment, and Mati-jai seemed to reconsider. He picked up one of the green fruits he'd offered Arias before, examining it with a thoughtful expression.

"Well, perhaps I should apologize. I am sorry for how our introduction went, and for trying to force you to divulge the secrets of your past. About that—I merely wanted to know whether I could trust you or not. When you live as long as I have, you tend to get a little jaded. Thanks to living here, I've become accustomed to having a difficult time getting what I want, but I do *always* end up getting what I want. The whole process of getting there, however, makes me a bit... irritable."

Arias didn't expect the sudden shift in the elder, and he wasn't sure whether to feel more relaxed or more attentive. He decided to choose the safe option of remaining chary, and was careful not to let any of his thoughts register as emotion. It didn't seem to matter as the elder Kirin wasn't even looking at him; instead he was taking great care to remove the seeds from his fruit.

"Anyhow, you didn't follow me up here to listen to me complain about my kind," Mati-jai continued on, his tone lightening. "We came up here to discuss how I may be able to help you, if you can help me."

Arias leaned in, curious. He felt as if he didn't

really have a choice in the matter either way, but he couldn't pass up a chance at helping Hlaena. Not after coming so close.

"Hlaena isn't dead," Mati-jai said. "That became clear to me quite soon after I took her from you and your friends. So long as she is kept where she currently is, she won't be visiting death for a time yet. You can't use mana, but considering you were raised by creatures of notable magickal capabilities, I'm assuming you've at least heard of mana before?"

Arias nodded, grateful that Hlaena had given him a brief explanation. It was incredible that he'd never thought to ask, but he'd been more concerned with adventuring with Brynne for most of his cubhood. "How do you know I can't use magick?" he asked. "You don't seem to know much about Gryphons besides that you don't like us very much."

"Don't take it personally, young flesh eater," Mati-jai said with an exaggerated roll of his eyes. "I can see that you can't grasp its usage, although I don't want to get into that now. One concept at a time, hmm?"

Arias didn't complain. Mati-jai went on.

"Some sources contain more mana than others. Think of mana as the substance that allows magick to be used in the first place. It can be depleted, and often is after enough usage. It can be held in plants, places, even in creatures themselves. Hlaena would recover a bit if she were conscious to eat some of the plants I've placed around her, but it would take a fantastic concentration of mana to cure her of whatever has happened to her. An event I'm sure you may know something of in your memories."

Seeing Arias's mood sour again, he quickly said, "But I digress! The plants we Kirin chose to grow in this garden were all selected specifically for their concentration of mana; they are quite useful in studies, particularly when the young fawns are just learning to control their magick for the first time. What I'm saying is, the sheer essence radiating from the plants I've picked for her will be enough to sustain her for a while."

Arias nodded again, listening intently. He recollected how Hlaena had voraciously eaten silver spangle and not much else, and he was about to ask if his suspicion was correct when Mati-jai said,

"There's a place north of here that contains an area of powerful mana. Simply coming into contact with its source may be enough to repair whatever injury your adoptive mother has sustained. I've never seen the place for myself, mind you, and I'm afraid that I can't risk making the journey at this time. My place here as an elder keeps me occupied, and, if I leave the temple for long, I'll lose what little progress I've made in trying to get new studies approved. It takes constant effort." He took a few bites of his fruit, and pulled a face as he chewed it. "I always forget how tangy these things are, but they are still one of my favorites. Anyway, I should say that I really don't have much more that I can add regarding the place you'll be seeking out. I've shared all that I know. My interest in this subject is academic, although I'd definitely follow in your wake should you return with a confirmation that the mana pool exists."

Mati-jai dug a small hole with his magick, tossed the core of his fruit in, and covered it with a stamp of his hoof. "I hope that through working together, you'll also come to trust me enough to at least tell me what you've blocked me from today. I'll also admit that I have a deep interest in learning from Hlaena if our plan works out, but that can be thought of as an aside."

Arias was in disbelief. There was still a chance to fix Hlaena after all! And Aaga the Phoenix had been right; there was help to be found to the north, just not in the form he'd expected. Between Mati-jai's words, which he honestly didn't trust, and Aaga's, there had to be *something* worth looking into. "I'll do it. I should leave now, though. I'll go find my friends first."

"Now, hold on," Mati-jai said. "You should take some time to rest. You won't get very far with the way you are right now. Your friends will be out hunting on the easternmost outskirts of our territory. It'll be marked by a thicket of white-barked trees; you won't miss it. If you're willing, I'll meet you tomorrow morning, near the entrance where Blu-shi obviously wasn't doing his job today. Ah! And I almost forgot. Don't leave any blood, gore or guts behind after your hunting. I doubt any Kirin would wander beyond the border of our territory, but I don't want to hear complaints from the others if they should chance to come across anything. I'm sure you won't have any trouble finding something fleshy to kill out there; our land is absolutely teeming with every shape and form of creature. We chase most flesh eaters out, as you may have guessed."

Arias nodded, and his stomach echoed the sentiment.

Mati-jai idly plucked another of the green fruits he'd offered Arias earlier, taking a bite and working his jaw back and forth while he stared at Arias with his strange, vertical pupils. Despite his obvious existence as a plant eater, there was something predatory about those eyes.

"I'll be sending my apprentice along with you tomorrow," Mati-jai said, tossing his half-eaten fruit into the thick jungle of undergrowth. "She won't slow you down. You may even find her abilities quite helpful. After all, you can't sense things within the ether, but she can."

It made sense that he'd send someone he trusted along, Arias thought. And if she was even remotely close to Mati-jai in her abilities, the elder Kirin didn't have to worry about her safety.

"Good. You can actually exit through this portion of the wall. See you tomorrow." He said the words with a warm enough inflection that Arias couldn't believe he was the same Kirin that had been forcibly trying to tear his way through his memories not too long ago.

"I'll see you then." He walked out through the indicated section of wall, shook some of the now-dried mud from his coat, and spread his wings to head east.

CHAPTER SEVEN

The edge of the Kirin's territory wasn't hard to find, just as Mati-jai had said. Arias hadn't flown far past the forest of white-barked trees before he found Brynne and Tybrake. Tybrake had an absolute monster of a wriggler hooked between his talons, its scaled body so large that even he couldn't swallow it whole. His slow progress at eating it, and the scattering of scales surrounding him, were strong testaments to the fact that it wasn't the first thing he'd caught. Brynne had already finished devouring some sort of wooly beast with huge, curling horns. In fact, its wool and horns were practically all that were left behind. Both blinked up to stare at Arias's mud-caked plumage when he arrived. The pair seemed oblivious to Mati-jai's requirement about not leaving any blood or ichor behind, and Arias supposed that Mati-jai was right. He doubted any Kirin would venture this far in the first place, especially if they were as prone to not leaving their temple as Mati-jai had made them sound.

Arias didn't feel hurt that his friends hadn't thought to catch or save him anything. Unless a Gryph said they'd bring food back, you were expected to catch your own. The only real exceptions were when you were in an eyrie or part of a bonded pair. It was lucky for Arias that Mati-jai had also been right in that prey was plentiful here. Like the peryton on the island, the ones here were just as naïve when it came to predation. It may have helped that Arias was still ruddy and brown with his coat of mud, but either way, it was a good day for him and a bad day for the sizeable buck he plucked with ease.

Finally eating under the light of sunset, Arias dared to believe it was possible he was having good luck after so long without it: food at last, a potential way to help Hlaena, and both his friends safe. He lounged for a while, also realizing that Mati-jai had been quite correct in that he wouldn't have gone far on the journey had he left today. It felt safe enough to relax, and fatigue set in with a vengeance the murm he did. He considered sleeping right then and there, but figured he should at least bury the remains of the peryton.

Kicking a last clod of earth over the picked carcass of the peryton, Arias decided that he probably wouldn't need his coat of dirt to blend in with his surroundings any longer. He remembered that Larin had shown him how to find water, and instead of heading back toward the river by the Kirin temple, he spent a little time seeing if he was any good at locating another source of water. It took longer than he wanted, but he was ecstatic when he was able to find a pond of decent size. Considering how many wrigglers were leaping over the water in the waning light, it wasn't hard to figure out where Tybrake had caught his feast.

Arias stared down into the water, trying to convince himself that there was no Kelpie waiting below to drag him to an early doom, and he settled on splashing in the shallows instead of jumping in as he'd planned to. Having restored his normal color, he studied the figure looking back at him from the still water. The reflection was distorted and unclear, but he could see the scars that crossed his neck, flank, and chest. They stood out as jagged pink lines, peeking out from beneath fur and feathers like dull reminders. It was amazing that the keythong staring back at him was actually him and not some forbidden stranger he was gazing at from the edges of Glendale's forest. It had taken him time to gain his size, but the pink skin and eyes—and the missing tail—confirmed that it was definitely him. It was shocking that he'd lived to see himself this mature. Maybe he'd had good luck, after all. He took a sip from the pond, and the movement sent ripples across his image, warping it. He took off to find his friends.

***

Brynne and Tybrake were both half asleep when Arias rejoined them. They were no doubt made drowsy by the amount of meat they'd eaten, as Brynne was stretched out in the lower branches of a huge tree, and Tybrake was dozing down below on the ground. Neither seemed to have bothered taking guard duty for the night.

They both opened an eye and trilled a greeting when Arias reappeared, however, and perked up when he told them what had happened to him and what he had found out. They were especially joyous when he told them Hlaena was still alive, at least for the time being, and then they became indecisive when he explained the deal Mati-jai had presented to him. When he explained how the elder Kirin had been able to enter his mind through the process he referred to as "Witnessing," his companions' eyes widened.

"He *what?*" Brynne exclaimed. "They can just do that whenever? And there's one of them coming with us? No! I say we go without them; we don't need some mind-reading gizzard trying to go through our thoughts while we're asleep!"

"He seemed to require my consent to do it," Arias said, although he wasn't totally sure whether that was true. "He also made it sound like there were things that he could do that not all Kirin can do. Either way, I understand if you don't want to come along. You have already stayed with me through so much, I don't think I could ask anything more of you. You'll have to go around the Aquila's nesting grounds to get back to the ocean, though. That, or wait until their young hatch, which could be a while."

"Ey, don't count us out just yet!" Tybrake said, sounding offended. "We didn't nearly die by lightning strike to turn back now. Although I'll be the first to admit that I'm not too excited to be travelling with creatures that have abilities like this."

"Yes," Brynne agreed. "That, and… well, those Kirin obviously can't be trusted. Even if using us helps them, I have trouble believing that a creature with their abilities would ever stoop to asking us for help. Mati-jai didn't do anything terrible to us when we were caught, but I feel like there must be some sort of catch."

"That's part of why I'd feel better if you two headed back to the shore," Arias said. "I have to at least see if there's any truth to what he's said. If I don't, it'll fester in me every day that I live after this. That, and Mati-jai has Hlaena. I really don't think that I can just march back into that temple and demand to take her, and leave."

"You don't have to explain yourself," Brynne said. "We'll come along. But we should probably rest for tonight, and head north early tomorrow. Unless you're really insistent on leaving tonight?"

It *was* still tempting to leave immediately, but Arias shook his head. "No, we won't be any good if we're tired. I think I see the perfect spot to sleep, up there next to you on that branch."

Brynne shimmied over so that Arias could fit at the broad end of the branch she was on, and he pressed himself against the crook between the thick limb and the trunk, letting a lower leg dangle. The forest seemed safe enough, but he knew better than to be fooled by appearances. He heard Tybrake yawn, and even though he didn't see it, Arias yawned, too. Brynne tried to stifle hers, burying her head under a wing.

"I'll take first watch," Arias said. "You two get some sleep."

There were no complaints as Brynne and Tybrake slipped off to sleep, and Arias had to battle his own lowering eyelids as the night deepened. He eventually settled into resting with his eyes closed and ears alert, listening to the droning of the early spring nocturnal chorus. A rustle cut through the noise, silencing half of the insects, and while he immediately dismissed it as a prey item of some sort, he opened his eyes regardless. There was *movement* in the brush adjacent to the tree. He blinked, now fully awake, and was grateful for the dim light of night as he focused on the shadow slipping through the fronds and leaves. It was clearly headed in the direction of him and his sleeping companions, and he was on the cusp of raising an alarm when he recognized the figure. It was the Kirin he and Brynne had originally tried to hunt. Ly-ra. That's what Mati-jai had called her. But why was she just standing there?

Arias continued to watch as the Kirin pulled some thin bark out of the gourd strung across her shoulder and started to dabble with it. The longer he watched the oddity, the stranger it seemed. He nudged Brynne, and the orange hen immediately jumped to her feet, a breathy hiss on her tongue. Arias pointed out their intruder, and she frowned. Ly-ra froze as she realized she was being watched, then darted off into the woods. Arias and Brynne shared a glance.

"Should we move somewhere else?" Arias asked.

"No. She can do that thing where she runs on the grass, remember? If she wanted, I don't think we would've heard her at all. And even if we do move, there's nothing to keep her from finding us again. Maybe she doesn't mean any harm— maybe—but I'll stay awake and keep watch with you just in case. Let's not wake Tybrake. Sky's end, he's bitter when he doesn't get enough to sleep and eat."

"You don't have to stay awake," Arias protested.

"Well, I don't want to risk anything happening."

The two stayed up, more alert than they probably needed to be, because Ly-ra didn't reappear. Nothing else happened. After a few hours, Arias started to nod off. Brynne didn't disturb him when he did fall asleep, somewhere long before the milky hours of morning.

***

Arias awoke later into the morning than he'd wanted to, but felt much better than he had for days. Brynne and Tybrake were similarly rejuvenated, and they all set off for the Kirin temple, eager to begin their journey. Mati-jai met them at the entrance and seemed particularly amiable as he led them into the temple, past scores of scoffing Kirin and wide tunnels, until they were back in the garden. Ly-ra was the only other Kirin present there, and was using her magick to hold a floating globule of water with which she was watering a plot of seedlings. She didn't look up until Mati-jai spoke.

"While it's very responsible of you to see to your chores, you were supposed to have been at the entrance and ready to go by now," he told her.

She blinked. "I thought my assignment was simply to observe these three last night. I did so. Are you saying you want me to go along with them north?" She wrinkled her nose. "I'd really rather not."

"You told her watch us last night?" Arias asked. "Why?"

"Because the best information is obtained when the subject isn't aware it's being studied," Ly-ra replied without breaking her stare at Mati-jai. The elder Kirin continued on as if Arias hadn't interrupted. "As you are my apprentice, you don't have the choice," Mati-jai said, prompting the younger Kirin's shoulders to rise and fall in a silent sigh. She dropped the water in a splash.

"Fine. But the flesh eaters had better behave themselves."

Mati-jai's bearded muzzle twisted upwards as Ly-ra suppressed a scowl and trotted past him. He, Arias, Tybrake and Brynne wordlessly followed her to the entrance of the temple. They'd nearly reached the exit when two older

Kirin stepped forward to block their exit. Judging by the way the other Kirin parted to get out of their way, and by the fact that their horns were several times longer than Mati-jai's, Arias guessed they must have been ancient.

"Mati-jai, stop!" one of them bellowed in a voice like a low rumble. "Your trespasses have been noted by the elder council. You'll submit to questioning at once!"

Mati-jai seemed to be on the verge of a sarcastic remark but his voice remained calm as he answered, "I've been very clear regarding my intentions with my studies, and no one has outright opposed them, even if some may find them unnerving. I'll be happy to have yet *another* meeting with the rest of the elder council about my proposal to learn more about the creatures you've no doubt seen over the past few days, and I assure you that the consensus will once again be that my studies pose no harm. I propose that we shouldn't allow our own wary misconceptions to diminish our ability to continue learning and growing, my fellow Kirin!"

Most of the Kirin replied with silence, but their expressions showed what they thought about the flesh eaters standing in their midst. The two elders glanced at one another, and then nodded.

"You'll be allowed to present your case, Mati-jai. We must listen to anything that may increase the learning of our kind, but if we decide that whatever this is must cease, you must abide by our decision."

"Of course I'll abide by the decision of the council," Mati-jai said, finally allowing a touch of sarcasm to slip into his tone. "Have I ever not done so in the past?"

The other two elders didn't reply. They were staring at Arias and his companions, their eyes lingering with a discomforting intensity on Ly-ra. Mati-jai hurried over to his apprentice's side, and kept an eye on the other elders as he muttered a hurried, "Take our friends outside and continue with our research, Ly-ra. I'll send for you as soon as I have word of the council's decision."

Ly-ra turned and started on her way without replying, and Mati-jai nodded for Arias, Tybrake and Brynne to follow her lead. They did so, happy to leave behind the tension of his clash with the other elders.

Once outside, Ly-ra pulled a thin rivulet of water from one of her gourds with her magick and, in an unenthusiastic voice, said, "Ready?"

"Aren't we going to wait to hear back from Mati-jai?" Arias asked.

"Ha! No. Who knows how long that council meeting will last? We'll get to our destination and back before they adjourn, probably. And if they end up not agreeing with him… well, as his apprentice, I'd prefer to just see whether this place he's mentioned is real or not. Research is more important than personal opinions."

"Are we going on claw the whole way?" Brynne asked. "I know you have your little way of skipping around, but it doesn't compare to flying."

Ly-ra scoffed and, with a flourish of shining water, leapt skyward in a massive puff of steam. With each step upward, a small cloud of warm mist rose and dissipated, propelling her upward. Arias, Tybrake, and Brynne watched in awe as they watched the fantastic feat. As she got further away, Ly-ra called back, "Hurry up! I can't exactly hover like this." The three snapped out of their staring and rose to join her.

"How are you doing that?" Tybrake asked. "I've never seen any creature fly without wings before."

She glanced over her shoulder at him and said, "It's probably not worth it to try to explain; I doubt you'd understand."

"You pretentious little pile of—" Brynne started, but the Kirin cut her off by saying, "Well, maybe you are smarter than you look. I'll try to explain it in terms so simple, even a fawn could understand them." She seemed not to realize her insult as she continued, "We Kirin can use magick, obviously, but we also have an affinity for water and for fire, which is similar to how Alicorns are drawn to healing magick. Kirin can take a small amount of water and heat it quickly, then jump off the rapid expansion of the steam to stay aloft. I usually try to create these expansion points where I'll be stepping next; the heat doesn't hurt my hooves, but I'm not exactly fireproof, either. We like to call this 'wind walking'."

Arias nodded slowly as he considered what she'd said, even though he didn't understand all of it. He wasn't going to let her know that. He decided to ask a different question.

"Can creatures that don't use magick gain that ability?"

Ly-ra slowed her leaping, falling into place beside him in the sky. "What an interesting question! So you *do* think beyond fighting and killing! Well, I can tell you that the answer for centuries has been a firm, 'No.' None of my reading has indicated anything other than that answer, ever. But my master is studying the topic extensively, with some promising results."

"I'm sorry, none of your *what* has indicated it?" Arias asked, curious. "Reading what? The stars?"

"It's—ah. Right. Your kind probably don't do that. It's where you make markings containing information so that you or others can know a piece of information exactly as it was meant to be understood, even if the creature who made the markings isn't around."

"We do that," Tybrake said, seeming confused. "Like when you're on a guard run, and you claw a tree so you know where you've been."

"Or to let others know to stay out," Brynne offered.

"Err... not quite the same as what I meant, but a very similar idea," Ly-ra said. "Anyway, regarding the magick, Mati-jai's research is so important because the possibilities resulting from it could be endless! It would be interesting to give other intelligent life the means to use even basic magick, for instance. Entire new cultures could arise as a result! Or, imagine one of our elders passing on his extensive collection of knowledge to his chosen successor! Oh! I get excited just thinking about it!"

Arias ignored Brynne's look from just off his side; she was indicating that the Kirin was insane. He agreed a bit, but if they were all going to be travelling together, he'd rather they try to get along. And, maybe Ly-ra would say something that he could use to understand and help Hlaena. "So what did you learn from studying us last night?" he asked. "You ruined our sleep, making us suspicious of you like that."

"Well, you weren't supposed to see me," she pouted. "I underestimated your hearing and vision, which was impressive in itself, and went into my notes." She used her magick to tug a sheet of bark out from her gourd, holding it rigid so that it couldn't blow in the airstream. Arias, Brynne, and Tybrake all tilted their heads as they regarded it. There was a miraculous depiction of two Gryphs drawn in a tree, with a third on the ground. Surrounding the images were other strange markings that were incomprehensible. Arias whistled in awe despite himself. He'd seen similar pictures before, scrawled crudely on the walls of Shadowbane's cavern back in Arborochre, but they'd been nowhere near this detailed. Even Brynne couldn't hide her astonishment at the accuracy of the image.

Ly-ra rolled the bark back into a thin tube and stuffed it back among the other sheets, using her magick to tie them together with a length of vine. "If I'm to be honest, my master sent me out to spy on you three, just in case you were trying to escape, or discussing an attack of some sort. I'm happy to see that even unintelligent flesh eaters are smart enough not to consider such foolish actions."

Arias snorted, and Brynne's eyes flashed, but she maintained her silence. Ly-ra seemed surprised by their sudden disengagement, but didn't fight it, either. They travelled for quite a distance in silence, stopping for water at around midday, at a small green pond. Arias wasn't thrilled as he stared down at the film of algae floating on the surface. He half expected to see the Kelpie staring back at him, its ugly form hidden just below the surface. Tybrake and Brynne said nothing, but he could sense their caution in their movements.

Ly-ra saw the way they were looking at the water, and used her magick to separate out a clean pool amid the muck. "I'm not a huge fan of the flavor of algae either," she said brightly, taking a delicate sip. Arias and his friends were grateful as they dipped their heads to drink after she'd had her fill. Suddenly Tybrake made a choking sound, his eyes growing huge. Arias and Brynne looked at him in alarm, until he cried, "Look at the size of those wrigglers down there!"

Ly-ra released her magick hold on the water, and it immediately mingled with the haze surrounding it to resume its prior color of green muck. Tybrake gasped, offended. "But did you see the size of them?" he asked, eyes still darting desperately across the surface.

"Didn't you just eat?" Ly-ra demanded, annoyed. The Ardeigryph's reply came in the form of a sad look and a nod.

"You're pretty much just a stomach on legs, Tybrake," Brynne said. She laughed as he thrust his long bill into the water to try his luck, each attempt becoming more frantic than the last, until finally she dragged him away by his tail. Arias let out a chuckle, and, despite the circumstances, he thought he saw a shimmer of amusement flicker across Ly-ra's face as well. The lighthearted mood didn't last, however, because the murm everyone was preparing to leave, Ly-ra asked, "You aren't going to murder anything before we go, then?"

Brynne snorted. "Depends, are you offering yourself up?"

Ly-ra flattened her ears. "I was just asking. It's a legitimate question."

Tybrake tilted his head. "We only have to eat

every few days, although I wouldn't turn down eating every day if the opportunity arose," he said. "And you don't seem to be aware of it, but you have a very rude way of regarding others."

"I'm not trying to be rude. Do you not murder creatures so that you may consume them?" Ly-ra asked.

Tybrake blinked. "You act as if you don't kill things when you eat them."

"I do not!" the Kirin replied, aghast. "It grows back. And it doesn't mind being eaten, otherwise it would run away when I go to take a bite of it."

"Sometimes weak or sick prey doesn't run," Brynne said.

"And I hope you don't eat tubers, or seedlings, or roots, because if you eat those, they don't come back," Arias added.

Ly-ra took a breath in as if she were going to argue, then stopped and blinked in consternation instead. After a while she said, "Plants, I assure you, have a different presence in the ether than other living things do. But you wouldn't know that. I do believe I see your point."

"Have you never thought of that before?" Arias asked, perplexed.

"No." she said. "I haven't. It's actually quite an interesting point. In my twenty-five years of life, I've rarely spoken to anyone aside from other

Kirin. Why would I ever bother to think about my eating habits? Everyone at the temple eats what I eat, and we tend to view ourselves as superior to common beasts... er, no offense. You're not the way I expected you to be."

"Twenty-five?" Arias proclaimed, shocked. "I thought you were barely older than those fawns we saw. Hold old is Mati-jai?"

"Four hundred and twenty-five. Or near about there. Why?"

Arias shared astounded looks with Tybrake and Brynne. "I'm still young at two, but I don't run around looking like a cub or anything."

"I have my horns thank you very much!" Ly-ra said, huffing. "They'll just take a while to get as long and as regal as an elder's. I hope mine bend on either side of my head when I reach my first century. It's such an elegant look!"

"I didn't know Kirin cared how their horns looked," Arias said, hoping to continue to learn more about his new companion. He opened his wings, and Tybrake and Brynne took his signal that he was ready to take off. Ly-ra was only too happy to continue chattering; she hastily refilled her gourd and leaped upward in a fantastic plume of steam, her conversation filling the sky.

***

Arias found sleep to be evasive, and so he opted to take first watch when he and his companions settled in a large conifer for the night. Tybrake was lying on the ground below, wings askew as he slept on his back, and Brynne was perched on the lower branch opposite to Arias, her ears still pricked high as if listening even as she slumbered. Ly-ra had chosen a spot higher up in the tree, her lithe form allowing her to balance on the thinner branches with ease. It was beyond strange to see an animal with hooves perched in a tree, but she appeared comfortable pressed against the trunk as she rested.

Somehow, under the cover of night, all the thoughts that were drowned out by the activities of the day—flying, solving problems, trying to help navigate, and conversing with others—returned with urgency. And in the still of the night, with nothing else to distract him, Arias's neglected thoughts demanded his full attention. He pushed down both the feeling that he was wasting time and the anxiety-inducing thought that it was possible there was nothing to the north at all, or that he'd find help for Hlaena too late. He sighed and let his legs dangle on either side of his branch, staring up into the wide disc that was the moon above. He always found the sight to be peaceful, despite the fact that it reminded him of Arborochre. The sight was so peaceful, in fact, that he nearly shot off his branch when he heard a whispered, "I guess overthinking is common in other creatures as well?"

Arias traced Ly-ra's outline, made pale by the moonlight, and gestured to his branch with a claw. "Feel free to come lower, if you'd like. We aren't going to bite."

"I don't know," Ly-ra said, leaping down on a cloud of steam to land with silent footing on the bark next to him. She glanced toward Brynne's sleeping form. "Sometimes I think that she's serious about it."

"Well, neither of us were joking about it when we first saw you on that plain," Arias said.

"Thanks for waiting until I came down to sit next to you to say that!" she said. "So, can I ask you a question?"

'What's that?"

Ly-ra slowly pulled a sheet of bark from her gourd. "Does bright light hurt your eyes?"

"Yes." He watched her scribble something down with something small and pointed, taking her time with making the markings into neat rows. "I assume you've been watching me more closely than I thought?" he asked.

"Not particularly closely. It's a common trait of albinos."

"Well, you might know more about me than I do, especially if you're as old as you say and spent all of that time studying."

"Not all of it," she said. "Just most of it." She lowered her voice as Tybrake shifted below, mumbling something in his sleep. "We Kirin like to enjoy ourselves, too. We spend time creating things, exploring new ways to grow our crops, recording history, singing songs, and even dancing. What do Gryphons do with their free time?"

Arias mulled her question over. "It depends on the Gryphs," he said. "Some groups like to hunt together, or to sit under the sun and preen one another. I've seen Gryphs make pictures the way you do before, just not as nicely as you can. And then there are Gryphs that find ways to use the hides from the creatures they hunt to use as bedding later. It sounds odd, but it's surprisingly soft and comfortable. Some flocks have interesting rituals that I don't even know about. I kind of had one with Brynne and her mother when we first began to learn to fly. It's called 'branching,' and you get used to using your wings by jumping from tree limb to tree limb. There are other things, too, like… like if some of your flockmates die…" He trailed off as he remembered the way that Tybrake and the other Ardeigryph had solemnly lined up to march in front of the lake. A shiver ran up his spine.

"What is it? Is something wrong?"

"No," he said. "Hey, you can't do that mind watching that Mati-jai did to me, can you?"

"Witnessing? Not at all. It takes many years of skill and practice to even begin to achieve such a high level of magick usage. One wrong move, and you could destroy the mind of your host. The magick user also probably has to be exceptionally good at using magick to even attempt to learn the skill. Mati-jai has always been gifted in that area.

I'm better than many of my year, but nowhere near as good as he was at my age."

Arias flicked an ear. "What does it feel like to use magick?"

Ly-ra wrinkled her nose as she thought. "That's actually really hard to answer. That's like asking me to try describing what it feels like to go from a walk to a run. Maybe it's difficult when you're young, but after a while, you can do it without even trying." She reached out with her magick to make the feathers in his crest stand on end, and he shook his head in reflex.

"Hey!"

"Heh, I wasn't sure whether you'd be able to feel that or not. Anyway, even fawns have some grasp of magick. I don't remember doing it, but not all that long after my birth, I liked picking objects up and throwing them as hard as I could, so I was watched pretty carefully. It's the reason I was placed with Mati-jai as an apprentice. And I'm really glad I was, because his research is always so interesting! If he finds a way to transfer the ability to use magick, you wouldn't have to ask questions like the one you just asked anymore, because you could just experience it for yourself instead."

"That would be pretty interesting," Arias admitted. He decided to dig a little deeper. "Ly-ra, why do Kirin hate us? I didn't ask to be born a Gryphon any more than you asked to be born a Kirin."

"Oh, I'm well aware of that," she replied. "It's just that it's a bit hard to feel good about a creature that slays others when we're so deeply entwined with the ether. We see the lines that connect all living beings, so killing becomes even more loathsome. Aside from that, well… we're very interested in our studies. Anything that detracts from that is an unwanted distraction for the most part, and I can tell you that having you three anywhere near the temple was a huge distraction for a lot of Kirin."

"I see."

Ly-ra continued to stare at Arias in the darkness. After a while she said, "So, I've had a question ever since I first saw you."

"What is it?"

"When it's cold, is your front half colder than your rear half? Or the other way around?"

"What kind of a question is that?"

"A good one," Ly-ra immediately said, rifling to grab another sheet of bark from her gourd. Arias ruffled his feathers, trying to detect whether there was any detectable difference of temperature in his body.

"Rear half, I guess. There's a reason down is preferred for lining nests."

Ly-ra made marks on her bark, seeming

interested and satisfied. Arias didn't have any more questions of his own, and, after a while, Ly-ra tucked the sheet away and stared at him through the darkness again. "Is that Alicorn really your mother?"

"Yes. She and the herd raised me."

"Why? Where are your real parents? I mean, you're lucky that you got to spend so much time with such amazing creatures, but there has to be some reason for it."

"Albinos are considered unlucky by a lot of the Gryphon flocks where I came from," Arias said. "I was never told who my actual parents were, and it doesn't matter, anyway. It's why I'll do almost anything to save Hlaena. She's all I have left of my family."

"You said Hlaena and the herd raised you. What happened to the rest of the herd?"

Arias closed his eyes, twitching his stub of tail. "I don't want to talk about it."

"It's okay," Ly-ra said quickly. "You don't have to talk about it. I'm sorry I asked. But, uhh," she used her magick to untie and riffle through her leaflets of bark, pulling something out from between two pieces. "I hope this isn't considered disrespectful to you, but do you want to have this?" She held the object closer to Arias, and he could make out a bundle of long, pale strands. He looked at her.

219

"I know it's a bit strange, but I wanted to study whether her mane had any interesting properties. Alicorns are mentioned often in our teachings, but without much detail. Umm… anyway. You obviously care about her. Maybe it will make you feel better about being apart from her. Do you want them?"

Arias reached out toward the delicate locks, but Ly-ra used her magick to tie them into a knot on the same cord as Naia's seashells. "This way, they won't get lost," she said brightly. He gently picked at the bundle of hair with his beak. "Thank you, Ly-ra."

"Heh. Sleep well." She curled up, growing still, and Arias went back to watching the moon journey on its nightly path. The breeze no longer held any hint of cold, and it rustled the early leaves of the tree, bringing him back to memories of watching spring flowers push up through the moist earth just outside Glendale, with Xio the Alicorn Sire next to him.

"Spring is a special time for most creatures, young one," the stallion had said. "It brings all manner of new things into existence, and drives away the cold of the winter so that the new can grow. In Glendale, our spring is eternal, but elsewhere, all plants and creatures celebrate the return of warmer times."

If Arias concentrated hard enough, he could remember the way the sun shone through Xio's mane, the way the sunlight dappled off his silver coat. He could see the way his muzzle pulled into a straight line whenever he did something to displease him, and he could hear his laughter, the way it rang out across the meadow. How much more could he have learned from the wise stallion if he'd only had him for a little longer? The memories made him just as sad as they made him happy. He found himself wondering whether he'd be able to visit the stallion in his dreams if he continued to think about him hard enough. Maybe he could even visit the rest of the herd as well, and Iba and Sheba, too. It wouldn't be real, but still...

Seeing them again would be nice.

***

Daybreak roused Arias from his slumber, surprising him. He must have fallen asleep instead of waking Tybrake to take his turn at guard duty. Arias was about to apologize, but Brynne and Tybrake had no regard for him at all. They were staring at Ly-ra, who was poised on the ground a little distance away from them, evidently impervious to their attempts to get her attention. She had her head tilted so far back that her horns touched the scales on her back, and her eyes were closed. Arias leaped down to poke her, but there was no response. He looked at Brynne, and she shrugged.

"How long has she been like this?" he asked.

"I woke up before the sun rose, and she was already like this," she said. "I think Mati-jai sent us a broken Kirin. Maybe we just have to try harder." She gave Ly-ra a sharp shove, and the Kirin slumped over onto her side. Then her eyes snapped open, and the irises flashed an angry gold.

"Is a little seclusion too much to hope for?"

"Sorry," Brynne said. "We didn't know what was wrong with you."

"Nothing was wrong," Ly-ra snapped, her eyes resuming their typical emerald color. "I was at Peace."

Arias remembered hearing something about that at the Kirin temple. "At... Peace?" he asked.

"Yes. At least once every day, preferably in the morning or at night, we attend Peace. You were all asleep, so I thought I had time. Obviously, I was wrong."

"But what were you doing?" Arias asked, curious. "I was wondering whether we should have been worried."

"During Peace, we concentrate on the ether and ponder our connection to the life source," Ly-ra replied.

"It's possible for you to live hundreds of years, and you're thinking about your death?" Arias asked, incredulous.

"It's more than that," Ly-ra shot back, then deflated. "It's not something I'd expect you to be able to understand fully. You'd have to know what it's like to draw upon the ether to even begin to comprehend what I mean. And no, I'm not trying to call you stupid by saying that. I'd just rather not explain. Anyway, if you are ready to leave, I am, too."

***

There was an abundance of thermals to take advantage of on the way north, and Ly-ra was impressed by the ability of the Gryphs, particularly Tybrake, to find the helpful pockets of air. Arias was happy to have an easy day of travel, but he didn't expect to feel something that wasn't air tugging at his wing tip. His first reaction was to glance sharply in Ly-ra's direction, but she was too far ahead to be the culprit. He looked around, and a small creature fluttered into view, revealing itself. It giggled mischievously.

"Looks like you've found a new friend," Brynne said, watching the Fae dart around Arias. Its skin glowed faintly in the sunlight, and its angular, translucent wings were flitting so fast that they were a blur. Apparently attracted to the flying of the Gryphs, it and another smaller wind Fae seemed content to follow alongside them. Arias remembered Xio once telling him that most Fae were benevolent creatures, and were happy to assist creatures in need if they were in a good mood. Typically aloof, these ones certainly seemed to be in high spirits. With the small figures darting to and fro, it was hard to capture their attention for more than a murm or two.

Arias blinked as the smaller of the two Faes perched on his beak, and climbed up so it was hanging onto his nostrils. He resisted the urge to brush it away. "You and your companion don't

223

know of any special areas around here, do you?" he asked.

The Fae nodded once, then spun away into the air, giggling as if it had been told the funniest thing ever. Arias tried again. "Would you be willing to show us where the place is?" he asked.

The Fae found its friend and the two looked at one another, ignoring him. Before long, they were dashing along and playing together, and Arias sighed as they went off to harass the others. The Faes poked at tails, grabbed at ears, and eventually settled for trying to untie Ly-ra's gourd, much to her annoyance. She lashed out with a tongue of flame, prompting them to go skittering back to the relative safety of the space around Arias. The larger of the Faes took interest in him again, opting to flutter in front of him, and after it was sure it had his attention, it returned to tugging on his wing.

"Uhh…" Arias said, not quite sure how to react. "Do you want a feather? Here." He snatched a bit of down from his chest, but the Fae was already shaking its head and pulling at his wingtip again. Arias sighed. "Of course you want one of the good ones." He tried to reach one of his secondary feathers, but it disrupted his flight too much to do so. Ly-ra saw him struggling and opted to help out by using her magick to rip one free in one swift motion. He hissed. "Not even a warning," he muttered, watching the now-excited Fae hurry to accept its gift. The two Fae proceeded to chase one another and fight over his feather, but after a short tussle, the larger of the two won the prize. Hugging the feather to its chest, it turned and pointed north with a resolute finger.

"Well, we already knew that," Brynne said. "But it's nice to have confirmation, I guess."

The two Faes laughed darkly. Then they dashed away on the breeze, vanishing.

"Faes can be such airheaded creatures sometimes," Ly-ra remarked.

"Airheaded, huh? I guess you'd know," Brynne said, prompting Ly-ra to turn her vertical pupils to her.

"I know you're still upset about not being able to catch and eat me earlier," she said, "but there's no need to always be so snippy. It must be exhausting to have such a tart attitude." She looked over at Arias and Tybrake, then asked, "Are your females this way all the time?"

Brynne snarled and made a dive for Ly-ra, striking close enough to grab a tuft of the fur in her mane. The Kirin had to burst into a gallop to escape, her fluffs of steam expanding into billowing clouds.

Arias noticed that despite the close call, she'd wagged her tongue comically the entire time. "Oh, leave her alone," he said. "Brynne is a good Gryph. And if you get on her bad side, she'll make you pay for it later. And I can assure you that she will eventually catch you. And it won't be pretty when she does."

"I was just having a bit of fun," Ly-ra said, slowing to prance next to Brynne. When the gryphoness ignored her, she added a much more candid, "I'm sorry. I'll stop."

Brynne snorted, which was probably as close as she got to accepting an apology.

"Do the oldest members of your society automatically become leaders?" Tybrake asked.

"Not every elder," Ly-ra said, "but yes, most. We are taught from fawnhood to respect and revere the elders for their wisdom, and every young Kirin has the hope that they'll be selected to apprentice under one. I was very lucky being placed with Mati-jai."

"So does he teach you only about magick?" Arias asked.

"Mostly. I've only been with him for ten years, but he will probably be my final master with the way things are going. We are appointed a new master whenever we outgrow our studies, beginning with our parents as the first level. Kirin believe that the familial bond only interferes with learning and growing, so we typically stay with them long enough to learn the basics, and then we are assigned to new teachers. My parents went as far as naming me in my fifth year, and that's it."

Tybrake frowned. "That seems a little cruel."

"Not really. Every Kirin knows the fate of any offspring they produce. It's for the good of our society that things are the way that they are."

"Would you ever want to have any fawns, knowing what will happen to them?" Arias asked.

"I don't know; I honestly have my nose far too deep into researching magick to have considered it," she replied. "And I don't think I can be too sad about it, because when I get old enough and learn enough, I'll probably have the opportunity to take on an apprentice of my own."

The group travelled on, with the Gryphs asking questions about the Kirin way of life, and in turn telling Ly-ra about their own experiences. Arias and Tybrake did most of the talking, but now and then Brynne added in a comment. Her words were much kinder since Ly-ra's apology.

The landscape changed until it was rolling grassland, a sea of soft, vivid blades. Arias noticed something hazy on the horizon, and at first dismissed it as an odd cloud formation. In the yellow light of the declining sun, it was hard to be certain of what he was seeing. He didn't like it, and his companions were also showing signs of unease.

"What do you think it is?" Tybrake asked. "Should we land?"

"Not until we work out what it is," Brynne replied. "We might have an advantage up here."

The group slowed, to give themselves some time if whatever was approaching turned out to be unfriendly. Arias tried not to focus on the thought that most of the creatures they'd come across in this new land had tried to kill them. He waited for his eyes to be able to pick out whatever they were about to face, his body tense. Whatever it was, there appeared to be a lot of it.

"Maybe we should land," he called out. "We might look less threatening if we give these newcomers the sky."

"And cut time off our escape if we have to flee?" Brynne asked. "I think we should stay up here."

"I can help if it comes to that," Ly-ra offered. "There aren't too many creatures who can resist the urge to scatter at the sight of fire."

The group landed, some more reluctantly than others. Arias pricked his ears high as he thought he heard a whinny, and his surprise was mirrored on the faces of his companions.

"By the tides," Tybrake said. "Are those what I think they are?"

Neighing seemed to confirm everyone's suspicions as the herd of creatures drew nearer. Arias almost couldn't believe it. A herd of Alicorns, out here?

But they weren't Alicorns, as he learned the

murm they closed in. The Pegasi seemed agitated as they landed in a wide circle, snorting and pawing. Arias couldn't get over just how much they looked like Hlaena, only without horns. To his relief, Ly-ra had relaxed considerably as soon as the beasts were identified. She whispered, "Mati-jai told me a story about these creatures before. They are said to be all talk and no—"

A big stallion reared up and pranced toward her, his pale mane falling around his shoulders. He swung his nose in Brynne's direction, his eyes suspicious as he flared his nostrils. "Outsiders!" he boomed, causing Arias to jump just a bit. "What are you doing on our land?"

"Just passing through," Ly-ra said. "We're sorry for bothering you, we will be on our way."

The stallion ignored her. He leaned toward another Pegasus as he eyed Tybrake. "I think they brought the big one along to intimidate us, don't you?" he asked, eliciting a vigorous nod.

"What?" Tybrake said. "That's silly, I—"

"I, Vander, will be the first to tell you that my herd and I will not be intimidated by such tricks!" the stallion went on. He flared his nostrils as he glared at Arias, Tybrake, and Brynne. "We know of your kind, Kirin, but why are you travelling with this pack of... *flesh eaters?*"

"I know it's strange, but we're travelling north together because I'm helping them to find something. They're trying to heal their friend.

And no, I'm not a prisoner, if that's your next question."

"Lies!" Vander boomed, whipping the other Pegasi into a frenzy. The pounding of their heavy hooves against the earth was almost enough to rattle Arias into flying, but he remained grounded despite himself. Pegasi weren't at all like Alicorns, it seemed.

"Flesh-eating beasts would never enlist the help of any aside from their own kind," a mare said, dancing back and forth with a nervous gait. She froze, eyes wide. "I bet they're here for our foals!"

A cacophony of whinnies and cries blared from the herd. Vander reared on his hind legs, snorting. "You aren't welcome here, so away with you! Go!"

Brynne flattened her ears. "All that high flying must have you lightheaded, grass-chewer. Why don't you try making us?"

"I agree with you," Ly-ra said, her green eyes flashing to gold. "We can't waste time here."

As much as Arias wanted to agree with their sentiments, he threw his wings out to stop them. "Wait!" he said. "Vander, what would it take for you to believe us? We can't go back. We don't want your foals. We just want to pass through, and we don't have time to go around."

"Hmm," Vander said, tossing his mane. The

other Pegasi quieted as he considered, and then a single voice cried out from somewhere in the herd, "First they get us to trust them, then they will keep themselves busy with hunting us in our sleep!"

"You're right!" Vander said, snapping his head in the direction the comment had come from. "Away with you! All of you! Do not return!"

The rest of the herd cried out in agreement, and began running, pawing and lashing out with their hooves. Arias flinched at the oncoming stampede, and then, with more urgency this time, he shouted, "Wait!"

Miraculously, the Pegasi halted their advance. They turned their small, pointed ears in his direction to listen to him.

"How about… a race?" he offered. Vander whipped his tail and trotted in a broad circle, his lips puckered as he considered. The other Pegasi seemed equally torn, and finally a voice from somewhere in the middle of the herd nickered, "Let's do it! Sounds like fun!"

Pegasi ran and jumped, taking to the air. Vander unfurled his wings to join them, pausing just long enough to say, "Four on four! Let's race! We'll start in that corner, where the foals are gathering!"

Arias was glad to have thought of something, but he hadn't forgotten the hardship his body and mind had endured over the past few days, either.

He doubted Tybrake or Brynne felt much better after flying through the Aquilas' storm, but they couldn't risk losing this race. "Wait!" he called out again, much to Vander's disappointment.

"No more stalling!" the stallion called down. "Race now, or turn back!"

"Let's make it one on one, then there can be no chance for a tie," Arias said.

Vander only nodded his agreement, impatient to begin. Arias sighed in relief, and saw the same feeling in Brynne and Tybrake's eyes. Ly-ra only chuckled. "Don't worry!" she said, "these Pegasi don't know what they're getting into."

***

If it were possible to prance in midair, Vander had perfected the technique. Arias watched him dip in wide circles around Ly-ra, tossing his forelock as his herd cheered him on. Ly-ra looked undaunted and bored as she leaped high on her puffs of steam and slowly drifted downward, waiting for the race to begin. Arias almost laughed at the contrast between the two. Almost, because if Ly-ra didn't win, they could lose their chance to help Hlaena. He, Tybrake, and Brynne would be a part of the race as well. If Ly-ra somehow lost, they would continue on as fast as they could with the hope that the Pegasi wouldn't follow them.

"The race is about to begin!" a Pegasus mare called, causing a hoard of excited foals and a swath of adults to scramble to line up around Ly-ra and Vander. Arias, Tybrake, and Brynne edged

232

their way toward them as the mare continued, "The first challenger to make it past the thicket bordering our grassland wins!"

"How far is that?" Arias asked.

"Who cares?" the mare replied, dancing on light feet. "I'm going to be even faster than Vander this race!"

It seemed that racing meant more to the Pegasi than Arias had originally thought. He hoped all the extra racers would mean he and his companions could disappear more easily amongst them if the race went wrong. He watched foals lean forward, tiny tongues licking their muzzles in anticipation.

"Let's go!" someone yelled, and the mass of bodies strained forward, only to rein themselves in once a condescending, "No, no, no!" made its way over the din. "Only I can give the starting signal!" Vander yelled. "Reorganize yourselves!"

Brynne rolled her eyes and Ly-ra gave Arias a look, but he only shrugged. As soon as everyone was in the right place, Vander shouted, "Hooves up! And go!"

The foals' eager squeals of excitement died away as Pegasi cut into the wind, wings churning and chests heaving. Vander and Ly-ra already had a lead, and every murm they drew further ahead. Vander didn't seem upset that she wasn't flying with wings. Arias was surprised that Vander could make keeping up with her look so effortless, but he was pumping his wings so hard that they made a roaring sound against the wind, and Ly-ra was burning through the water in her gourd so fast that the streaming water she was pulling from her gourd shone like fire in the orange sunlight.

Arias's muscles protested against the first part of the race, but it wasn't long before he'd paced himself next to a mare and forgotten his fatigue. The mare had her head down as she strained her wings, obviously trying to pull ahead of him, but the spirit of competition had awakened in him, and he stayed at her neck despite her best efforts. After a while, she peeked out at him with a pale gray eye, and he thought he saw the faintest smile twist her gaping muzzle before she lowered her head and leaned into the race again.

Brynne was somewhere near the front, racing a massive stallion, and poor Tybrake was stuck toward the back with the little foals. Ardeigryph were masters of the wind and waves, but speed was lacking for them. Still, he was close enough to be able to escape with them if Ly-ra somehow lost the race. Arias realized with a start that the Kirin had gained such a lead that she and Vander were no longer visible to him. That worried him a little. He wished he could ask Brynne or Tybrake if they could still make out whether she was winning or not, but speaking came a distant second to breathing. The mare gained a hair of a lead on him, and he snarled, redoubling his efforts. It wasn't often that he felt the thrill of wanting to win, but he embraced it now with the hope of closing some of the space between him and Ly-ra. Then again, the Kirin had said that she could cross enormous distances with her method of flying.

She's fine, he told himself. *Stop worrying.*

As it turned out, Ly-ra was better than fine. Arias was greeted by the sight of her and Vander still trying to catch their breath just beyond the thicket the mare had mentioned earlier.

"That," Vander panted as Arias drew near, "was one of the most rousing races I've ever partaken of! I won by such a narrow margin that I'd demand an immediate repeat-race if I weren't so tired!"

Arias couldn't hide his shock that Ly-ra had lost, but the Kirin looked smug as she started to talk to Vander about how she and the other Kirin would love to visit and race more in the future, and the stallion looked excited as he nodded in agreement.

"I look forward to our future races!" he neighed. "I cannot prevent such a brilliant competitor from continuing on through my land. Until then, go with my blessing. May the breeze carry you and your companions aloft!"

Ly-ra thanked Vander, then trotted over to Arias to wait for Brynne and Tybrake to find them. Arias nudged her and chuckled. "That was cunning for a piece of preymeat like yourself."

She laughed harder than was appropriate, then sat with her eyes twinkling. When Tybrake and

Brynne finally joined them, they set off on hoof and claw, telling stories about their races. Before they could get too far, Arias heard someone call behind him, "There's a small spring on your way out of here, you can't miss it! Come back some time for a repeat-race, alright?" He turned to lock his gaze with the gray-eyed mare, and he laughed.

"Thanks!" he called back. "We'll race again someday."

CHAPTER EIGHT

Despite how tired they all were, Arias and the rest of the group were cheerful after their race against the Pegasi. After stopping for a break at the spring the gray-eyed mare had mentioned, sunset wrapped the land in amber, and they all decided to bed down in a gorge nearby. Arias ended up taking last watch, and he marveled as the first vestiges of light began to streak across the horizon. Not all that long ago, he would've been closing his eyes to sleep the day away in Arborochre. He'd been so naïve back then… it was incredible that he'd survived to this point. He couldn't, however, forget the fact that countless others hadn't.

The high, keening cry of some predator off in the distance snapped Arias away from his thoughts, and he took it as a reminder to be more attentive. He was happy when Brynne, then Ly-ra and Tybrake began to stir, and no one complained when he set the pace for the day at a little faster than normal, especially considering the previous day's race. Tybrake found air thermal after air thermal, and the group moved quickly to exploit them, but Arias noticed that Ly-ra was still leaping along at the same rate as she always did despite the helpful updraft.

"The air thermals don't do anything for you?" he asked, and she shook her head.

"Not really. I've no wings to cheat with, like you have."

It made sense. Arias still felt a little bad, although the Kirin method of flying didn't seem to really tire her out. It was a little like eating a grand meal while a friend went hungry nearby. "What happens if the water in your gourd runs out?" he asked.

"I'm very careful not to let that happen," she said. "But if it does, I can pull a bit of moisture from the surrounding air. It's not the easiest thing to do, but it would probably save me from a life-threatening meeting with the ground below. Probably. I'm not too keen to find out."

"Hmm." Arias waited, but the Kirin didn't add anything else. She'd been unusually quiet today, and after her near constant chatter beforehand, he found her sudden silence unsettling. "Is anything the matter?" he asked. "I feel like I'm the one asking too many questions today."

"Heh. And no, not really."

Arias exchanged deliberate looks with Tybrake

and Brynne, and Ly-ra huffed. "Well, you don't have to be so obvious about it. It's just that... well, spending time with you guys and with the Pegasi has made me think of things I've never bothered with before. It's fun, in the way that learning how to extract the juices of potent Kremberries is fun. Now I'm just wondering what else I've missed out on, by never exploring beyond the walls of the temple."

"I see." Arias got the vague feeling that perhaps she'd expected more in response, but he had nothing more to offer. Finally he added, "I'm glad to hear that you're not finding this trip as terrible as you expected to begin with."

"Ah. I'm sorry about that."

The group fell into silence until around midday, when Ly-ra suddenly called out, "Let's stop here."

Arias and the others obliged, watching with interest as Ly-ra touched down and stood with her eyes closed. Every now and then, she turned her head in a different direction, and Tybrake risked asking, "What are you doing?"

"Silence, please," she said. "I'm good at this. And there's something here." A few murms later, her eyes sprang open victoriously. "I knew it! Stand back. I've never used this spell before for its intended purpose, and I'm not sure what will happen."

Arias frowned. "What spell?"

"Its purpose is to dispel." She glanced over her shoulder at him and added a haughty, "It only took me two years to learn."

Arias, Tybrake, and Brynne moved back far enough for Ly-ra to dabble in her magick, planting her hooves as she drew mist around her in a blanket. With the fog surrounding her and her eyes glowing gold, her visage was a little disconcerting. The mist coalesced into a sphere, and when it was small enough and dense enough, Ly-ra tossed it into the sky above her. With a sound like shattering ice, it met with something unseen. Despite squinting, Arias didn't see anything that it could've touched, but he could certainly feel a rising wind. Ly-ra seemed alarmed.

"Move further back!" she commanded, and Arias and his friends scurried to comply. The perfect illusion of their surroundings dissolved just a few murms later, revealing a swirling tempest of impossible proportions. Arias held onto the earth below him with his claws, tucking his wings shut against his body to keep the gale from tearing at them. Eyes narrowed against the grit being hurled at him, he could see Brynne struggling to creep backward from the howling winds, but the murm she lifted a talon, the gusts threatened to drag her skyward. Tybrake had hunkered down into a mound of fur and feathers, his narrow shoulders tense as he tried to keep his body firmly against the ground. He poked his lengthy bill out long enough to cry, "Is this part of your magick, Ly-ra?"

"No!" she cried. "I'm not sure what this is, but I think it's a trap! It's to keep us out!"

Arias couldn't see much past the maelstrom of grit, grass and dust, but he swallowed hard as he considered. "We can't crawl out of here," he shouted. "Maybe the only way out is through it!"

"Have you gone tweeter-brained?" Brynne screamed above the wind. "Going through that will kill us!"

"Or break our wings at the very least, unless it outright rips them from our shoulders!" Tybrake added in a panic.

"Any better ideas?" Ly-ra called.

No one answered.

"We can't sit here forever," Arias shouted. "If we crouch here until our grip tires, we're going to get sucked up anyway. We may as well try to ride it out, maybe it'll dump us somewhere safe on the other side."

"Someone created this," Ly-ra replied. "Whatever lies on the other side, I doubt we'll be alone. We might even have eyes on us right now. I can try to create a barrier between us and the worst of this. I had no idea that something so dangerous could've been on the other side of that illusion, I should've sent you all further back. I'm sorry!"

"No time to think about that now!" Arias

shouted back, wincing as a chunk of wood glanced off his forehead. He knew they were all thinking the same thought. It was possible that this was the last time they'd see one another. But no one said it.

"Halada guide us!" Brynne cried grimly. Arias and Tybrake both gave her a stiff nod, and Ly-ra took a deep breath.

"Ready..." she said. "At once... now!"

And they all let go.

***

Still squinting through the wind lashing him to and fro, Arias felt that his wings were as useless as wet leaves. He was pressed earthward then flung sideways and upside down. The maelstrom seemed to have a mind of its own, deviating into a crosswind before wrenching him down with terrifying force, and it was easy to see that Tybrake and Brynne weren't faring much better than he was. Ly-ra's unique way of staying airborne granted her more control, but it was impossible to tell whether her magick was helping to deflect any of the gale away from them. It was eerie to be in the midst of such raw energy and to see no clouds, no rain, and no lightning. All that existed was the scratchy gray of flying particles, just dense enough to strip away all visibility. At least the Aquilas' nesting ground had presented a real, visible threat. The source of this tempest seemed to be a threat that was felt more than seen.

Brynne tried to fight her way above the

screaming gusts but she was no match for the whirlwind. She was able to force her way up a few wing beats, but she plummeted a mere murm later. Her shriek of frustration was cut off as she was yanked head over heels, and she was dragged closer to Arias. Her beak moved, and although it was clear that she was yelling, Arias couldn't make out the words over the howling in his ears. Somewhere off to his side, Tybrake was spinning out of control and, before long, he vanished from sight. Arias called out for him despite knowing no one could hear him, and, with a spike of panic, he realized that Brynne was no longer near him either. He tried to peer through the grit blasting his eyelids, but it was impossible to spot his two friends anywhere. It was just him and Ly-ra, continuing on a blind path into the unknown.

An eternity seemed to pass, an eternity in a bleak, shapeless world where stinging beads of sand and lacerating wind passed him back and forth in a cruel embrace. Muscles burning with effort, Arias used every ounce of his strength to prevent himself from being blown asunder. Ly-ra was having trouble staying within view, but each time she disappeared, she found a way to reappear by his side. Effort etched into her features, she kept a grip on her gourd, using what little precious water she managed to prevent the storm from ripping away from her to stay aloft. Without warning, a stream of air ripped them upwards, so high that it felt like they wouldn't ever touch the earth again. Arias couldn't hear his own screaming as he tumbled, and part of him wanted to perish. At least then this would end. But a small part of him reminded him that, only a few days' flight away, Hlaena was barely hanging on. He had to try to save her.

Arias began a downward descent, and before he could gather his wits, he was being whacked all over with something wet and flexible. His speed slowed, and he realized he was no longer caught in the clutches of the evil windstorm. Instead, he was falling through a forest of broad leaves, and he instinctively opened his wings to catch himself—not soon enough to soften his collision with the ground, but perhaps soon enough to save his life. He heard a sickening crunch as he met solid ground, and the subsequent pain kept him from answering the figure that was moving toward him, crying out a number of what sounded like furious insults.

Arias found it hard to focus on the sounds the figure was making, because the words seemed to grow further and further away as he tried to make them out. There were little stars dancing at the edge of his vision, and a searing pain tore through his body. Unconsciousness seized him like a welcome mercy.

***

Arias gasped, struggling to flop over onto one side. It was unusually hard to breathe. He became aware that he wasn't alone; there was a huge, shaggy and menacing creature nearby him. His alarm grew as it moved toward him, but it seemed to sense his fear and stopped a small distance away. It viewed him with suspicion, and the sounds it made were of a harsh, brassy language. Arias blinked, eyes wide, not daring to speak. Talking would use precious air, air he needed to not feel like he was drowning despite the fact he wasn't near water. The creature watching him softened its gaze, and moved to sit across from him in silence. It seemed a lot less intimidating that way, despite its size. It had a huge, broad chest, and two long horns that branched out on either side of its head, ending in sharp, upturned tips. Thick fur graced its entire body, but especially so on its head, hanging down over its eyes in long tendrils. The odd, upright stance it had used earlier seemed to belie that it had cloven hooves. For whatever reason, it wore a covering of gold wool that hung loosely around its hips, and it was festooned with a variety of items on woven cords. A rod made of a sleek material was grasped in one of its thick, three-fingered hands. With the other hand, it slowly reached out toward Arias, and he hissed despite the circumstances. The creature laughed in response, its square teeth glinting in the sunlight.

"Ready to fight me when you can barely stand, eh?"

Arias's eyes widened as the creature slipped into using the common tongue. It seemed to pick up on his change in demeanor, because it continued, "You're a fierce one, I can say that much. I'm Byson. I don't know how you passed through that spell alive, but I'm guessing you were blown off course while you were migrating or something?"

When Arias didn't answer, the creature tilted his head. "Ah, poor thing. Perhaps you won't make it another day. You were lucky enough to crash into those Besthestamus leaves, though. Without those to slow your descent, you'd be dead right now. Maybe your good fortune will hold out."

Arias blinked again, still trying to figure out what he was looking at. Maybe if he was careful about his breathing...

"What... are... you?" Arias asked.

Byson didn't hide his surprise. "So, you *can* talk! Well, I'm glad I didn't say anything weird or embarrassing!" He flashed his teeth at Arias, not unlike the Mermaid had done before. "I'm a Minotaur. My kind have lived here in Dantzik forest for many years. I can't imagine why a Gryphon would try to pass through here, though. Most creatures see the wind barrier and decide to stay out!"

Arias had a look around. He wasn't out in the forest, though he could see it from where he was lying. He was in a sort of den, made of dry blocks of earth. He was lying on top of a thick mat of wool, large enough to cover most of the floor. A material he couldn't place crossed over his chest and around one of his wings, and was tied so that he couldn't undo it. Trying to stand sent pain across both his shoulder and chest, so he stayed down. He gave a soft whimper though he didn't mean to, and the Minotaur half stood in concern.

"I'll go fetch you something for your wounds," he said, turning to depart.

"Wait," Arias grunted. "I... came here with friends. Where... are they?"

Byson rubbed the tip of a horn. "Others... of your kind, I imagine?"

When Arias didn't reply, he added, "No. I haven't seen anyone else. I'm sorry. But you have quite a few worries of your own with your injuries. Stay here. I'll see what I can do for you. And if it makes you feel any better, I'll ask some of the herd to go looking for them."

Arias wasn't satisfied with that answer, but he couldn't very well object. He watched as Byson stepped onto a small platform at the entrance of the den, turning so that his eyes winked in the light. "I feel comfortable leaving you here, now that I know you're a reasonable creature. But know that you may not leave this place, so please don't try to. Spend your time resting." He disappeared from view before Arias could attempt to reply.

Not that Arias minded much. He felt as though he'd been crushed by a log and then dragged out to continue with his day. At least the floor was soft. Softer than hides, even. He closed his eyes, fatigue quieting his thoughts before he could get too anxious. Before long, Byson returned and crouched low in the corner opposite to him. After a few murms of clacking sounds, a fire started to dance to life there, and Arias recoiled away, the shriek on his tongue only silenced by the warning ache in his chest. Byson held his hands up in a reassuring gesture.

"It's alright. The fire lives in these coals. I'm sorry I didn't warn you beforehand, though. I guess it makes sense that you aren't used to something like this. The warmth will make you feel better, you'll see."

Arias calmed as he realized that, indeed, the fire wasn't advancing. It never reached beyond the stony cage Byson had put it in. Arias felt safe enough to resume dozing, until something grabbed him, pulling at tufts of fur and feathers all over his body. His eyes shot back open, beak open with defensive intent.

"Out!" Byson roared, sending a group of lively Minotaur calves out of the space. He snorted, arms crossed. "I'm sorry about that. I told the calves they could look at, but *not* touch, you. I guess after the first two commented on how fluffy you were, I should've taken the hint and sent them away."

Arias gave a weak huff of amusement, watching as some of the braver calves peered at him from just beyond the entrance. Byson followed his gaze and snorted again. "He's not a pet. Be respectful." The calves nodded, still watching with interest, their legs primed to run the murm Byson yelled at them again. Seeing that they weren't going to leave, Byson added, "I imagine that our guest will be staying for dinner. Go select one of the older lioshi to have prepared for him."

With dejected sighs and downcast eyes, the

calves departed. Arias wasn't sure what a lioshi was, but he felt bad seeing how sad the youngsters were upon receiving the order. He looked up at Byson with a quizzical expression.

"The lioshi are raised mostly as pets," Byson said. "Our calves do most of the rearing, although we adults do most of the shearing. There's no end to the uses for good wool, and it makes a nice sleeping mat, as I'm sure you'd agree. We have a few beasts in their twilight years, though, and although we typically let them pass on of their own accord, we may as well not let them go to waste if you'd benefit from them. They become fertilizer for the plants under other circumstances."

"You... don't have to do that," Arias said. "I can... find my own food."

"I very much doubt that," Byson said. "Besides, I'll make sure it's a swift end. You'll heal up much faster if you're eating right. I figured with those claws and that bill of yours, you must enjoy your meat quite a bit. Don't worry about it."

Arias didn't argue further. He took interest in mysterious bunches of dried herbs that had been hung from the roof and were waving in the breeze. There were also clear containers of something that glowed, and it was a shock to realize that whatever was inside was *moving*. Arias stared more closely at them.

"Will-o-wisps," Byson said, tracing the

movement of his eyes. "We let them go and find new ones every night. They sure like to hide during the winter when we need them the most, of course. It's a good thing the calves are almost always happy to go search them out. Anyway, it's time that I made you that potion. Sorry. I'll be back."

Arias watched him head away, the staff ever-present in his fingers. Were all Minotaurs that huge? He was lucky Byson seemed to be in a good mood about his unintentional intrusion.

It took Byson quite a while to return, but, when he did, he had a huge bouquet of fresh herbs in his free hand. Arias didn't see most of what he did to the plants, but, by the end of it, he had a steaming, earthen container of brownish liquid flecked with bits of floating greenery.

"Here," Byson said, pushing the mixture toward him. "Drink this. It'll help you feel better."

Arias stared at the herbs floating in the mixture, and it reminded him of the potions Hlaena and the other Alicorns used to make. He watched the remedy steam, confused. Water and other liquids didn't steam. Instinct told him to remain careful, and he wasn't sure why until a sip revealed that it was burning hot. Crest raised in alarm, his eyes flew over to Byson.

"You have to wait until it cools off or it'll scald you. Again, I should've told you. I'm sorry. I'm not used to having guests who can speak, but also aren't used to these things."

Arias nursed his sore tongue as he waited for the curls of steam to stop rising from the potion, then he took another sip. The liquid had a mild flavor, and he drank it all in a few swallows. If Byson had wanted to hurt him, he had already had ample opportunity to, and besides... the Minotaur seemed sincere enough. A pleasant warmth flooded through his body, dulling the insistent aching of his injuries. He flicked an ear at the speed with which the effects had taken hold. "That works... really fast."

Byson nodded, seeming proud. "I wish I could say that it was because yours truly crafted it, of course, but that's not it at all. The plants around here have properties the likes of which I've never seen elsewhere. Excellent for herbal remedies and food. Lucky for you, eh? We'll have you back in the sky in no time. Just take it easy, though. That potion may take away most of your pain, but your injuries haven't disappeared. You'll make yourself worse if you don't rest."

Arias nodded obediently. Then he yawned. Byson laughed.

"Yeah, that's the other great thing the mixture does. Puts you right to sleep, like a calf after its night's milk. Sometimes I'll whip myself up a little just so no one can ask me for anymore favors for the night!"

Byson was showing his teeth again, evidently amused at his own clever ruse, but Arias was too sleepy to entertain his words. He nodded twice, and then was asleep.

***

The murm Arias awoke, Byson was there to offer him more of his herbal mixture. After he'd drunk it, Byson settled a serious gaze on him.

"We didn't find anyone else out there," he said.

Arias frowned, and stood up on unstable legs. Byson rushed forward with hands outstretched, but evidently Arias was just big enough—and perhaps menacing-looking enough—to cause him to pause mid-stride. "I'd like to go looking myself," Arias said, glad he could at least get out a full sentence without rushing to breathe again. "But first, I'd like to thank you for showing me the kindness you have so far. And I must tell you why I'm here. I need to find a way to heal someone, and I was told the answer might be here in this forest."

"Well, you've risked a lot for this individual," Byson asked. "Who are they?"

"Her name is Hlaena. She's an Alicorn, and part of the herd that raised me."

Byson took in a breath of air, his eyes wide with disbelief. "An Alicorn? They still exist? I don't believe you."

"It's true," Arias said, still confined to speaking slowly. "The hair tied into this necklace belongs to her. If whatever I need to help her is around here, I'd be happy if you let me seek it out and look for my friends. We won't bother you again afterward."

Byson peered at the bundle of pale strands that had been pulled into a tight knot alongside the shells. His eyes lingered on the item for quite a time, and he pulled at his bearded chin, thoughtful. "An Alicorn would possess a wealth of wisdom if they're anything like they are in our stories. And... it's hard for me to imagine a creature such as yourself lying—no offense intended. Hmm. I'll have to meet with the elders on this one."

"How long until then?" Arias asked.

"After we eat, so just after sundown."

"I can't wait that long," Arias said. The sun was still high up in the sky. "I've already wasted enough time."

Byson crossed his arms. "And I understand that. But I'm afraid this cannot be changed."

Arias sighed. "Can I at least look around until then?"

"No. I have my own duties, and I can't spare anyone to follow you around all day. My herdmates are still looking for your companions. If anyone is found, regardless of whether they are alive or dead, I'll let you know. For now, try to rest. The calves will come to fetch you for food later tonight."

"You don't have to feed me," Arias said. "The young ones seemed sad about it."

Byson stared at him with a long, expressionless gaze. "You're strange, for a predator."

"I know. I'll be fine for a bit longer. Don't make the calves kill one of the lioshi just so I can eat it. Not if they mean something to them."

"Well, then. I guess it fits into your whole story of being raised by Alicorns, that you act like this. Would you like some other assortment of dead critters to eat?"

"I won't say no." The entire time that they had spoken, Arias had kept his eyes glued to the rod the Minotaur carried. There was something about it that, like the steaming liquid, made him wary. He wanted to stay on Byson's good side. He stiffened as Byson leaned down and took the shells Naia had given him in his fingers, turning the smooth objects over and picking at the strands of Alicorn hair tied there. The Minotaur snorted and headed for the doorway again. His voice drifted back just loud enough that Arias could make out him telling someone, "Watch the newcomer. I need to speak with Nandi and the others. Don't let him leave your sight, we don't know enough about him or his kind."

***

Arias awoke to Byson gently shaking him. The Minotaur backed away the murm he opened his eyes. He was showing his teeth again.

"The calves are intrigued by you. Most of them have never met another creature that can speak the way that we do, even if it isn't in our native tongue. They want to put on a performance for you tonight."

Arias didn't care to see a performance. He wanted to find his friends and whatever Hlaena needed to get better. He must not have hidden the emotion very well, because Byson sighed.

"The elders haven't made a decision yet. They outrank me whether I can use magick or not. I'm sorry. I'd like to help you right now, but I can't. You understand that, don't you?"

Arias took a murm, and then he nodded. Byson's face lit back up.

"Good; follow me. Do you feel well enough to walk?"

Arias nodded again. He trailed Byson to the outside of the dwelling, and found himself in the midst of a number of other Minotaurs all going about different tasks. Byson's home faced many others of the same appearance, all in a circle around a clearing. Smoke rose from most of them, indicating that fires were living in most of them. Minotaurs looked at him with curiosity as they noticed him, their gazes lacking the judgment that had been held by most of the Kirin back at the temple when they'd first seen him. Arias's eye was drawn to the interesting looking creatures that some of the Minotaurs were leading around, and he judged them to be lioshi by their golden wool. They were small creatures, perhaps coming up to his chest at their tallest, and had thick, spiraling horns, pointed faces, and round ears. His attention was ripped away by a group of lanky youngsters that ran by carrying sharp sticks, and an adult whose booming voice yelled at them to stop playing and to get to their evening tasks. Arias stared at the glittering, smooth hoops and studs that adorned the ears, forearms, and sometimes noses of the Minotaurs he passed by. The way they gleamed was pretty, but he couldn't figure out what purpose they had.

Arias followed Byson to a small hillock overlooking a patch of forest, where they sat and waited while other members of the village trickled in to sit alongside them. Someone dumped a sizeable pile of deceased creatures next to Arias, and he thanked them as he examined them. There were bigger longear than he'd ever seen before, something with small ears and a bushy tail, and a couple of fat, squat creatures with huge orange teeth. "Byson," he said, "what do you call these? I know what these ones are, but I've never seen the other two before."

"Ah. We call those hoppers, these squileaps, and the big ones are brimels. They all raid our gardens quite often, so I don't think the calves felt too bad about their fate tonight."

Arias could see why the Minotaurs might call longears "hoppers", but he still preferred calling them longears. He picked one up and swallowed it whole as the calves gathered along the tree line at the base of the hillock. They were passing along branches that were on fire, and he watched with interest as they handled the burning wood with a blasé lack of care. It would seem they were comfortable around the destructive element from a young age.

He reached for another creature, the one Byson had called a "squileap", and paused as he became conscious of the fact that pretty much every Minotaur in attendance was watching him. He almost put it back down to ask whether something was wrong, but his audience must have become aware of their own behavior, because they diverted their eyes instead to a cow that was carrying a large container. The steam rising from it indicated that whatever was inside was warm. As she approached, the Minotaurs all took something from the wool covering at their hips, and, as the cow drew near to Byson and he reached for a similar item, Arias could see that the things they were holding were hollow horns. He looked from the horns growing from Byson's head to the one he held in his hand. They were the same.

"It's Minotaur tradition to honor your mother and father at least twice a day," Byson said, seeing the look Arias gave him. "For mothers—he tapped at a pale horn, still tied at his hip—it is during the mornings, and for fathers, during the evenings." Arias stared at the dark, sleek horn grasped in Byson's fingers and decided not to ask how the horns were collected. The idea seemed a bit strange to him, but he was sure the Minotaurs would also find a lot strange about Gryphons. He ate another of the creatures he'd been given as Byson stood, filled the horn in his hands with whatever was in the cow's container, and sat down again. The Minotaur sniffed at it before taking a sip; he seemed pleased with the flavor.

"What's that?" Arias asked, and Byson lowered the horn so that he could see the dark liquid glinting inside.

"Brigberry slew... that is, fruit that has been left to sit in a wooden container for moons and then made warm to ward off the chill of the night," he said. "Do you want a taste?"

Curious, Arias took an experimental gulp, and he immediately regretted it. The acrid taste made him recoil, and it even burned going down. A panic rose in him until he heard Byson let out a hearty laugh. Arias swallowed hard, feeling the urge to cough, but resisted because he knew how badly it would hurt if he did.

"Not your favorite, I see," Byson observed, taking another hearty swig. "You know, it's kind of interesting, but calves usually hate the flavor, too. I guess it takes a well-seasoned adult to enjoy the stuff." He took another long swig, and Arias rolled his eyes, then tilted his head as he noticed that the metal rod Byson kept with him was lying just a bit away from him in the grass. It was smooth, so polished that it was almost reflective, and was inlaid with a single, sparkling stone. There was something interesting about it... almost as if it were making a sound he couldn't hear. He reached a talon out toward it. He just had to touch it, whatever it was.

"Hey, claws off," Byson said, picking the rod up with his free hand. "That's mine."

"What's it for?"

"I wouldn't expect you to understand, but it channels mana when I use magick," he said. "Do you know what magick is?"

Arias nodded. "I was raised by Alicorns, remember?"

"Well, every Minotaur has a weapon of choice, forged either by themselves or by the herd's master smith. Guess who this herd's master smith is?" He flashed his teeth again, something Arias was slowly beginning to get used to. It would seem that the showing of teeth wasn't something to fear so long as it wasn't accompanied by a snarl or hiss. "Anyway, my magick is stronger with this staff than without it. The item itself was created from the minerals hidden beneath Dantzik, and they don't disappoint with their properties. We Minotaurs believe that a weapon forged by oneself will always perform better than one made by someone else, and it's been true for me and this staff." He held it out and flicked an ear. "You can touch it if you want to."

Arias did so, and marveled at how smooth the metal had been made. Looking around, he also noticed that many of the Minotaurs carried a variety of intimidating contraptions with them: wedges of stone attached to wood, wood that ended in sharp tips, and other, more complicated creations that he had trouble understanding the use of. "I didn't know you could use magick, Byson. Can all Minotaurs?"

"No, not all. A few who can are born to our herd every now and again. I'm the only one right now."

"And it takes something called a smith to turn minerals into things like that staff?"

"Mmm, kind of. It takes a lot of hot fire and skill, as well."

Arias shrank back a little. Fire reminded him of what had happened at Arborochre, at Naugi's death. He thanked Byson for the explanations, happy to go back to watching the young calves, all of whom were waving their flaming branches now. The herd rose to their feet in response, and drank from their horns as they watched the calves begin to skip and jump. Arias ate one of the brimels to get the taste of Byson's drink out of his mouth, his ears rising as the calves' lilting voices filled the air with a haunting chant. Some of the adults joined in, stomping and chanting in unison with the youngsters' melody. Arias's feathers rose as goosebumps rippled across his skin, his eyes glued to the shadows cast by the fire in the failing light. The tune increased in speed and volume, and some of the calves dropped to all fours in their dancing; their torches held in their muzzles. Arias found himself joining in as well, his voice more akin to a crude crowing alongside the crystalline voices of the Minotaurs, but they seemed happy for his participation.

When the calves ended their performance with a huge flourish, smothering their flames against the ground, everyone cheered and slapped their hands together. In the excitement, Arias hadn't realized that Byson was no longer beside him, though he didn't feel particularly uncomfortable among the rest of the herd. The Minotaurs seemed to be a sensible and likable species, and he thanked the calves for their performance as they surrounded him and began to fuss over him, patting his feathers and peering at his scars. They asked a myriad of questions as well, but before Arias could answer any of them, his ears shot up and swiveled toward the tree line below. He turned his head to follow the source of the sound, and the calves backed away from him with uncertainty. Arias kept his eyes on the forest below, listening to the soft crunching of something on the move. He didn't want to get his hopes up, but...

Ly-ra trotted out of the forest below and onto the hillock and they locked eyes. She started to run toward him in excited leaps, crying, "Arias! You made it!" But before she was even halfway across, the Minotaurs sprang into movement, collecting up the calves and scurrying away. A cow placed her hands a little too tightly around Arias's neck, and he looked up at her in confusion as she barked, "Get the calves to safety! Seize her! And guard *him!*"

Arias froze as Minotaurs rose and brandished their contraptions, beginning to charge down the hillock toward the Kirin. Ly-ra had stopped her advance, one leg still held aloft as she tried to determine what was happening. Even from the distance between them, Arias could see her eyes flash to gold.

"No, Ly-ra!" he shouted. "Run!" The cow jerked him backward into the arms of a waiting bull, yelling, "Take her down!" Most of the Minotaurs had already made it partway down the hillock, and were eager to comply. They reeled back, sending their sharp sticks through the air with such force that Arias could hear them whistle through the air. Ly-ra wind walked over one and twisted past the other, fleeing back into the cover of the trees.

"After her!" the cow bellowed, taking off to sprint down the hillock herself. "You can't dodge them all, serpent! Take that Gryphon to the elders, and don't let him out of your sight!" came her fading cry.

The bull holding onto Arias grunted an affirmative, and dragged him off, back toward the village.

"Let me go!" Arias cried. "What did she do? Why are you trying to kill her?"

The bull shifted his piercing gaze to him. "Quiet! We should have known you got into here somehow."

"We're just trying to help someone!" Arias pleaded. "I already told Byson that."

262

"You failed to mention you were travelling with one of those thieving liars. No more talking! We'll decide what to do with you later."

With each interaction, the bull's grasp around his neck seemed to strengthen, so Arias decided that lapsing into silence was a smart move. Arias was led past the various dwellings to a part of the village he hadn't seen yet. A round structure made from clay rose up from the ground, decorated with huge insignias that had been carved into the entrance. The entrance itself consisted of a simple opening covered by a hanging of wool, and inside, a fire roared in a stone box that had a considerable amount of soot and ash built up around it. If Arias had thought that the wool mat he'd slept on before had been soft, the entire floor here was much more so. The fleece was so deep that he couldn't feel the hard ground beneath. He might've enjoyed the sensation if he wasn't fearing for his life.

The fire was the only light in the space, and it illuminated two figures sitting side by side, drinking from their ancestral horns. One was a cow, her bottom lip drooping low with age, her hooves cracked and splintered in places. The other was a bull, wizened and gaunt, his eyes hidden by the curly fur on his head. One of his horns had been broken off at the tip, and the jagged edge had a harsh glint in the firelight. He snorted when he saw Arias, then looked at the accompanying bull for explanation.

"Much respect, and my apologies for

disturbing you, Nandi and Argus. This is the one who arrived through the spell," the bull said. "He mentioned having come with others, but he neglected to mention that there was a Kirin among them."

"A Kirin," the old bull echoed, glancing toward the cow. "What say you, Nandi?"

The cow nibbled at her lower lip, revealing that she was missing quite a few teeth. "We can't have a Kirin among us regardless of the reason, Argus. You know that. Was the Kirin killed?" she asked.

Arias's guard shook his head. "It went on the run, but the herd is tracking it as we speak."

Argus crossed his arms, eyes smoldering beneath his forelock of hair. "You, Gryphon. Why did you omit the fact that you were travelling with a Kirin?"

"I didn't know it was important to you," Arias said. "The other two are Gryphs like me. I didn't know it would cause trouble. I promise I'm not feigning ignorance; the Kirin is a new companion of ours. If there's any danger regarding her or her kind, I didn't know."

Nandi tilted her head, still nibbling at her lip. "It's possible he's telling the truth, Argus."

"The Kirin elder has been made clever by the years. We would do well to be suspicious," Argus replied without taking his eyes off Arias. Arias flicked his ear at the mention of a Kirin elder. "You wouldn't happen to mean Mati-jai, would you?"

The Minotaurs all seemed to tense at hearing the name. "So you know him," Argus said. "I'd advise you to speak truthfully and carefully in regard to your relationship with him."

The bull holding Arias tightened his grip in warning, and Arias tried not to wince. "Things will be easier if I tell you the story from the start. I want you to understand how we came across the Kirin in the first place." He looked at his guard out of the corner of his eye. "I know my word doesn't mean anything, but I'm not going to try anything stupid. Moving fast isn't exactly a strength of mine right now." The last comment came out more snark than he'd intended, but the bull thankfully relaxed his hold enough so that it no longer caused discomfort. Arias sat down—slowly so as not to cause any alarm—and launched into the tale of his journey. He didn't leave out the fact that Mati-jai had forced him into the arrangement, and, at the end of his tale, both elders were staring down into their ancestral horns with thoughtful looks on their worn faces.

"It sounds as though you've been tricked, Gryphon, and perhaps through no fault of your own," Argus mused. "Mati-jai was alive when I was just a bullock. Back then, he wasn't the elder he is now. He was a curious scout, searching for viable ingredients for his potions. Our ancestors settled on this land long ago, and we guard it fiercely to protect the amazing concentration of mana here. As it turned out, because of Mati-jai, we learned that it's best to keep others out.

"Mati-jai's initial visit here was peaceful. We gave him ingredients, and he gave us many fine things in return. I dare say he and I even developed a sort of friendship over the years. We were particularly fond of the jewelry he created from the metals here, and he taught our sorcerers magick the likes of which we didn't know was possible. But Mati-jai's interest in magick darkened with each passing moon. When we realized he was studying how the addition of sacrifices could enhance his abilities, and learned of how his studies in Dantzik would involve the permanent alteration of the land and its properties, we requested that he cease his activities here. Of course, he ignored that, leaving us with no choice but to oust him. The other Kirin didn't seem particularly eager to accept him either, but he'd grown to power with both age and capability. The wind barrier went up to keep him out, and up until now, it appeared to be successful."

Nandi nodded, adding, "We would have lost our home long ago if we weren't lucky enough to have sorcerers born into our herd every few generations. This time is unusual in that Byson was the only bullock born with any significant ability. The worry is that if you and another Kirin made it in, Mati-jai certainly can." She looked up from her ancestral horn with droopy eyes. "Under the circumstances, I imagine that you agree that to maintain the peace, this 'Ly-ra' must be disposed of. Am I correct, Gryphon?"

"What?" Arias exclaimed. "No! She hasn't done anything wrong. I mean, I don't know her well, but we should at least give her a chance to explain herself."

Argus and Nandi raised the ridges of their eyebrows at him. "You act as though lying isn't in the nature of every intelligent beast," Nandi said. "If she comes without a struggle, she will be given the chance to speak freely, but it will be viewed with the suspicion the Kirin deserve."

"That's not fair," Arias said. "She's not going to come without a struggle when you have half a herd of armed Minotaurs chasing after her. Let me speak to her at least."

Argus snorted. "Don't be foolish. For all we know, you're working together."

"We are, but not in the way you're thinking!" Arias said, exasperated. "Imagine what will happen if she doesn't return to the Kirin temple at all. She already got in, probably with a spell that Mati-jai taught her for this very purpose. Mati-jai will certainly come himself, and possibly with other Kirin if he thinks she's suffered an ill fate here. If there's any chance at all that she is ignorant of his plans, she should be given a choice to make her own decision. Ly-ra is strange, all Kirin are. But in my time with her, it seems that she never left that temple. She is many years older than me, and certainly intelligent, but some part of her intelligence is more akin to that of a cub. Please. At least give her a chance to explain and decide for herself."

"Hmm." Nandi nibbled her lip again, but this time, she didn't speak. Argus sipped from his horn, his dark eyes once again hidden under the hair on his head. The guard holding Arias spoke up, saying, "Apologies, my elders, but I have a question. If Mati-jai was truly studying how to use mana to strengthen his own abilities, what does it mean that this Gryphon delivered a being as powerful as an Alicorn to him?"

The dwelling was quiet before, but now it seemed even more so. Arias stiffened. "I have to go back—" he started to say, but Argus silenced him with an annoyed growl. "So that what, exactly? Mati-jai isn't going to let you just stomp back in; he's using you for a specific purpose. If you don't fulfill it, you are useless to him. And if he has somehow managed to use the mana of the Alicorn, there may not be nothing to return to save, anyway. Besides, you wouldn't make even half that distance in a decent time frame with the condition you're in."

"However, if she lives yet, we may be able to restore her," Nandi said. "And I doubt even Mati jai could rival the power of an Alicorn. There's a great chance that he hasn't killed her, if he can help it. Doing so would mean the end to exploring the power she possesses."

"She's at the Kirin temple," Arias said, "and there's only one creature here that we could even think to send there."

Argus barked a tart laugh, eyeing Nandi and the young guard. "First he wants us to consider letting the Kirin live, and now he wants to send her back to her master after meandering throughout our forests. Shall we all kill ourselves and lower the barrier for Mati-jai ourselves, then?"

"It sounds like there's nothing to lose, unless you want to sit around and wait for Mati-jai to arrive on his own. And if all he could do when you knew him was to wind walk and play with a little fire, I have bad news regarding what he's capable of now," Arias said.

"We'll prepare our defenses," Argus said, setting his jaw. "If we all die, it'll be with honor and glory."

"No, it won't," Arias said. "He took my two friends and me and flung us across the sky as if we all weighed less than a feather. It will be the senseless slaughter of your herd, and I suppose myself as well, since I can't leave here. If every other option is exhausted and it comes to that, then I suppose that's one thing. But what would it mean to pass up the one chance that might be everyone's salvation?"

Argus narrowed his eyes as if he'd been threatened, but Nandi sat her empty ancestral horn down on its side in her lap and sighed. "The Gryphon has a point. But we must take things one step at a time, and the first step is to not let that Kirin escape."

"No one escapes me." Byson walked triumphantly through the entryway, flanked by an equally victorious looking gathering of bulls and cows. At the back of the group were two big bulls, each holding Ly-ra by a horn. "Down, serpent!" one of them spat, wrenching her sideways toward the ground. She resisted, tail lashing, but folded under his weight with a grunt. A cow rushed forward to go through her meager belongings, tossing aside the empty gourd, unbinding the bark leaflets and passing them around. Byson's eyes widened as he snatched at one of the sheets, holding it up for all to see.

"Markings in the shape of our homeland!" he announced. "She must have been searching for the Crowning Point. A traitor, just as we expected."

"I knew it!" Argus called out, creeping to his feet. "Execute the traitor!"

The bulls holding Ly-ra forced her into a sitting position, and one muttered, "Make any fire, and know that you'll just be hastening your own death." Her eyes burned gold, but no flame issued forth. Instead, she looked over at Arias, and her expression was plain. *I'm sorry,* it said.

"Wait!" Arias said, moving forward and tensing as a myriad of sharp sticks were swung in his direction. "This isn't fair. Of course she would have something like that on her, that's the whole reason we came this way. But that doesn't mean she's still loyal to Mati-jai." He glanced at Ly-ra again. *Please,* he thought. *Give me something to believe that you're not who they think you are.*

Ly-ra lifted her head the tiny bit that the bulls allowed her to, leveling her gaze on the two elders. Her eyes didn't lose their gold flicker. "I'm who you think I am," she said. "I'm Mati-jai's apprentice, and he sent me here first to see if his spell would work on the barrier, and then to locate the mana well and relay the information back to him."

So much for that. Arias stared at her in disbelief as rumbles of dissatisfaction rose from the gathered Minotaurs. The stone in Byson's staff took on an incandescent quality as he pointed it at her. "At least you're an honest serpent," he conceded.

"You could say that," she said undeterred. "And I wasn't quite finished."

"What more is there to say?" Argus hissed. "You've just admitted to being guilty."

"I never imagined a world outside the one I experienced when I lived in the temple," Ly-ra said. "All I cared about was being a good apprentice. And, while Mati-jai's studies do interest me, I began to realize that there's a reason the rest of the council looks down on them. What he's hoping to do would destroy this place. No Kirin needs as much power as he's hoping to achieve. The way to change the minds of others shouldn't be through force, but through understanding. It's not easy for me to denounce my master. I'd like to believe that he's still good inside, just… confused somehow. The same as I was, before spending time with Arias and his friends. They opened my eyes to things I'd never considered before. They certainly aren't the mindless, aggressive beasts I originally expected."

She locked eyes with Arias, and they slowly bled to their former emerald color, sparkling in the firelight. "I owe you and your friends an apology, Arias. Originally, I was told to act as though I wanted to learn more about you so that you'd trust me. But then at some point, I realized I wasn't acting anymore. I'll be honest and say that I'm not completely sure I'm doing the right thing one way or the other. And I'd be lying if I said I wasn't trying to save my own life as well." She glanced at Byson. "I'm surprised you didn't kill me just now in that ambush. So thank you. I can't promise my heart is in my alliance to you, but I can promise that I want to help Arias. Hlaena is real, I've seen her with my own eyes. I'm afraid of what Mati-jai may have done with her, but if she's still alive, I'll do what I can to help. That's all I have to say. I know you have no reason to believe it, but… thank you for letting me say it anyway."

Arias released a breath he didn't know he was holding. The Minotaurs shuffled and mumbled among themselves, but Argus wasn't having any of it. "She has openly admitted to doing Mati-jai's bidding, and we pause in her sentencing because she has a feel-good story about realizing other creatures may be more than bumbling fools?"

"We've discussed this, Argus," Nandi said

softly. "Think past the immediate and into the future." She stood on feeble legs to address the rest of the Minotaurs, resting an unsteady hand on the shoulder Argus offered her. "Without an envoy back to the Kirin temple, we risk having Mati-jai return on his own to this place. If his magick has advanced to the point that his apprentice passed through the wind barrier with one of his spells, we can only imagine what else he can do. The Gryphon has told us some of the nature of his new abilities, and it isn't good. This Kirin may hold the key to our survival…. Or our destruction. It appears that unless we choose to leave our home, the outcome will probably be the same whether she dies or betrays us. I, Nandi, choose to take the chance she may save us."

"Our numbers are too large to survive as nomads as our ancestors once did," Argus grumbled. "We would be consigning any who leave to death."

"It's a chance," Nandi said. "Perhaps the coming of these two is some small fortune in disguise. Had Mati-jai come, I doubt he would have bothered with formalities after the manner in which we cast him out from here."

Argus fell into silence, fingers cupping his drinking horn. The rest of the Minotaurs all looked at one another, shaken. Byson finally took a deep breath, staff still pointed at Ly-ra. "Please, depart so that the elders may convene in privacy," he told the others. "Spread the word among the rest of the village. And you, Kirin… don't try anything."

"I won't," Ly-ra replied, and the two bulls holding her released her, allowing her to shuffle back to her hooves. The Minotaurs filed out of the dwelling with anxious hands gripping their contraptions, and Ly-ra used her magick to tie her empty gourd over her flank again. She left the sheets of bark where they'd been left, discarded, on the ground. "I can reach the temple in only a few days' time," she said. "If Hlaena lives, I can carry her with my magick, and if she can be helped, maybe this place stands a chance. If she can't, I vow to return and await the coming of my master. I'll defend this place with my life in exchange for being spared now. If I can, I'll let the other elders in the council know what's going on, too. It's possible this can all be stopped at the source. But to be honest... they fear Mati-jai's abilities even though they outnumber him."

Byson's staff stopped glowing, and he held it upright in his hand again. "It doesn't bode well that you'd turn against your master so willingly. Even if it's to my benefit, all I see in you is someone who serves only herself."

"I'm not happy to do this," Ly-ra said. She gave no further explanation, and Argus grunted under his breath, but made no comment. Arias crossed to stand beside her, and enveloped her with his good wing. "I didn't expect you to say the things you did before, but I hope you know that I believe in you," he said. She nodded, swallowing hard. "I'll look for Tybrake and Brynne on my way out there. I'm sorry, Arias."

"It is not your fault," he said. "And they're tougher than they look, don't worry. I'll be looking for them around here while you're gone." He replied quickly, because he could feel dread creeping into his gut again at the mention of his friends. Passing through the barrier had incapacitated him, so what had become of his friends? Were they out there now, alone and injured?

"I'll take you to refill your gourd," Byson said, though his tone was harsh. Ly-ra thanked him and, with one final glance at Arias, followed him out of the dwelling.

CHAPTER NINE

Ly-ra flew high and fast. Byson had lowered the wind barrier for her, and she'd wasted no time after refilling her gourd. She would burn through the water before noon, but that was far from being a concern of hers. She knew that once she entered Kirin territory, she'd have to take care not to be noticed by anyone from the temple. She also kept an eye out for Tybrake and Brynne, but the land below remained devoid of signs of them. Throughout her flight, she tried to stay out of the part of her mind that had remained doubtful about the whole situation.

What are you doing? You had clear instructions from your master…

Those Minotaurs could have killed her. She knew the reason they hadn't was that she was their only hope against Mati-jai, but still. It was disheartening that they wouldn't have let her plead her case until Arias spoke up. If anything, she wanted to do the right thing. She couldn't ignore that there had been something off about Mati-jai's disposition in these recent years. It also wasn't her job as an apprentice to judge, though, so—

You'll know what the right thing to do is when it counts the most. Just focus on flying for now.

Mati-jai had never treated her like her real parents had. She remembered that much about them. He took care of her in the sense that he never let her go hungry, and treated her when she was sick, but she never felt comfortable asking him questions beyond their practices in magick and potion making. It was supposed to be an honor to be selected as an apprentice to an elder, and it was, but Mati-jai had been explicit in telling her that he'd selected her for her promising skills. *And only your skills,* she reminded herself.

Still, she cringed as she imagined what the other Kirin would think of her after learning of her actions. Would they disown her for conspiring against her master in favor of lesser creatures? Or side with her, despite their fear of Mati-jai's power? Could she live with herself if she were cast out from the temple permanently?

Ly-ra's thoughts were like a relentless storm cloud, rumbling urgently with every step she wind walked across the sky. To drown them out, she buried herself in the details of her plan.

And then, three days later, she acted those details out exactly as she'd laid them out in her head.

277

***

Night enveloped the temple in a shroud of wet darkness as rain pelted down onto the land below. Ly-ra crept through the forest surrounding the temple, leaping with silent, careful hooves over the sodden, leaf-littered ground. She'd set her trap up, and now needed to wait until the appropriate time to act. She hoped that all the time she'd spent studying tracking would be useful today. It wasn't wondering whether her skills were up to par that was feeding her anxiety, though. The waiting was the worst part.

Two guards had been placed at the threshold to the main entrance, and they weren't bothering to hide their disdain at being stuck with the job. Both around Ly-ra's age, they chatted in lazy voices about assignments. After a while, they shifted to discussing other young Kirin they'd taken a fancy to. Ly-ra felt her ears lifting with curiosity, but then she shook her head, focusing on her task. She closed her eyes and took a deep, slow breath, examining the ether around her. Then she focused on the temple, and the Kirin within blazed to life with color. Ly-ra examined the gold glow of the guards posted by the entrance, and, satisfied that they wouldn't interfere, blinked to return to the physical realm. She could feel a prickle of excitement such that she hadn't experienced since Mati-jai had tested her fawnhood ability to levitate objects. The real gravity of the situation hadn't taken hold of her yet. Somewhere in the temple, Mati-jai existed as a crimson conflagration in the ether, a vibrant radiance that made the other elders' signatures seem paltry by comparison.

Ly-ra carefully dug up a wad of earth. She'd run out of water long ago, and, while she felt compelled to refill her gourd at the river, she was convinced that she wouldn't make the trip in time. She couldn't risk missing the switching of the guard. She used her magick to funnel as much rainwater as she could into her gourd, then closed her eyes and entered into Peace to stop her racing mind. The second guard change would be happening soon, which was when all the younger apprentices would return for the night from their assignments. She'd go back to worrying then.

***

The sound of the guards changing over was Ly-ra's sign to break Peace. Senses taut, she watched as those posted at the temple door turned and headed back inside, then were replaced by a couple of Kirin who appeared to be a few years older. The first of the apprentices started to trickle back into the temple not long after. Ly-ra recognized most of them, though she didn't know all by name. They were sharing their studies among one another, while the shyer ones walked in silence, reading their texts by the light of their own flames. Ly-ra watched them carefully, rejoicing inwardly when she realized a few weren't among the group. After all, it wasn't the prompt, more astute apprentices that she needed for her plan.

Ina-mu was a friendly enough Kirin, but he never finished his work in time. On multiple occasions, Ly-ra had come across him scrambling in the night, hurrying to collect bundles of mushrooms and leaves and scribbling down terrible representations of creatures from memory instead of observation. His attempts to cheat were futile, but he and his teacher got on so well that she kept him as her apprentice despite his shortcomings. Of course, his lazy ways meant he was years behind the other apprentices of his age; he didn't even know how to make a flame whip yet, which meant his teacher had to accompany him during his assignments for his own safety. Predators were known to take the occasional careless fawn, and while the Kirin tried their best to protect their young, there were a few cases every few years.

Ly-ra prowled through the southern border of the temple with her mud wad firmly held in her magick. She knew Ina-mu would be here with his teacher, struggling to finish his assignment. He'd been stuck on his toxic flora studies for half a season, and she doubted he'd suddenly passed in the time she'd been away. It didn't take her long to hear two voices drifting through the foliage, speaking about their favorite flavors of fruit. One of them evidently had said something hilarious, because their laughter rolled through the air. *Must be nice,* Ly-ra thought to herself. Softening her wind walking, she shortened her stride and set her path to intersect with them in a matter of steps.

As Ly-ra moved, she became conscious yet again of the fact that she could easily turn back. She could tell Mati-jai of the Gryphs' betrayal, let him know his shield against the Minotaurs' barrier worked as intended, and continue on with her life as a hero in his eyes. It was hard *not* to want the adoration of such an accomplished elder, but she'd had the entire journey here to consider her actions. Whether she liked it or not, there was something wrong with Mati-jai's methods. She loved his work, but he'd sent her on a mission without waiting for the council's approval. He'd continued his own studies on the transfer of magick when he knew how unpopular they were, and instead of trying to convince them that it could be helpful, he'd instead freely admitted to her that sometimes others had to be forced to see reason. With the power he could draw from Dantzik, he would do just that, and there was no way the Minotaurs would give it up peacefully.

There was also the quiet thought that she'd always pushed to the back of her mind, that Mati-jai didn't share his knowledge with her to ensure her generation was educated, but for his own gain. The thought had nothing to do with her relationship with him as an apprentice, and thus she'd ignored it, but... Even Ina-mu had conversations with his teacher that veered away from the studies at hand. She'd never had that with Mati-jai.

If he honestly cares about more than just himself, if he cares about the betterment of all Kirin, he'll make it clear after this is all over, Ly-ra told herself.

Or he'll catch me and he won't.

Ly-ra lunged forward and let loose with what she hoped was a decent impression of the snarl of a hunting fangjaw. She used her magick to fling her mud into the eyes of the two Kirin she'd ambushed, seizing Ina-mu. Ignoring the terrified cries of the pair, she splashed back toward the temple, trying her best to be noisy as she tore through the brush; she didn't want Ina-mu to notice that her steps sounded more like they belonged to hooves instead of paws. She also understood that it would be rather unbelievable for a fierce predator to leave no marks on their prey, and so she sent a silent apology to Ina-mu as she grabbed his fur in her teeth and ripped a sizeable patch free in a swift motion. His screaming achieved a higher pitch than she thought possible, and he redoubled his feeble attempts to fend her off, but he was so weak that it was almost laughable. His spurts of attempted magick usage felt more akin to being tickled than being attacked. Ly-ra actually found herself having to concentrate not to laugh.

Ly-ra didn't have to run far to come across fangjaw prints on the ground, already beginning to grow indistinct as they filled with rainwater. They were her own brilliant creations, of course, and she wind walked over them so her own tracks wouldn't be visible. Then, hoping that Ina-mu hadn't noticed the lapse in her running, she reeled back and released her magick hold on the buck, throwing him hard enough to send him tumbling through the underbrush. She gave another snarl for good measure, but Ina-mu was doing an even better job of wailing and fleeing than she'd anticipated, and the desired effect was immediate. The guards sounded the alarm at the temple, and Ly-ra dashed for the entrance. She waited until the rush of concerned Kirin waned before slipping through the entry, head down, hoping she would remain unnoticed in all the commotion. The familiar walls of the temple encased her like a tomb as she sped down to the lower levels of the structure, taking the lesser used passages whenever she could. She hoped Ina-mu's master didn't face any trouble before she had time to explain her actions.

It took a certain level of focus to look into the ether of the world, and although the unease seated in Ly-ra's mind reminded her to check for Mati-jai's signature every few steps, she couldn't risk stopping now that she was in. She just hoped she blended into the ether alongside all the other apprentices. Every moment she was here was more time for a Kirin to recognize that Mati-jai's pupil, who had been missing for quite a while, had mysteriously returned at the exact time another apprentice was attacked by an unconvincing fangjaw.

The clatter of Ly-ra's hooves against the stone floor seemed deafening as she hurried along. She wished she had gone to refill her gourd after all. Her apprehension prodded at her again, and she skidded to a stop, panting in the dim light of the underground tunnel. She squeezed her eyes shut, and the world of ether shakily dotted itself into existence behind her lids. She focused harder, and the ether obeyed by solidifying into its rivulets of flowing color. As quickly as she could, she cast about, noting the orange presence of most of the Kirin milling about upstairs. On the level just below her, Hlaena's signature was where she expected it to be, though instead of the hazy blue it had been before, it had deepened into a dull indigo blur. *That's not good.* But her attention was drawn away from Hlaena, to the area above her, where Mati-jai's crimson glow was located high above the main floor of the temple. Only now it had a strange quality to it, and, instead of just being bright, it also flashed with fragments of other colors that she couldn't make out. Had the other elders done something to him as part of their punishment?

Mati-jai was being very still despite the ruckus. It was almost as if he were asleep, but there was no way anyone could have slept through the guards' alarm. Ly-ra blinked, unsettled. The area above the temple was never used, because... she gasped. Her master had been imprisoned in the bastille above the temple! As shocking as the realization was, Ly-ra couldn't help but feel that it was a lucky boon. The other elders must have finally stood up to him after he sent her and the Gryphs to Dantzik. She resumed running, her heart soaring. She was going to make it out of here.

Ly-ra edged into the chamber where Hlaena lay. The greenery the Alicorn had been placed on had started to wilt, the edges a limp yellow in color. She supposed that with Mati-jai imprisoned, the other Kirin had opted to let nature take its course. Ly-ra took the Alicorn in her magick, straining before she achieved a firm grasp on her. She'd originally thought Mati-jai had been cruel when he'd trained her to levitate more than her own body weight. Indeed, other masters had referred to his teaching methods as unreasonable, but now she appreciated the effort she'd expended back then. Mati-jai had taught her to be a tool for his own use. He'd probably never expected that tool to turn against him.

Ly-ra crept back into the tunnel and began her escape. She knew she couldn't sneak out of this place with an entire Alicorn in her grasp, but she'd determined she might draw less attention if she went out through the garden. She could refill her gourd at the stream there, too. There was no way she was wind walking all the way back to Dantzik carrying a load this heavy without water.

Reaching the garden was a reassuring achievement. Ly-ra took a careful look around before entering and placing Hlaena on the ground. She drank deeply from the cool stream water, dipping her gourd in at the same time, and took a murm to check on Mati-jai again. He wasn't in the same place as before. In fact, he was moving at a frighteningly fast pace, directly toward her. Flushed with panic, Ly-ra took Hlaena in her magick and skittered for the exit, not caring who was on the other side of the wall. But before she could reach it, she hopped backward in horror, her clouds of steam vanishing in a thin sheet of mist. The entire wall of the garden was bubbling and shifting, even the parts that were solid rock. Ly-ra froze as she realized Mati-jai's form was melting into existence before her. His eyes glowed a blazing white, and parts of his body seemed to have melded into a pale haze, seemingly no longer part of the physical realm.

"What have you done, fawnling?" Mati-jai

hissed in a voice that was strangely disconnected from his body.

Ly-ra regained control of herself and held on more tightly to Hlaena. She dodged sideways past Mati-jai and through the nearest section of the exit that she could access, and was greeted by open sky pouring over her. The small fragment of relief she felt was ripped away as Mati-jai bolted after her, and she hardly registered the gasps of shock from nearby Kirin as they looked upon the sight of the elder. The ground below her flew by as she burned through the water in her gourd, wind walking with all her might away from the abomination that was Mati-jai. And somehow, impossibly, despite the fact that she should have been many lengths out of his grasp, he reached out with his magick and plucked her from the air.

"You think you know magick," Mati-jai growled, drawing her nearer to him and jerking Hlaena away from her. "But you haven't the slightest inkling. None of you do!"

Fear, cold and icy, raced through Ly-ra. She couldn't even begin to pry her way from the unbreakable hold he had on her. How had his magick grown so strong that she couldn't even move? She opened her mouth to form a flame whip, but he clenched her tighter, forcing the air from her lungs. Murmurs of fear rose up from the other Kirin. The other elders were indignant, but none stepped forward.

"This is true power!" Mati-jai shrieked, somehow managing to ascend without wind walking. Energy crackled around him as he flipped Ly-ra, catching her in his magick so that she dangled by a hind leg above those assembled. "Look upon me with envy, my timid kindred," he cried, fixating the elders with his blank eyes. "You could have ascended as well, if you had just followed reason. I'll give you all a chance to renounce your stupidity, but those who don't will suffer the same punishment as this traitor."

Ly-ra felt a pull on her limbs that increased in force, dragging her in opposite directions. Tears sprang to her eyes as she cried out, but fear had rooted every other Kirin into place. What sensible creature would risk such a fate to save one apprentice that wasn't even their own?

Ly-ra felt a popping along her spine as the horizon lit with a brilliant radiance, and she realized that this would be how she ended, torn apart in front of an entire community that was too afraid to stop the monster that had existed among them for decades. The light grew brighter, and she wondered if this was how it felt to die. It had come more swiftly than she'd expected, but it strangely looked more like a wall of fire than anything else. The fire didn't burn her, but Mati-jai roared in agony, dropping her to the ground. Kirin began running in all directions as the fire started somehow spreading across both land and sky. It was no normal blaze; indeed, it took on a purple hue, something Ly-ra had never seen before. The wall of flame concentrated around Mati-jai, but left her and Hlaena unscathed.

"How are you doing this?" Mati-jai shrieked.

"You took the power in Dantzik for yourself, didn't you? You disgraceful clod of filth!"

Ly-ra didn't know how she was doing it, either, but she didn't want it to stop. She got to her feet and examined herself, grateful that everything still worked properly despite the discomfort that now accompanied every step. She grabbed Hlaena again, and an ember flickered to life in front of her as she prepared to flee.

"You have the right idea," it said. "Go, now. I can't hold him for long."

The flames parted, revealing a path northward, and Ly-ra took off along it. Explanations could wait. For now, there was no way she could let Mati-jai have his way.

***

Ly-ra was frightened enough that she didn't dare take time to search for her master in the ether. She pressed on until she was well into her second day of travelling, when exhaustion became a force she could no longer contend with. She circled over a dense thicket, noting that the branches of the trees were too thin to support the weight of her and Hlaena, and instead landed at the edge of the tree line. With an arc of her magick, she tossed up a pile of dead leaves, enough to conceal her and Hlaena. Then she closed her eyes and searched for rest. There was no hiding from Mati-jai, and flesh eaters could smell them anyway. If they found her, she'd deal with them then. It felt like she'd only just slipped off to sleep before a loud voice boomed in her head,

"Get up. We have to go!"

Ly-ra cracked her eyes open, leaves slipping from the sleek scales on her back as she lifted her head. She didn't have to look for the source of the voice, because the huge firebird flying toward her made it obvious enough. She couldn't believe her eyes at seeing a real Phoenix, and her intrigue at hearing his voice in her head almost detracted from the fact that he wasn't slowing his speed. Before she could object, he dipped down and snatched both her and Hlaena up from the leaf litter.

"I'm not complaining since you helped me to get away from my master," Ly-ra said, blinking past a groggy haze. The Phoenix's body seemed to switch between being feathered flesh and a fiery inferno, and it made her feel like she must be dreaming. "But who are you and why are you doing this?"

"You may call me Aaga," the Phoenix said. "I'm the guardian of this region, though you rightfully have no knowledge of that. It would seem that my reluctance to interfere in the lives of the beings that call my land home is the exact thing that has now threatened it. I had the opportunity to help this Alicorn, and I chose to stand by instead. But Mati-jai has used my disregard as an opportunity to empower himself. I have no idea how he's robbed this creature of what little remaining power she had left, but he has. If he reaches the Crowning Point, the place of power at the center of Dantzik, no creature will be able to withstand his might. Even now, I fear I can't hold him back for long. His presence in the ether is twisted beyond restoring."

Ly-ra huffed. "So you decided to show yourself when you did, and not before Mati-jai decided to try to tear me apart like a hunk of ripe fruit? I suppose I should thank you, anyway." Aaga's sense of amusement washed over her in an unexpected wave of emotion.

"You're quite cheeky, for a mortal who just had your life saved."

"You're not the first creature to tell me that. And are you saying that you really do live forever?"

"Yes. Unless I'm killed." The Phoenix's amusement faded to seriousness. He looked over his shoulder. "We need to go a lot faster than this if we're going to stay ahead of him. This may not be pleasant for you, though. You may want to close your eyes."

Ly-ra turned her head against the wind as a distorted roar crackled across the distance. She could just see a glittering smudge silhouetted against the horizon. Aaga ruffled his feathers, and they burned away in a burst of cinders, leaving Ly-ra to scream as the talons that had been holding her were replaced by flickering flames. A prickle of annoyance emanated from Aaga.

"I won't burn you. Now you know the first reason I suggested that you close your eyes.

Here's the second." Aaga leaned into his flying, his body stretching out until he was like a radiant meteor streaking through the air. If his voice hadn't been directly in Ly-ra's head, it would have been drowned out by the rushing of the passing air. Ly-ra used a bit of her magick to create a small barrier around herself, buffering the air a little so she could breathe. She thought of doing the same for Hlaena, but if the poor Alicorn had seemed lifeless before, she was especially so now, hardly possessing a signature that could be detected in the ether. With a sinking feeling, Ly-ra wondered whether death would have been preferable to whatever fate she was enduring now. In the distance, Mati-jai screeched again, and she peeked back to watch him *teleporting* at irregular intervals across the space. The sight made her tense despite being clutched in Aaga's talons.

"So you're hoping to use the power of Dantzik to stop Mati-jai? What happens if you can't?"

"*I'm* not hoping to do any such thing," Aaga replied. "It's only a matter of time before Mati-jai overpowers me. However, if we can revive this Alicorn, she may be able to tip things in our favor. If not, perhaps you, I and a Minotaur spellcaster may be able to put a stop to this." He didn't sound particularly hopeful.

"Byson? Even I got through his spell, so I doubt he'd be much of a match for my master. And I know I won't be much help, either."

"Let's not worry about it until we have to,"Aaga said. "And I hope we won't have to."

CHAPTER TEN

Arias felt like he was sinking into a warm, soft abyss, the pain of his wounds forgotten. He sighed, grateful for the calming effect the herbal remedy the Minotaurs had given him had on his mind. Thoughts that would normally consume him for hours were only passing considerations in his current state, but, as he'd come to expect, no peace lasted forever.

An uproar began outside. The bull that had been posted to guard him darted outside without a second glance at him, sharp stick at the ready. Arias dragged himself from his stupor and stumbled after him, joining other members of the herd as they gawked up at a spot of red that was glowing just outside the wind barrier. Arias feared that it was Mati-jai, and Byson must have thought the same thing because he yelled for everyone to take cover before snatching Arias up and depositing him inside a nearby dwelling. It was only murms later that a ball of fire came screaming through the wind spell, and impacted the ground with an eruption of earth. Arias cried out for joy when Ly-ra's head popped up from the dirt like a fresh spring bloom. With her magick, she held Hlaena.

The sense of relief that flooded Arias's mind was stifling, but before he could open his mouth to speak, Aaga the Phoenix materialized into physical form. He shook dirt from his feathers, and shouted,

"Any of you who can't wield magick, flee! You're all in danger here, you—" His voice was drowned out as a wave of wind and dirt cut through the group in a blast strong enough to knock grown Minotaurs to the ground. When Arias crawled to his feet and looked up, the wind barrier was gone, leaving an eerie quiet in its place. Mati-jai landed in their midst, and was immediately met with a lashing of fire from both Aaga and Ly-ra. Without waiting to hear the story, Byson rushed over as well, his staff raised high above his shaggy head. With a flourish, he sent a crescent of wind careening toward the Kirin elder, and it combined with Aaga and Ly-ra's flame to form a force great enough to stagger Mati-jai. The rest of the Minotaurs edged closer to the battle with uncertainty, but Byson sent them all scattering with a wave of his staff. "No! Run!" he screamed. "Get out of here!"

***

Mati-jai had an unearthly calm about him as he regained his feet. He looked about, searching for Hlaena, and then he closed his eyes, focusing past the fleeing forms bustling around him. Even with his eyes closed, he side-stepped another attack.

"He's looking for her in the ether!" Aaga cried, rushing toward Mati-jai. "Don't let him! Ly-ra, you're too weak! Go help Arias!"

Mati-jai shook his head, ignoring the small part of his brain that tried to alert him to the threat of another impending attack. He only had one goal right now, and that was... the corners of his mouth curled upwards into a grin. There she was, moving through the forest alongside the mundane presence of lesser beings. *Arias,* he thought, grinding his teeth. Who would've known that such a worthless beast could cause him so much trouble? He had lost a good apprentice to his own stupidity, though. He'd been wrong in thinking that Ly-ra would never have fallen to such base desires of wanting acceptance from anyone other than himself. None of that mattered now, however. He'd end both the Gryphon and Ly-ra, take back the Alicorn, and have a new, better apprentice under his teaching in due time. There was no need for this blunder to mar his legacy. He'd lead the Kirin into a new era, an enlightened one to rival the great period of knowledge that had changed them from forest dwelling heathens and into knowledgeable and powerful scholars.

Mati-jai grunted as Aaga bore down upon him, wrapping him in a sphere of burning fire. The purple flames burned as they licked at his flesh, but the intensity wasn't nearly as great as he'd expected. His body seemed to be accepting of the mana he'd infused himself with. Who would have known that the mana Alicorns used for healing could be so useful in other ways as well? He dispelled Aaga's magick fire, then teleported after Arias and Hlaena. The Phoenix and Minotaur spellcaster were minor inconveniences at this point. He couldn't risk letting that Alicorn take the reservoir of power in Dantzik for herself. He teleported high into the sky, and decided to try something new. He'd always enjoyed the spell he'd developed, the one that flung his foes into the very heavens themselves to live—or not—far from the point he'd tossed them from. He wondered how it worked in reverse, if he threw them toward the ground instead of into the sky. He chuckled and reared back, his magick encasing any creatures he could find. Their screaming was a beautiful sound he reveled in. "You probably should have stayed home, dear Aaga," he said, holding on extra tight to the struggling form of the Phoenix. Then Mati-jai plunged downward, releasing his hold on his screaming captives as he did so.

***

Sheer determination prodded Arias to drag Hlaena through the forest toward the Crowning Point. Ignoring the cries of the rest of their herd, Argus and Nandi had broken off to help him the murm they'd seen him dart for her. Even with the help of the two Minotaurs, most of Hlaena's weight rested on him. For all their courage, Nandi and Argus were old and feeble, many years past their prime. Still, they carried on alongside him, faces contorted with their effort. They'd already passed the lightning-struck tree bent at a right angle, a sign they said meant they weren't far from the lake. Beneath the masking effect of the potion he'd taken, Arias's ribs sang out with pain, but he ignored the feeling. There'd be time to worry about himself after this was over… or when he was dead.

The sound of something moving through the brush ate a hole of panic into the small group, but the sight of Ly-ra made Arias feel a rush of hope. She didn't stop as she bore down upon them, grabbing Hlaena up in her magick and straining to keep up her pace. She glanced back as she galloped. "Keep up! I need to know where I'm going!"

Argus and Nandi shared a look. They both turned to Arias. "Dead northeast," Nandi panted. "There's a spell over the lake; you have to mix water with the earth at its shores to see the Crowning Point. Smear the mixture over your forehead. Now go!"

Argus reached out and touched him on the shoulder, quickly saying, "Spirit of your ancestors be with you. If you do not succeed, there will be nothing left for any of us to return to."

Arias didn't pause to reply, but turned and sprinted to catch up with Ly-ra, the pain in his chest dragging tears to his eyes. He was barely within a few lengths of her when he heard her yell, "He's close! Don't stop running!"

Dread edged into Arias as he wheezed, wishing he had the use of his wings. He could hear Mati-jai crashing through the undergrowth, getting closer to him and Ly-ra. He could barely draw the breath to call to Ly-ra.

"North...east!"

She didn't look back. It felt like they'd been cutting through the forest for eternity, but then they burst through the trees and found themselves on a sandy bank. Ly-ra looked back at him with a wild expression.

"Water," Arias wheezed. "Pour... it into the sand."

Ly-ra responded with an incredulous expression, but he growled, "Do it!"

She drew some water from her gourd and threw it into the sand, and Arias used his talons to smear the mixture over his face. "Do the same!" he croaked, eyes widening as a beautiful lake shimmered into view. Its surface reflected the sky, its depths undisturbed by waves. Ly-ra gasped as the same image revealed itself to her, and she turned to him again, her voice urgent. "What now?"

"I... don't... know," Arias said, drawing in quick breaths. He looked about, but there was no time; with a shriek Mati-jai burst into the clearing behind them.

"Traitorous disgrace!" he cried, leaping toward Ly-ra. "All those Minotaurs are dead because of you... but I have to thank you, as well. The power of a Phoenix is truly an amazing thing. You could have shared in it with me, apprentice. You could have experienced what it feels like to be a legend!"

"You chose to let your own desires corrupt you," Ly-ra said, placing Hlaena on the ground. Arias glanced up at Mati-jai, but the elder Kirin's eyes were trailing Ly-ra. He heaved against the Alicorn's body, and the water of the lake sent a shock through his body; it was still frigid despite the coming of spring. The adrenaline rush from trying to outpace Mati-jai had worn off, and it was impossible to ignore the pain that blossomed in him with every attempt to drag Hlaena further into the water. He kept one eye on Mati-jai as he struggled as quietly as he could, his talons leaving long red lines on Hlaena's pelt. He didn't know how the Crowning Point worked, but he knew he only had murms to figure it out.

"You were easily the most gifted in magick among us, and it still wasn't enough. You've stolen from others to play pretend with all the power and influence you wish you had. If you want to talk about a disgrace, you should look at yourself... I'm ashamed I ever looked up to you," Ly-ra said, creeping sideways.

Mati-jai laughed. "Goodbye, Ly-ra. Or rather, goodbye to your potential. I was never too satisfied with the rest of you." His horns glowed ominously, and Ly-ra yelled, "Wait! You don't know where the Crowning Point is, and I do. You'll never be able to take its power without me."

Mati-jai paused, finally looking at Arias. With a cold, deliberate finality, he said, "Then I certainly don't need him."

And he vanished from sight.

***

Arias froze. The forest, empty except for him and Ly-ra, deceived him, but he knew that in the next murm, his life would end. He clutched Hlaena tighter, knowing that somehow, some way, he had to save her before he died.

"Don't let go!" Ly-ra screamed, leaping toward him in a massive cloud of steam. Her magick trickled over him, warm in comparison to the icy water, just as Mati-jai faded back into existence wielding the largest, hottest flame whip he'd ever seen. The blistering heat had just touched him when, still holding Hlaena, he was wrenched sideways and up into the air. The brightness of Mati-jai's attack lit up the shoreline in a dazzling firestorm of light, and then Arias saw and heard nothing more of it as he crashed into the lake.

Arias gasped as the glacial chill of the Crowning Point raced across his skin. He wasn't far below the surface, but he had already breathed in the water, and his panic grew as his frenzied movements brought him no closer to the surface. A small distance away from him, Hlaena was slowly sinking into the depths, her eyes half open as her mane spread out in an undulating ribbon behind her. Arias choked, numbness setting into his limbs as gravity dragged him after her. The dark pit below swallowed them up.

CHAPTER ELEVEN

Hlaena followed Xio deeper into the lush grasslands. It was warm and inviting here, totally different from the dreary chill she remembered leaving behind. Everything before now all seemed so vague. It was hard to remember.

"Where are we going again?" she asked Xio, and he turned, bright eyes twinkling.

"You'll see," he said.

Playing coy, Hlaena thought, still trotting after him. He'd always been that way, but that was part of why she loved him so much. "Where are the others?" she asked. "Shouldn't they come, too?"

"They're waiting for us, now. Come on! You're always asking questions." He started to canter, and Hlaena was about to join him, but something stopped her in her tracks.

What was that?

"Wait," she called out, half turning. She pricked her ears, but the forest behind her offered no answers. But that feeling... had she imagined it?

"Come on, Hlaena!" Xio whinnied, slowing to a walk. "Let's go."

"But—" Hlaena shifted on her feet, confused. She couldn't smell the fresh breeze of this place. She took an uneasy step backward. Now that she thought about it... just where was she *really?* Why couldn't she remember anything? Xio had stopped moving, his eyes filled with worry.

"Hlaena?" he called.

"Hold on," she said. "Go on without me for now. There's something I need to check first." She raced back in the direction she'd come from.

Xio didn't follow after her.

***

Hlaena's eyes fluttered open in darkness. She was immediately aware of the sensation of water, and of the muck she'd settled into. The faint light flickering from above indicated the surface, and she instinctively used her magick and wings to propel herself upward.

She *used her magick.*

As she rose, snippets of things that had occurred around her in the past days trickled back to her. She hadn't been fully conscious, but she'd heard plenty, and some part of her had been present enough to make sense of the conversations and sounds around her. As she tried to compile her memories, she became aware of the excess mana in the water around her, leeching into her like a precious life spring until there was nothing left. By the time she burst through the surface of the lake, shattering its illusion, she was filled with a sense of urgency… and of anger.

Hlaena breathed in air that she'd felt she'd been without for eons. Mati-jai was standing over charred remains, his mouth hanging open as the spectacle of the lake revealed itself to him. When he rested his eyes on her, he growled.

"The lake was hiding here under a pathetic illusion all along, and now you've wasted its power on yourself!"

"You act as if power is eternal," Hlaena replied. "Only a fool believes such things."

Mati-jai smirked. "Under my rule, it will be. I haven't come this far to let you stop me. I already took what I needed from you, and from that useless Phoenix, too. I *am* eternal."

Hlaena tilted her head. She was aware of her fury for this miserable creature, but a greater sense of calm controlled her senses. It was an interesting sensation. "Then please," she said, beginning to walk toward the elder Kirin, "allow me to show you how wrong you are." She investigated the surplus of mana surging within her, curious that, instead of the frailness she expected to find after such a long period of dormancy, there was a vitality she'd never felt before. She prodded the raw power, exploring the extent of its potency, and it unlocked at her touch. Mati-jai noticed the change in her demeanor and vanished into the ether. Hlaena snorted. It was no wonder Mati-jai's teleporting was choppy. He was doing it wrong. All one had to do was…

Hlaena winked from existence in a flash of light, leaving the physical realm to join Mati-jai in the ether. Their forms were no longer tangible, but she could still detect his disbelief at finding her alongside him. With an outpouring of energy, she threw him back into the forest, and then leaped so that she was ahead of him. Then she shifted all her weight to her front legs, and kicked as hard as she could. The crisp snap of her mana-infused hooves connecting with his skull rang out with a satisfying crack, and the subsequent sound of him crashing into the greenery behind him was even more satisfying. A murm later he jumped out from the mess of collapsed boughs and splintered trunks; he was so imbued with mana that he was virtually unscathed.

"The power is wasted on you," he snarled, "and you know it."

"Just as it is wasted on you, Mati-jai. Now, I'd like you to return what you took from me."

Mati-jai's eyes widened, and he summoned his flame whip. Hlaena waited until he reared back to lash out with it, and then slipped back into the ether for a murm to avoid it. She gave an unimpressed whicker as the purple flame set a swath of trees aflame, instantly darkening the trunks a singed black.

"No!" Mati-jai shrieked again, scrambling to his feet. "You're an Alicorn! You're forbidden to kill!"

"That may have been true in my past life," Hlaena replied, still moving toward him. "But it doesn't look like that will be true for this one."

"I could bring them back," Mati-jai blurted, backing away. "If you spare me…My studies can show me how to bring Arias and Ly-ra back. I've already mastered the techniques I would need."

Hlaena stopped moving as hatred flared to life within her once again. She lowered her horn toward the elder Kirin, and, incredibly, he started to laugh.

"My whole life—to end like this… such a pitiful waste," he said. "But in the end, I still won, Alicorn."

Hlaena poured everything she had into wiping Mati-jai from existence. The resulting explosion was so great and so bright that she had to close her eyes against it. When the light finally faded, all that was left of the elder was a broken fragment of one of his horns. She felt no guilt or pity for the creature. Frantic, she teleported back to the lake, and examined the charred remains there.

Reverently, she traced out the blackened outline of scales among what was left, and of the two objects that must have been horns... it probably had been the one called Ly-ra. She bowed her head and gave a silent thanks to the creature for her sacrifice, and then looked around the lake again. Where was Arias?

Hlaena's gaze was drawn past Ly-ra's body, to a deep scorch marring the earth, forming a clear line into the water. A sprinkling of half burned feathers were scattered across the sand, with more floating on the surface of the lake. She hurried to the edge of the shore, undaunted by the visage reflected back at her, of an Alicorn whose horn crackled with latent magickal energy and whose eyes wept with mana. Even her tail, formerly cut free to serve as a blindfold for Arias, had been restored. Bracing herself against the cold, she dove, searching the body of water in all directions. A single object was suspended in the depths, unmoving, and she used her magick to draw it to the surface.

Arias's eyes were open, but unseeing. He'd given up the fight to live, and she hadn't been there to save him. Hlaena carefully laid him next to Ly-ra, pacing and pawing as grief took hold of her. He'd been so insistent on helping her to recover. They both had. And now...

Hlaena started as an idea came to her, and she closed her eyes, focusing in the ether. A lifetime of learning to manipulate mana had given her the inane ability to detect it in the life around her, and she peered at the two fallen creatures before her.

Ly-ra, rest her young presence, had already departed, but a faint blue essence still clung to Arias's form. Hlaena whinnied with hope, her eyes springing open. She couldn't accept a conclusion wherein she had no Xio, no herd, no Arias, and dozens of innocents dead partially because of her. She wouldn't.

There were certain practices that no creature, no matter how gifted in magick, ever attempted for fear of loss of life. Her blind dismissal of the knowledge in an attempt to save Naugi was what had got her into her predicament in the first place. But if it meant even the tiniest possibility of bringing Arias back, she was willing to try. She aimed at the spot just under his wing and behind his foreleg and, taking a deep breath, thrust downward with her horn. The barest remainder of his life force wasn't much to work with, but she patiently wove threads of mana into his broken body with all the care a giant would use to not crush a dry leaf. She used her magick to draw the lake water from his lungs, and to fix the other injuries he had, too. She didn't know how long he'd been unconscious, but he was still holding on to the thinnest thread of life. She didn't have to bring him back from the dead, she just had to coax his life source back into a body that was stable enough to support it.

Hlaena stood at the water's edge for a period of time that felt indeterminate. She refused to let her concentration wane, even as the thick scent of smoke began to fill the air. The mana trickled from her at a lethargic pace, like sap from an old tree, but the process couldn't be hurried. Hlaena could see flickering orange from behind her eyelids by the time she felt she couldn't spare anymore mana. A part of her wanted to continue anyway, but then the sacrifices that had been made by so many would have been worthless. She'd learned that lesson well enough in her old homeland, when she and the rest of her herd had tried to save their guardian Hydra, Naugi.

Hlaena opened her eyes again, and leaned down to nuzzle Arias's limp body. The fire she and Mati-jai had started in the forest had grown, coloring the sky an acrid orange. Eyelids drooping with exhaustion, she used her magick to pull water from the lake. Her ability to jump through the ether and teleport had vanished when the mana she'd taken from the Crowning Point had been emptied out in trying to heal Arias. She opened her wings, resisting the temptation to leave the blaze to fate. She couldn't let it run amok, not when there were sure to be survivors in Dantzik. Grunting with effort, she took to the sky, and smothered the worst of it. Then she returned to the lake and tried to gather Arias and Ly-ra up in her magick, but exhaustion brought her to her knees. She folded her legs and lay on her side to rest against the gritty sand. Sleep was immediate.

***

Hlaena sensed that she wasn't alone. Waking up was a fight in itself, and she battled to open her eyes. She half-peered into the ether, and found that a figure with a magickal presence was moving toward her. She managed to push herself into an upright position, shaking the sand from her mane. The morning light was too bright, and she squinted to make out the form of a Minotaur bull limping his way across the shore. He carried a metal rod in one hand, and leaned heavily on it with each step. Though the creature gave no indication of being aggressive, she regarded it with wary suspicion. He seemed to realize this, and stopped, calling out, "I'm Byson, and I know you as Hlaena. I only mean to help you, don't be alarmed."

Hlaena could see that the right half of the bull's face was caked in blood and dirt, and if his gait was any indication, he was too lame to pose any real danger. She coaxed her legs into allowing her to stand, though even that was a feat. "I didn't know there were Minotaurs here. Mati-jai mentioned killing a Phoenix... did he do this to you, as well? Are there more of you?"

Byson's eyes were glued to the albino Gryphon lying in the sand next to her. His muzzle twisted into a grimace, and Hlaena answered his unspoken question. "Mati-jai is dead. I believe there is hope yet for Arias, but we must wait and see."

Byson looked across from Arias, and his gaze became somber as he realized what the charred object next to him was. "Poor thing. So she really did stand by her word."

Hlaena knickered softly. More words weren't spoken between her and Byson, but she gathered up Ly-ra's remains and he hefted Arias's body over his shoulders. Together, the two made the long trip back to what was left of the village of

Dantzik.

***

Hlaena heard the wailing long before she saw the remains of Dantzik village. The Minotaurs' homes were heaps of crumbled earth, and, here and there, dotted along the ground, were the remains of what used to be the Minotaurs themselves. Lioshi were scattered about, calling out with faint sounds. Red feathers drifted in the breeze, though Aaga's body was nowhere to be seen. A few gasps rose from survivors when they saw Hlaena return with Byson, and she had to resist the urge to avert her gaze. Since most of the dwellings had been destroyed, Besthestamus leaves had been strewn across what was left of walls to enclose the spaces within. Byson approached one of the dwellings that was mostly intact and passed Arias to an able-bodied cow. He took Ly-ra's remains from Hlaena, placing them inside a partially shattered earthen container, and limped off, presumably to store them elsewhere. Hlaena called after him, "I'm strong enough to mend your leg, perhaps. Then at least you can get around a little easier." Byson paused, looking at her over his shoulder with his good eye.

"Worry about yourself," he said, shifting his staff between his hands. "You look like you've been to the afterlife and back. My leg will be fine, my herd are good healers. Is there anything that can be done for Arias?"

Hlaena shook her head. "No," she said. "Only the gift of time can help him."

***

That night was merciful in Dantzik, holding

310

the warmth of spring and sheltering the survivors of Mati-jai's attack. The floor in most of the surviving dwellings had been lined with what lioshi wool and woven mats could be scavenged from the wreckage of the village, giving a bit of comfort to those within. Nandi and Argus helped as best they could, persistent despite being slowed by age. Hlaena likewise stayed busy, fetching water, helping to build fires, and gathering food and herbs from the surrounding forest. She occasionally took time to search the wreckage for stragglers who may have survived, encouraged by the fact that a few survivors had trickled in over the course of the day.

"Without a barrier between Dantzik and the rest of the world, any hostile creature could move in on us," Byson said, fatigue sinking his low voice into an even deeper rumble. He and Hlaena had just finished carrying a last load of water up to the tents, and it felt like they finally had a murm to rest. Both had shuffled a little further away from the others, out of earshot. "You and I have magick to protect ourselves should anything attack. Any of my herd who are well enough to take watch would be better served helping the others, and the bulk of the immediate work is done—much thanks to you, I'm sure you know."

"I agree," Hlaena said, stifling a yawn. "I'll take first watch while you rest."

"You've done enough here, Alicorn. I'll take first watch."

"You shouldn't be on that leg in the first

place," Hlaena scolded. "It helps me to be busy. I'll sleep when you take next shift."

Byson opened his mouth as if he wanted to argue, but the comment didn't make it to his tongue. He limped back into the tent without another word, and Hlaena started to make her rounds around the occupied portion of the village. After the first pass, her strides started to shorten, and her hooves dragged with every step. The still, muggy air lulled her, and she shook her head to keep awake, only snapping back to attention whenever something crunched in the distant forest. She folded and refolded her wings, insistent on keeping them from drooping down, but, before long, their tips were grazing the ground anyway. The night was still young as her head slumped lower and lower, and soon she was slumbering peacefully on her feet.

***

"Hlaena."

Hlaena jumped awake, eyes darting. One of the elder Minotaurs, the one called Nandi, was backing away from her with her hands held up. Hlaena sighed. "I must have drifted off, I'm sorry. I just blinked... and now I can see that it's been quite a while."

Nandi's deep-set eyes held an eagerness as she waved toward the tents, pointing at one in particular. The one where Arias was.
"Something's happening," she said in an excited whisper.

Hlaena's ears pricked at the words, and she

turned to gallop for the tent as fast as she could. Then she remembered Nandi, and she turned back, lying down so that the elderly cow could ride on her back. She had to force herself not to run, keeping her gait at a fast walk so as not to jostle her load, but the murm she'd deposited Nandi outside the tent she rushed inside.

Arias hadn't moved from where he'd been placed in a corner and on a bundle of soft wool. In fact, he looked unchanged from when he'd been brought in, but every few murms, he drew in a long, wheezing breath. Hlaena edged closer, and Minotaurs shuffled out of her way so that she could lie next to him, tucking him under her wing.

"I'm here, Arias," she said, gently nuzzling the feathers and the base of his neck. "You'll be alright. I'm here."

Arias took another breath, and Hlaena gave a hopeful whinny, gathering him in closer to her. The Minotaurs leaned in with interest, chattering with muted excitement, and offering their own bedding to make the two more comfortable. From just outside the tent, standing with her arms folded, Nandi gave a relieved sigh, feeling hopeful for the first time in days.

CHAPTER TWELVE

The Minotaurs were slow to rebuild Dantzik after Mati-jai's destruction of it. The dead had been buried. The forest surrounding the village continued ushering in the coming of spring, but somehow the plants seemed less vibrant, and the leaves and needles reached up toward the sun without the vigor they once had. Hlaena and Byson, along with the other Minotaurs who were able, kept busy with meeting the needs of the village, but the ordeal they'd overcome took its toll on them, and there were days when they simply languished in the shade of the leaves strewn over the dwellings, resting in the warmth.

Arias was up on his feet, but the Minotaurs wouldn't let him help with anything—neither would Hlaena—even though he was finally feeling well enough to do so. It had been many days since the devastation of Mati-jai, and despite him looking every chance he could, there was still no sign of Brynne and Tybrake.

314

"The Crowning Point may return to its former glory," Nandi said to Argus, her voice hushed but by no means hiding secrets from the others. "The land is still viable, and without Mati-jai, we will be left in peace to rebuild..."

Arias lowered his ears, no longer listening to the conversation. Naia's shell pendant still hung limply around his neck, though the strands of Hlaena's mane, that Ly-ra had tied in with them, had been singed away when Mati-jai had attacked him. He stared at the satchel made of lioshi wool that was at the side of the dwelling, away from everyone else. He knew what was inside that satchel, the bag that was crudely held closed with a length of fiber knotted at the top. He closed his eyes, his heart heavy again. Hlaena watched him from across the space, and after a while he heard her shuffle to her hooves and walk over to stand next to him. He peered up at her through half-open eyes, and she whickered at him to get to his feet. The crack in her horn shimmered like quicksilver, mended by her extraordinary encounter with the Crowning Point.

"I was out early this morning," she said, "and I spotted half a tusker in a gully not too far from here. Why don't we go try to find it? You haven't eaten in a while."

Arias wiggled his stump of tail and closed his eyes again. "I'm not hungry."

Hlaena lowered her head and blew warm air on him through her nostrils. "Even so, you should eat. Maybe you'll be hungry later?"

Arias doubted that, but he ruffled his feathers and got up to follow her anyway. The sun was high in the sky outside, and he squinted and used his wings to block out the brightest of the light. He felt light on his feet, lighter than he should have, and walking too fast made him feel faint. Hlaena was careful to keep pace with him, pausing if she ever got too far ahead. He'd felt strange ever since waking up in what was left of Dantzik, but everyone assured him that he just needed more rest, and more food, and more water. Maybe they were right. He blinked as he and Hlaena entered into the cool cover of trees, and he lowered his wings. He and the Alicorn mare hadn't talked much in the past few days. He was happy that she had recovered, unimaginably so, but he also felt responsible for what had happened to Ly-ra… and for whatever had happened to Brynne and Tybrake. He felt he couldn't return to the rest of the flock without the two Gryphs.

Hlaena slid down the slant of the gully, then turned and used her magick to place Arias next to her. There out in the open, not even covered to keep it hidden from other predators, was the rear half of a tusker. Not very long ago, Arias would have been excited to find such a feast. Instead, he glanced at Hlaena.

"Are you going to stay here? With the Minotaurs, I mean."

"I was thinking about it," Hlaena replied. "After all, without Aaga to watch this region, I'd feel better knowing Dantzik is safe."

Arias tilted his head. "You said the abilities the Crowning Point gave you left you."

"They did. I'm not particularly worried about that, though. I don't think there is much out here that I couldn't handle."

The droning of some creature sounded through the air, joined by a few others of its kind. They quieted as a breeze blew through the brush.

"I'm going to leave soon, Hlaena. I want to take Ly-ra back to the other Kirin. And then I need to find Brynne and Tybrake."

Hlaena flicked an ear, not looking at him. "Larin and the others will be wondering where you are. It's possible Brynne and Tybrake made their way back to them. Without knowing what lies in the lands beyond, travelling alone may not be the best choice."

Arias sat down, annoyed. She was right, of course. "You won't come back with me?" he asked, and she finally fixed her maroon gaze on him.

"Not yet. I'm happy that you have others of your kind, who love and appreciate you, to return to, but my place isn't among them."

"You know you're always welcome in the flock, Hlaena. I know a few Gryphs said some things after the sea serpent encounter, but—"

"That's not quite what I mean, Arias," Hlaena cut in, her tone remaining friendly despite the interruption.

"Are you going to try to find other Alicorns like yourself?"

"No." She answered so fast that Arias paused. She took a deep breath, and continued, "The Minotaurs will be good company, and I want to help them rebuild. Regardless of whether the Crowning Point returns or not, Dantzik will still make a good home for them. Maybe my thoughts of seeking out others of my kind will change in the future. Maybe not."

Arias nodded. "I think I understand. But regardless, I'll come to visit you as often as I can."

Hlaena chuckled. "I'll do the same. I dare say I'm a little faster than you on the wing."

Arias snorted. "We've never raced before on the wing, but I think you'd find victory a little harder than you'd expect, Hlaena."

"What you have in youth, I more than make up for with years of experience in flying," she replied, a combative twinkle in her eye.

Arias laughed, edging closer to her, and she nibbled playfully at him. When he tried to dart out of her reach, he lost his balance, toppling sideways, and she pricked her ears in concern.

"I'd better be careful," he mumbled, righting himself. "I'm still not as nimble as I used to be."

"As you will be," Hlaena corrected. "You know, you'll get there faster if you—"

"Eat and rest like I'm supposed to?" Arias said, rolling his eyes. "I know, Hlaena."

The mare swished her tail, content. "I'm glad you agree. You should stay here at least until you feel completely well again, little one."

"It means I get to spend more time with you, so of course I will."

Hlaena didn't hide how much she reveled in the statement, and Arias trilled softly at seeing her happy again. They spent a little more time at the gully together, and then took their time returning to Dantzik, their steps matching as they walked through the forest with tusker in tow.

***

Arias ended up staying in Dantzik much longer than he'd intended, but he didn't regret the time spent. Much of the village was rebuilt, including a new pen for the lioshi. Argus was vocal with his concerns when he noticed Arias had a deep interest in the creatures, but Arias assured him that he just liked to observe them. It wasn't often that he encountered prey that didn't mind letting him sit close by and watch as they went about their lives. Really, it was one of the rare murms he got any peace and quiet. Half of his days seemed to be spent being trailed by Minotaur calves who begged him for flights over the forest whenever the adults weren't watching. More often than not, they were dragged away by their older peers before succeeding, but occasionally he indulged them. He was so used to flying that the mystique of it had mostly left him, but he could still remember how wonderful it had felt to spread his wings and soar with the Ardeigryph for the first time. So long as the calves were careful of where they placed their hard little hooves, he didn't mind letting them experience what it was like.

It hadn't taken long for Arias to get back to feeling like himself. His plumage was taking its time shedding its burned feathers, but the physical reminder of Mati-jai's attack faded a bit more with each passing day. His strength had returned quickly when he had started eating again, and it hadn't taken much convincing from Hlaena to get him to agree to flying out with her every morning to search for herbs. The outings reminded him of the way he'd scamper around Glendale in his cubhood, searching out plants alongside the rest of the herd while he tried not to get trampled underhoof by accident.

Hlaena was quick to use her magick to help injured Minotaurs who would accept it, but a surprising number of them respectfully declined, only trusting their own traditional remedies. Byson was one of those who'd declined, despite the fact that Hlaena had been quite sure she could save his injured eye. The Minotaurs' mixtures were sound and effective, though not nearly as fast acting as magick. Arias was sure that the method by which Alicorns healed others played a part in the herd's hesitance as well. It wasn't exactly a pleasant thing to watch or to experience.

***

Arias awoke one morning to the beautiful sound of the early morning chorus, and stepped out into the milky fog of early sunrise. Hlaena was awake, lying just outside a newly-constructed dwelling, and staring into the distance. She nickered a muted greeting to Arias, and didn't seem surprised to see that he was holding a woolen satchel in his mouth. He placed it on the ground reverently. "It's time for me to go."

The Alicorn mare stood and opened her wings to embrace him. "Travel safe, little one. Tell everyone that I send my blessings. And Arias… I'll keep my eye out for your friends. I hope that Brynne and Tybrake are waiting for you with the rest of the flock."

"Thanks, Hlaena."

"You're not going to stay to say goodbye to the Minotaurs?"

"I'm afraid the calves will want last-murm rides on my back." Hlaena's eyes danced with amusement, and he added, "I'll be back sometime soon."

"I'm no calf."

Arias and Hlaena looked up in surprise as Byson walked down to join them. He snorted, crossing his arms and feigning indignation.

"I didn't mean it like that, Byson," Arias said, but the Minotaur was already chuckling, his good eye winking in the early sunlight.

"I know you didn't. Here, I have something for you. I thought of giving it to you a while ago, but the time never seemed right, and... well, here." He reached down and placed something on the ground, and Arias immediately knew what it was. Ly-ra's sheets of bark were deeply creased and no longer bound together, but the markings Ly-ra had made on them were still as fresh as the day she'd made them. Arias couldn't understand what the scribbles meant, but his eyes settled on the drawings she'd made of him, Brynne and Tybrake. He looked up at Byson.

"Thank you, Byson. I'd love to keep them, but I don't know how I'll take them with me."

"Leave that to me," Hlaena said, trotting off. Arias and Byson watched her leave, then sat and spoke as the sun sent rays down that cleared away the morning mist, keeping their voices low so as not to wake the other Minotaurs. Before long, Hlaena returned with a bundle of waxy leaves and long grasses, and Byson made haste to fulfill her request for a bundle of lioshi wool. Hlaena carefully surrounded the sheets of bark in a thick layer of the leaves, then secured them by tying the grass around the entire bundle. She shaped the wool around it, and used more of the fibrous grass to tie the pouch around Arias's neck.

Hlaena examined her work, then said, "It shouldn't make any noise if you go hunting between now and reaching the eyrie. The leaves should keep the bark from getting wet, but you should still stay out of the rain as much as you can, just in case."

"I will. I can't thank you two enough." Arias bowed deeply in appreciation, and Byson flashed his teeth at him. Hlaena leaned down to give Arias one last affectionate nuzzle, and he trilled happily before taking Ly-ra's satchel in his beak again. He flew off in a rustle of wings, and, when he was high enough, he circled around Dantzik one last time, looking over the scorched forest that would someday be green again, and at Hlaena raising her wings in farewell. And then he headed south, toward the Kirin temple.

***

Arias kept an eye out as he crossed over the grassland that was home to the Pegasi, and, as expected, they rose up like a cloud on the horizon to meet him. Vander and the herd were confused upon seeing him alone, and Arias tried not to let his voice betray him when he asked them whether they had seen Brynne or Tybrake. He didn't mention what the satchel he was carrying contained, and Vander didn't ask. The stallion dipped and twirled in a wide circle around Arias, but he seemed to have picked up on Arias's somber mood, because he didn't ask him to race. Instead, he asked whether he wanted to stay in the grasslands for the night, which Arias politely declined. "I have somewhere important to be," he told the Pegasus stallion. "But if you want to race a fair match against someone who can fly faster than you, I know where you can find her."

Vander froze in midair, flapping closer to Arias. "Nonsense! Blasphemy! Who and where? Send her here at one!" he demanded. Arias was more smug than he'd intended as he said, "You'd have to go to her. Her name is Hlaena, and she lives in Dantzik."

"Dantzik? There are no flyers in the land of the Minotaurs, only a terrible windstorm that keeps the land secret from outsiders. Do you take Vander for a fool?"

"No, no!" Arias said, keeping a firm grip on the wool satchel with his talons. "The wind barrier is gone. There's an Alicorn in Dantzik now."

He tried to keep his amusement in check as a collective whinny went up from the Pegasi, and they began to discuss the prospect of a race with a new stranger. In the din of their excitement, Arias allowed himself a snicker. He was sure that Hlaena would have some choice words for him upon their next meeting, but he also knew that, while she'd never admit it, some part of her would be secretly just as amused as she was by the entire situation. Then he dipped his head to Vander. "I have to get going, but I'll see you again sometime soon. It's been nice speaking to you again."

Vander likewise dipped his head, and then turned and cried out, "Any who believe they can keep up, follow me! To Dantzik!"

***

Travelling back to the Kirin temple was lonely

without companions. Every now and then, Arias called out for his two friends despite knowing that the chances of either of them hearing him were small. He never heard a reply.

The temple was quiet when Arias reached it. No guards were posted near the entrance, and he walked right up to the main entryway without anything happening. He waited around for a bit, watching the cliff for any sign of activity, and even considered walking in, but decided against it at the last murm. Instead, he sat down and yelled, "I need to speak to one of you! My name is Arias; I'm a Gryph—" He cut off as a shaggy head beset with a set of twisting horns poked through the rock to peer at him. The elder looked him up and down with a pair of mismatched eyes, one brown and the other green.

"You came back. Why? And where is your master, Mati-jai?"

"He was never my master," Arias replied, trying not to focus on the drastic difference between the creature's eyes. "I'm glad to say that he's dead, erased from this world with the help of one of the creatures he tried to exploit. I came back because she should be returned to her home." He nudged the wool satchel forward, and the elder's eyes narrowed with understanding.

"You may come in. Behave yourself, flesh eater. Antics won't be tolerated here." He disappeared back inside before Arias could say anything in response. Arias carefully picked up the satchel and, after a murm of hesitation, followed him through the deceiving entrance.

The Kirin within the temple stared at Arias as he walked past them, their whispers filling his ears. The elder led him down a short chamber just beyond the main entryway, and indicated a sheer rock face before walking through it. The Kirin seemed to love their deceiving thresholds, and Arias felt that he'd never get used to the feeling of convincing himself to walk into a solid-looking object. He felt his way past the illusion by sending a single talon through first, followed by the rest of him. The sight of what lay just beyond made him gasp in awe.

A high ceiling formed of pinkish crystal looked down on a jewel-encrusted floor. The tiny pieces of mineral glinted as Arias entered the chamber, and he was directed to stand at the center by his guide. Soon after, a dozen other Kirin found their way to the assembly hall, each flanked by their apprentice. The way they held their sheets of bark at the ready reminded Arias of Ly-ra. The marked leaflets Byson had given him, wrapped protectively in wool and leaves, suddenly felt heavy with memories as they rested against his breast. The Kirin settled at the far edge of the hall in a manner that in no way fully utilized the sheer size of the space. No one spoke, and after a long and uncomfortable silence, Arias took the initiative.

"I don't know what your customs are, beyond what I was told by my friend, Ly-ra," he said, ignoring the indignant grunts that eked from the throats of some of the elders at his choice of words. "I do know that Mati-jai was held in high esteem by many here, and that he was also criticized, for good reason. I want to start my story from the beginning, and you can do what you will with the information. But before all of that, I think that Ly-ra should be respected and attended to in whatever way your kind dictates. Without Ly-ra, I, the Minotaurs, and the Alicorn Hlaena would not have survived. I'm afraid to say Aaga the Phoenix wasn't so lucky." The gasp of shock that spread throughout the space was only amplified as Arias carefully untied the satchel, and the Kirin beheld what was inside.

The same elder that had led Arias into the assembly hall composed himself, and, standing up straighter, said, "You have our attention, Gryphon. Please, explain."

"My name is Arias," Arias replied, "and I fully intend to."

***

Arias watched the sun set, tinting the blue sky with shades of orange and purple. Here at the edge of the forest, just beyond the river that bordered the temple, stood a new sapling: Ly-ra's sapling. One day it would be a towering tree, free to spread its limbs up to the sky, the place that was as much a home to the Kirin as the ground below was. Arias didn't know what happened after creatures died, but he figured Ly-ra would have liked the idea of being laid to rest here in the woods. The elders had given him permission to hunt their territory, but he wasn't hungry. They told him he was free to spend the night in the temple as well, and he decided that he would. He

327

knew he wouldn't feel safe sleeping under the stars all alone.

The elders and their apprentices had remained in the assembly hall after Arias had finished telling his story and answering their questions. They appeared to have wrapped up quite some time ago, however, and the one who had first spoken to Arias, To-shin, had asked the apprentices to keep an eye out for his return. The murm Arias was within sight of the temple, a young Kirin buck posted at the main entrance leapt to his hooves. His horns were just spikes on his head; obviously he was quite a bit younger than most apprentices.

"Are you ready to head in for the night?" the buck asked, his tone far too formal for Arias's liking.

Arias nodded, trotting after him. He managed not to flinch as he crossed through the illusionary entrance this time, and he stayed on the buck's heels as he led him higher and higher in the temple via interesting passageways. Arias wondered how much of the temple itself was the work of magick, and how much was real. "Why are so many of the entrances here hidden?" he asked his guide, who slowed to a walk and replied,

"To-shin was one of the founders of this temple, and he was very fond of deceptive magick as a younger buck. He favored illusions, and enjoyed tricking others so much that he decided to hide all the entrances in this manner one night while the others were asleep. It would seem that many of the elders had a sense of humor when they were younger, because they kept them this way."

Arias scanned the wall of the passageway they were passing through, wondering if he could spot any inconsistencies where an entry might be. The apprentice noticed and chuckled. "Trust me, I've done the same. They're *really* high-quality illusions. And there are no other entrances besides the one at the end of this passage."

"So this 'To-shin' is the one who has been giving me anxiety about walking into rocks since I got here…" Arias muttered accusatorily, and the fawn's resulting laughter rang off the solid walls. The passageway turned upward at a sharp angle, and there was enough space for Arias to open his wings and fly up instead of walking. The apprentice stared at him in wonder, and, noticing that he was gawking, quickly directly his gaze to the ground. Arias landed, again, chuckling. "My friends and I looked the same way when Ly-ra flew with us for the first time. Wind walking is really interesting."

"Ha! You think so? I'm just learning."

"At least you're getting an early start on it," Arias said. "It took me a long time to learn to fly."

"Really? Is it hard? I mean, it must be kind of like running, right? Because you're not using magick?"

"Well…" Arias answered question after question from the fawn, inwardly amused by his curiosity. Like so many other things here, it reminded him of Ly-ra. While it saddened him to know that the lively doe was no longer here, he was happy that most of his memories of her were good ones. To the very end, she'd trusted and been trustworthy. To honor her, he decided that he'd try to be the same. He'd find Brynne and Tybrake, no matter where they were.

"Here we are," the buck said, returning to formality. "Let me know if you need anything. I'll be just out here."

Arias stared at the solid wood door. The irony that it belonged to a trickster who hid every other doorway wasn't lost on him. He frowned. "Why don't you come in?"

"Oh! No, master To-shin probably wouldn't appreciate having me in his private quarters. Besides, I have studying to do." Then, oddly enough for a creature possessing magick, he announced their presence by headbutting the door.

Arias blinked, looking from the fawn's tiny horns to the fawn itself. "Does that not hurt?"

"Not even a little bit."

The door swung open, and To-shin nodded to the buck. "Thank you. Come in, Arias! I have so many questions to ask you."

Arias saw a majestic vertical space beyond the doorway, made of expertly cut stone in interesting formations; it contained a roaring hearth that would've frightened him if not for his time spent with the Minotaurs, and a small stream even cut through the space, vanishing beneath one of the walls. He tore his eyes away and looked at the fawn. "Can he come in, too?"

The small buck froze, but master To-shin only gazed at them with a curious expression on his face. "Why not? Tradition would not approve, but I suppose these past few days have been anything but traditional. Come in, both of you!"

The fawn hardly hid his excitement, nearly bounding into the room before controlling his enthusiasm. Arias followed him, and cried out in surprise as he stepped on the stone floor. Soft... rocks? He sent a reproachful look at To-shin, finding pure amusement on the elder's face.

"First the entryways, and now this!" Arias said, to which To-shin laughed outright.

"It's been too long since I've led any creature astray," he said. "And don't worry, it's only the floor. You're welcome to perch on some actual rocks, over there."

Arias regarded him with a flat expression, but after a few more steps, he was used to the misleading feeling of the ground. He settled in a corner, next to the hearth. To-shin watched him with interest.

331

"Not afraid of fire, eh?"

"Just used to it," Arias said. "The Minotaurs were quite fond of having it around."

"Ah, the Minotaurs. How are they these seasons? Is Argus still around?"

"Yes, and he's probably one of the surliest beasts I've ever met," Arias replied.

To-shin paused for a long time before saying, "Maybe I'll visit them sometime. See if they need help with rebuilding."

Arias's eyes sparkled in the firelight. "I think they'd like that," he said. "But I hope you wouldn't try anything. You'd have an Alicorn to answer to if you cause any trouble."

"Me? No, not at all!"

Arias looked from the ground back to him, and the elder snorted. "You know what I mean. Most of us aren't like Mati-jai. How we let that monster spring up among us, I'll never know. Some of us spoke out against him, but we were so wrapped up in who-knows-what that no one did anything. I'm not exempt in that regard. It's interesting that it took you, a flesh eater—I don't mean any offense in that—to show us the error of our ways." His eyes shifted over to the fawn, who was going through his notes studiously. "And we lost not only the guardian of our region, Aaga, but also one of our brightest apprentices," he added sullenly.

"No group of creatures is without its problems," Arias said. "We all just have to make sure we learn, and try to ensure the same things don't happen again." He thought of Hilda, still out there somewhere with the Pale, and felt an itch of urgency to get back to the flock as soon as he could.

"You shouldn't be that wise at only two!" To-shin cried, sitting across from him next to the hearth. He picked up a dried stalk of something, and started to gnaw on it, closing his eyes. He had to work it back and forth in his mouth for a little while before finding suitable teeth to chew it with. Arias hadn't before noticed just how many of his teeth were missing.

"I'd offer you some, but I don't think a creature such as yourself would enjoy sweetcane. Honestly, I'd probably have more of my teeth if I stopped hoarfing it down whenever I can get my hooves on it. You, buckling! Do you want one?"

The fawn looked up in surprise, and nodded gratefully with wide eyes. To-shin took a stalk with his magick and tossed it over to him without looking. "I have three apprentices at this very moment, and they all only stay with me for a matter of seasons before they move on. I like teaching youngsters to wind walk—they're always so excited to get it right for the first time, and they aren't stuffy like the other older codgers around here. I'll be darned if I can remember any of their names, though." He munched down the last bit of the sweetcane, then reached for another.

"So, if you're going to go see the Minotaurs, does that mean you Kirin will go back to exploring again?" Arias asked. "Ly-ra made it sound like no one ever left the walls of the temple these days."

"Ah," To-shin said, his sweetcane drooping in his lips. "That'll be up to each individual Kirin. I'm hoping that, as the years pass, we'll be more open to the concept. I'm sure you know that, after what's happened, your kind are more than welcome here. The council is still divided even on *that*, by the way, but I think those of us in favor outrank those against."

Arias nodded. Mati-jai aside, he enjoyed the company of the Kirin, more so when they weren't busy looking down at him. He figured they'd come around, or they wouldn't. Either way, he was sure that the majority of the other Gryphs would be excited to meet the Kirin if they ever got the chance.

The rest of Arias's night at the temple was spent talking to To-shin, and eventually to his apprentice as well. They talked about the future and about traditions, as well as asking too many questions to keep track of. When Arias left in the morning, it was with the glowing feeling that he'd made true friends during his stay.

***

The Aquilas' territory was beautiful when there weren't storm clouds and bolts of deadly lightning arcing across it. Arias initially cowered when the two huge thunderbirds descended upon him, but, recognizing him, they stopped short of their assault on him. They inquired as to what had happened to Hlaena, and he told them; they didn't ask about Brynne and Tybrake, but he nevertheless asked them if they'd seen them. They both shook their heads. Arias prepared to continue on his way, not wanting to test the patience of the two large creatures, but they both insisted that he see their chicks before he did so, evidently proud of their creations.

Arias flew to the top of one of the sparkling towers that the Aquila had built their nest atop, and there beheld one of the most unsightly beings he'd ever rested eyes on. The chick was featherless save for a few sparse sprinklings of down, and its eyes were sealed and appeared too large for the size of its head. He could hear the occasional cries of the other two from their respective platforms despite the distance.

"Oh," Arias said, looking it over. The parents stared at him as if waiting for more, so he hurried to add the first thing he thought of, which happened to be, "…Interesting."

"Two males and a female," the hen said happily, adjusting some down around the chick with a loving touch. "I can't wait until they open their eyes."

Arias blinked. He realized he'd never seen a newly-hatched Gryphon before, and he wondered if they were just as hideous. The chick squeaked, struggling to lift its enormous head, its equally-as-huge mouth gaping open. He supposed there was something tragically cute about how helpless it was. "Your first?" he asked, to which the male nodded emphatically.

"Have you any offspring of your own, Gryphon?" he asked, and Arias shook his head.

"No."

The two Aquilas nodded and gave one another knowing looks before going back to their doting. Arias tilted his head, but they no longer addressed him, and so he took to the sky again. Before he got too far away, he yelled, "Good luck with raising your little ones! Thanks again!" The pair went as far as to cry out in farewell to him, and he felt a strong updraft that hadn't existed before. He peered back, wondering if the Aquilas had done him a small favor, but they weren't looking at him.

He hoped if he met the thunderbirds again, it would only be under good circumstances.

* * *

Arias flew directly over the entire swath of territory where the bonebrancher had been. There was no way he was willing to risk dealing with that again. He eased into the pattern of sleeping during the day and flying at night, feeling more secure with his ability to see and detect danger in low light. It took a few nights to reach the Kelpie's lake, and, although thirst tried to convince him to land, he decided that he'd rather go without water all the way to the coast than tempt the horrendous beast.

The night was beginning to streak with the first blues of morning when Arias heard the roaring of the ocean in the distance. Excited, he flapped his wings harder, hoping to find Brynne and Tybrake along with everyone else, waiting for him. Cries of alarm pierced the air long before he reached the coast or saw anyone, and he was inwardly pleased that the flock had done such a great job of setting up guards. He supposed he shouldn't have been all that surprised, especially with Larin around, but he was impressed all the same. Before long, a few Gryphs rose to trail him, calling out in eager greeting to him. He called back, and the first bits of the eyrie they were creating became visible to him in the form of a long network of dens and structures that reached all the way from the beach and up into the forest. Gryphs busy with sorting preymeat, casting for wrigglers, and digging new dens all stopped their activities to come up to meet him. He'd barely touched down on the ground when a figure darted into him and knocked him to the ground, winding him. Larin engulfed him in her dark wings and subjected him to a particularly affectionate embrace, and he laughed, wrapping his wings around her.

"I'm glad to see you're alright!" he said, righting himself. "I missed you!"

Larin waved her wings, her tail quivering in her excitement, and bowled him over again, garnering a few chuckles from the others.

"Arias?"

Arias's ears pricked up at the voice, and he picked Lue out of the crowd. She stepped forward, her movements tentative. "Where's Tybrake?"

Arias's heart sank. "He's not here? What about Brynne?"

The happy atmosphere of the murm rushed away. Lue blinked at him, as if expecting some further explanation. "I was hoping they were both here," he said, scanning those gathered around as if his friends would somehow appear among them. "We were split up days ago, and I couldn't find them. I tried, I promise I tried. I just couldn't find them—"

"Hold on now," Bala said, walking through Gryphs to stand next to him. "You've only just arrived back. Let's listen to what happened, and maybe we can help you to find them. They're alive as far as you know, yes?"

Arias nodded, then shook his head. "I'm... not sure."

Gryphs lowered their heads and murmured with uncertainty, but Bala hushed them and nudged Arias toward the beach. "Calm down, everyone. Give him a murm to collect his thoughts." He turned his eyes back to Arias. "Let's get you something to eat. And something to drink too. Come on now, this way."

***

Sunset tinged the horizon as Arias sat near the water's edge, watching the waves. He'd told the flock his entire story, and already there were a few parties out searching for any sign of Brynne or Tybrake. Lue had been one of the first to volunteer and set out. He felt terrible about the entire situation, and had tried to head out himself, but pretty much every Gryph had forbidden him to go scouting before resting. He'd been awake all night, and all day, and now it was night again. He wasn't tired, though.

Hilda hadn't been a problem since the flock had begun to establish itself at the beach. Food had been abundant, and the development of the eyrie itself was going well. Everyone had been happy to hear that Hlaena had pulled through, and had been incredibly interested to hear about the Bonebrancher, the Kirin, Aaga the Phoenix, and the Minotaurs. He carefully unwrapped the markings Ly-ra had left on her sheets of bark, and every Gryph gathered around to peer at them curiously. Arias had been counting on telling the stories alongside his friends who'd been there with him. He sighed, staring out across the sea. There was one thing in particular that had bothered him ever since his return, a hole in the details everyone had shared and received. No one had any idea of how the Strigigryph were doing, and, in the flurry of activity, of course no one had gone to check on them.

Arias reached down with his bill and lightly pecked at the shell ornament still tied around his neck.

He was planning on changing that.

Thank you for reading! If you enjoyed this book, please consider leaving an honest review for it. Also, consider joining the mailing list:

https://www.kathrynobrown.com/

Read them all!

The Quill and Claw Series:

Book One: A Gryphon's Journey

Book Two: A Gryphon's Trial

Book Three: A Gryphon's Mercy

THE ADVENTURE CONTINUES IN BOOK THREE…

A GRYPHON'S MERCY

A curious sound reverberated through the tunnels, like the groaning of a large tree's roots begrudgingly losing their hold on the earth. A scattering of dust and grit showered across Arias as he sat there listening, trying to pinpoint where the sound had originated from.

"What –" Brynne started, but Roarick cut her off sharply.

"Shh! Listen…"

After a long murm, the sound came again from somewhere high above their location, and with it came the unmistakable sound of rock moving against rock.

"We have to move!" Roarick said, abandoning his post in front of Arias and the others. Arias shook his head as more of the grit drifted down, sharp and irritating against his eyes. He darted off behind Brynne and Roarick, and he could feel Larin at his heels.

"What's that sound?" Brynne demanded, grunting as she grazed her wings in her haste to keep up with Roarick, who was suddenly moving through the tunnel with the hectic grace of a Gryph half his size.

Roarick barked a quick, "jump here!" and Arias heard the Barbagryph, and then Brynne, clear some sort of ledge before them. Arias miscalculated his own leap, managing to catch both ankles against the sudden rise in the terrain. He hissed at the sharp, unexpected pain, but didn't stop.

"It sounds like the mountain is shifting," Roarick finally replied. "I've never seen it or heard it before, but smaller tunnels have caved in before down here. We don't want to be in here if this one goes."

www.ingramcontent.com/pod-product-compliance
Lightning Source LLC
Chambersburg PA
CBHW051604100726
47898CB00001B/220